The Half Killed

QUENBY OLSON

World Tree Publishing

The Half Killed is a work of fiction. Names, characters, places and incidents are products of the author's imagination or are used fictitiously. Any resemblance to actual events or locals or persons, living or dead, is entirely coincidental.

ISBN-10: 0989446069

ISBN-13: 978-0-9894460-6-8

Published in the United States of America by World Tree Publishing.

First Edition: August 2015

1 2 3 4 5 6 7 8 9 POD B1532

To Tim, for believing I could do this.

Prologue

It wasn't your fault. Mama forced you to do it, one hand on your sleeve, the other combing through your curls, and all while she whispered in your ear, saying it would be all right, that it would please her so much if you would just show yourself in front of the guests. And with such enticement, what choice did you have? So you said yes, and adjusted the bow in your hair, and waited for the uneven smile to tease the corners of her mouth.

The planchette sat in the middle of the table, Mama's favourite one, carved to resemble an ivy leaf, the slender veins aligned to the placement of her fingers. She took such good care of her hands, always aware of how often they would be on display. Papa never complained about the amount of rings she wore, though he had to have known how much of his fortune decorated her pale skin. You remember he mentioned it to her, and she laughed in that way of hers, with her head thrown back and her eyes closed, and he was so charmed that he never introduced the subject again.

There were several people around the table, their faces warmed by the light of the candles. And they were so large to you, then. You, The Little Darling, as Mama called you, her fingers still in your hair, then sliding down to your back, pushing you forward against your will. But you didn't stumble, and the shadowed faces around the table were not the least bit frightening. Even in the faint illumination, you recognised Father Crusoe, and Papa, the both of them lending a sombre contrast to the light Mama seemed to pull into the room.

And Aunt Anne was there, too, still in black and crepe, as if her Roger had passed away only two months before, instead of a dozen years. It surprised you, after all her complaints about your

I

demonstrations, that your gifts should have been put to better use. She smiled when she saw you, the familiar light gleaming in her hazel eyes, her eyelashes fluttering. But you failed to return the unspoken greeting. Mama had already warned you not to smile, or to laugh, or to appear too frivolous. There you were, barely nine years old, carrying the expression of one five times your age. And so Aunt Anne's grin faded away, and you wished you would have committed that last smile to memory, the details of it: the deep dimple in her left cheek, the curve of her mouth. It would've pleased you to remember her that way.

Mama begged you to sit, so benevolent in front of others, and she gave you a moment to smooth your skirt, the pale blue satin shining under the light of the candles. Her own dress was a deep red colour, maybe burgundy, but it has been years since you could remember the exact shade. Her hands glittered as she moved them over the table, and you wondered if she had done something to her skin, treated it in some way that made her very flesh pick the light out of the air.

The prayer came first, six heads bowed at once, but you kept your eyes open, stealing glances at Mama to your right and Aunt Anne to your left. And then they placed their hands on the table, their fingers spread apart like a fan, Mama's rings glittering even while her hands stayed still. She said something, a few words, barely audible, and they crept across your skin, settling at the base of your throat, curling around it like the cold hand of some deceased thing.

You had done this before. Sat still and calm in the circle, the voices ringing in your head, nearly drowning out your own voice as you asked questions to the darkness. But what was different this time? Why did the shadows twitch and writhe at the corners of your vision?

Your hands slipped off the planchette. Mama kicked your leg with her foot, and you knew there would be a bruise, but you refused to obey. The little triangle of wood trembled without your pressure, agitated by your refusal to cooperate. And all while the cold tightened its grip around your throat, spreading across your shoulders, down your arms, prickling in the tips of your fingers.

And when you looked up at Aunt Anne, you realised she sensed it, too. There was no smile on her face, only an increasing horror, and as she pushed her chair back and stood, you cried out to Mama that you wanted to stop, that you wanted to go back to your room and hide where the voices could not find you. But she wouldn't allow it, and the planchette continued to move beneath her touch, and her head tilted back, her eyes closed as she began to laugh.

Except it wasn't her voice. And yet you had heard it before, though the memory of when and where would elude you. But the familiarity of it stole through you, though you could not give it a face, as if it had chattered to you in your sleep for some time, years perhaps, pressing at your consciousness, at your sanity. And now it came from your mother's mouth before she bit down on her bottom lip, and you saw the blood, black in the faltering candlelight, trickle down the side of her chin.

Beside you, Aunt Anne cried out. Her fingers clawed at your shoulder, tearing at the sleeve of your little dress until you swatted her away. But the room became darker, and though the candles continued to burn, it was as if their light was smothered. And you looked at the walls and the ceiling, at the darkness spreading across them, down to the floor, flooding the carpet like water.

In your head, the voices—your constant companions—laughed at you. And they grew louder until you couldn't see, and you couldn't think, and with your hands pressed to your ears, as if the vile sounds came from outside of your head instead of within, the first sobs broke free of your chest, and the hot tears spilled down your cheeks.

Mama remained at your side, and her hand was on your head, toying with the ribbon in your hair, before it slid down to your throat, and her fingers wrapped around your slender neck, pressing down until you couldn't breathe. So you struck out at her—something you thought you'd never do—her flesh beneath your nails, and the warmth of her blood, but you told yourself not to fret, because it wasn't Mama

3

anymore. The voices told you she was already dead, and it gave you some comfort to believe them.

Chapter One

The body doesn't move. I don't expect it to, and yet I'm transfixed all the same. My eyes search the thick block of a neck for the slightest vibration that would indicate a flow of blood beneath the skin. The skin itself is enough to intrigue me, cast in a pallor no virulent illness could begin to imitate. It is this shade, this absence of colour that makes the deep bruises beneath the jaw stand out, curving in a mockery of the smile that still graces the frozen features of the dead man's face.

A push from behind forces me to take a step forward, my heel slipping on the greasy cobbles before I regain my balance. It is a small group of onlookers that has gathered around the scene since my arrival, but no one lingers for more than a passing glance. The poor man has nothing to recommend him. See there? The scuffs on his boots? And look at the patches on his coat, the fabric worn so thin it could lead a double life as a strip of cheesecloth. And what about his face? Oh, it's not a handsome one. A face that could earn naught but a mother's love, as is often said. And so the pedestrian moves on, his pace quickening until the shout of a seller or the rumble of a passing dray erases the memory of the dead man from his mind.

I know I shouldn't stay very long myself. Another glance from the constable, and I wonder if I've already worn out my welcome. His uneasiness grows the longer I stand here, and when his partner joins him, there is a great deal of whispering, punctuated by more than a few looks in my direction.

Not only because I'm a woman, surely. But because I'm a young woman, in modest dress, wandering the streets before the first rays of the sun have touched the dome of St. Paul's. And most shocking of all, because the sight of a recently deceased man sprawled across the

5

edge of the pavement does nothing to disturb my feminine sensibilities.

And why should it? There's nothing particularly gruesome about the scene. No blood, no other visible marks or wounds apart from the row of dark bruises beneath the unshaven jaw. If the eyes weren't open, gazing up at the channel of brightening sky, I could almost fool myself with the belief he had simply passed out, and at any moment, he'll groan and grumble back to life, waving his hand to clear away the inebriated haze that settled on his mind some hours before dawn.

But he doesn't move, and one of the constables takes the liberty of borrowing a tarpaulin from a local shopkeeper, the better to shield the inert form from view. Move along, my mind tells me. Nothing more to see. And though I'm tempted to argue, I put on my best show of slipping into the crowd and allowing their rapid pace to carry me back towards home.

A simple left turn, the burgeoning river of pedestrians sweeping me along, and I couldn't stop if my next breath depended on it. This early in the morning and already the streets are swollen with people. And again I think of a river, ready to overflow its banks and spill into every crevice.

The coolness brings them out. This brief respite from the sun, before the light produces an unusual warmth that hovers over the city as thick as the brown fog that clings to the rooftops in winter. But it is summer now, and the stoves are cold, the hearths swept clean. Even the thought of a flame is enough to start a prickle of sweat behind the knees, and in the evening, after the lamp lighters have made their rounds, most people tend to skirt the dim circle of yellow light that illuminates the pavement. Light is heat, and heat is light, and both must be avoided at all costs.

It is one of the great topics of London conversation, the heat. In large block letters on the front of every paper—the ink so fresh it stains the skin—the headlines shout and complain, syphoning the thoughts direct from the minds of the general populace and printing

6

them out in black and white for everyone to read. For a pence, I have my own copy, and I tuck it under my arm until I can settle down with a cup of something and read through it without fear of being trodden underfoot by the passing crowd.

But the papers are not the only messengers, come to remind us of our current troubles. There are the missionaries, wandering the streets in their dark woolens and caps, brandishing their Bibles as a killer would a sharpened knife. The heat is a punishment, they cry. A punishment for our wicked deeds. Because we turned from God's path, and now He has sent hell onto the Earth, and we will burn in our beds, every one of us, until we bow down our heads and beg for forgiveness.

And there are the bodies, more of them now that summer has set in. They drop where they stand, mouths parched, eyes rolling back into their heads until their hearts cease to beat. The old and the young are the most susceptible. The heat whittles away at them, preying on their weaknesses until it finds nothing left with which to work, and so moves on to the next life.

It's as if the season gains strength from every soul it takes, every day warmer than the last. The fog of winter has turned into a foetid steam, blurring the horizon and changing it to a silvery haze, until it seems that the Thames itself will evaporate to nothing more than a ribbon of cracked dirt and mud.

And what of the bodies that do not perish? The figures that clog the streets and alleyways at all hours of the night? It is in them, in their surreptitious movements I find another popular topic of London conversation, though this one is spoken with many furtive glances thrown over shoulders, voices lowered to a pitch almost below breathing.

But even though I'm unable to hear their conversations, I sense their restlessness, their eagerness to leave all and be done with it. For it is an exodus they speak of, nothing so epic as the biblical tales drummed into their heads when they were children, but a slow, subtle movement out of the city. And how can I blame them? With word

7

coming back that the outer counties aren't suffering under the same drought that punishes us, who wouldn't be tempted to pack up their belongings and make a fresh start elsewhere? It is a question I've often taken to asking of myself. But I doubt my answer would find a match with many of those around me.

The church bells call out the hour as I turn the knob on number 121, the door letting out a half-hearted squeal of protest as I press my shoulder against it, careful not to disturb the knocker that glares down at me with its grime-encrusted eyes. Indeed, the great slab of painted oak sticks inside the frame today, the wood so swollen and warped it no longer closes properly. Today, a jolt from my elbow isn't enough to break it free. A kick from the heel of my boot does the trick, and I'm inside once more, the clamour of Chancery Lane blocked off as I make my best attempt at closing the door behind me.

My paper still pinched beneath my arm, I pull off my gloves and tuck them into the waistband of my skirt. It is now that I feel the difference between the heat of outdoors and within, as I fill my lungs with a season's worth of stale air trapped in a windowless room, the walls—what little can be seen of them—displaying tapered streaks of smoke from the candles and oil lamps tucked into every available space.

And there they are now, the yellow-orange pinpoints of light flickering dully as I pass through the room, my shoes leaving faint tracks in the dust that coats the buckled floorboards. If there is a window here, it is well hidden. Enormous bookcases line every wall, flanked by sideboards and wardrobes more suited to a castle on the moors, their cobwebbed cornices decorated with the vulgar countenances of demonic gargoyles. They would be enough to still the heart in ordinary light, but here, with only the paltry glow of a few candles to illuminate them, their bulging eyes and forked tongues carry the power to steal the breath of a healthy man.

The shadows fail to unnerve me, and after a few moments my eyes adjust to the dismal light. A longer look at the candles tells me they've been left to their own devices for some time. Great puddles of wax coat every available surface, trickling down the sides of crates and bureaus in greasy rivulets that dribble onto the floor, waiting to be hidden beneath another month's dirt and grime, existing without fear of ever being prodded with a broom.

My hand finds the rail, the wood worn smooth by the passage of a hundred hands before mine. And that is when, in the far corner of the room, a bundle of rags shifts to reveal the threadbare upholstery of an armchair, and beneath that, a dusky grey cat that licks at a claw with a feline fastidiousness.

"Good morning, Mrs. Selwyn," I say, my voice cracking from disuse.

The bundle rolls onto its side. A head appears above a flattened collar, lank grey curls peeking out from under a cap that defies the laws of physics in its perch on the side of the old woman's head.

"You're up early." A sniff, and she glares at me, her wrinkled face sandwiched between layers of fabric, all of them so out of fashion her wardrobe has long passed into the realm of curiosities.

"I was just going up to my room," I explain, while the fingernails of my right hand carve figures in the soft wood of the bannister.

"No work for you today, Miss Hawes?" There is something in the way she draws out my name, adding syllables that spring into existence on the tip of her tongue. "Ah, to spend my days lolling about, all ease and comfort."

I close my eyes, shift the newspaper beneath my arm and imagine half the front page smeared across my sleeve. A slow intake of breath, and there is nothing else to be done before her prepared speech breaks the silence.

"D'ye know what work does for a person? Honest, steady em-ploy-ment? Keeps a head twisted on tight, is what. The order of the days, the weeks, years in and years out..."

Her voice falters. Blinking, she seems to have momentarily lost her thread. And then her eyes brighten as if lit by a spark, her tongue running over her ivory teeth as if to remind herself where she'd been keeping them. "You've lost track of the time," she says. And when I make no immediate response, she sniffs again. "You owe me."

I lower my chin an inch. And there I stand, a study in penitence.

"I am sorry, Mrs. Selwyn. I had meant to pay you, but—"

"The first day of the week. Every week," she stresses, allowing her words to hang in the air for a moment before continuing. "I know you've not been here long, but I can't be playing the Samaritan, filling up rooms with folks who won't... who can't..."

"You'll have it tomorrow."

She sniffs a third time, and runs the side of her hand across her flaking nostrils. The grey cat slinks out from under her chair, rubs along the edge of my skirts, and stalks off.

"You were up again last night. I heard you knocking about, letting out a wail like the devil hisself was after you." She eyes me carefully. "But you wouldn't know anything about that, like."

I fiddle with the corner of my paper, already soft and wilting in the room's oppressive warmth.

"I'll go up to my room now. Good day."

"You'll be frightening off all my regulars."

An outright lie, that is. As if a few cries in the middle of the night would be enough to scare away the sort of individual to find himself sheltering under Mrs. Selwyn's roof.

"Yes." I clear my throat. "It won't happen again." And there it is. Another lie to match her own, only this one carries me up the stairs, my elbows bumping against the slanted walls as I lose and regain my balance. Onto the landing and I'm already warm from this slight exertion, my shoulders rising as a trickle of sweat runs down my spine. My room is at the top of a second flight of stairs, at the end of a narrow, unlit hall. Around me, I hear the rest of the household waking to life, and downstairs, Mrs. Selwyn is no doubt preparing another speech for the next unlucky soul to stumble across her doorstep.

I've no doubt Mrs. Selwyn considers me something of a witch, though her own inventive mind has probably exaggerated many of the details during the last five weeks I've lodged under her roof. By this time, I've become a regular messenger of Satan, dabbling in the black arts and scrawling pentagrams on her gritty floor. That she might say prayers for the condition and keeping of my soul, I can't bring myself to believe. For Mrs. Selwyn is the type of woman who prefers her religion to be a vague and distant thing, the good Lord and his angels residing comfortably in the stories she read out of a primer six decades ago. In her mind, God and his host must dwell somewhere near the Queen, cordoned off and quite unreachable.

But contrary to Mrs. Selwyn's belief, there are no allusions to the dark arts in my tiny room. A bed, a small chest that leads a double life as a wardrobe, a cracked washstand, and a chair that might have been salvaged from a dreary attic. There are few amenities here. The chair stands beside the bed, acting as a small table beneath its burden of a cup of water and—what would astonish Mrs. Selwyn—a creased and dog-eared Bible.

The book was here before me, no doubt left behind by the room's previous occupant, a young man who absconded in such a rush he left two socks—mismatched—and a pair of braces slung over the back of the chair.

The man never returned for his belongings, and the socks are now relegated to the position of stopping up a mouse hole in the baseboard. But the mice-chewed tufts of wool can't keep out the heat that insinuates itself into the room, finding no escape with the setting of the sun. The window, a small pane of bubbled glass that looks down on an alley without an escape, refuses to open no matter how much force I might use against it, and I spend too many evenings moistening the glass with my breath before I take to beating my head upon the papered wall.

But instead of abusing my head, I channel my energy into my fingers, and my right hand slides down the length of my left arm with a movement that has become almost instinctive. My fingers push at the cuff of my blouse until they've wrapped around the narrow span of my wrist, the pad of my thumb gliding over the fleshy welts of repaired skin that will forever prevent me from displaying my forearms in public.

With such a vain thought still tickling my conscious, I drag the paper out from under my arm and toss it onto the end of the bed, accompanied by the gloves I pull from my waistband.

Outside my window, several feet below, the morning traffic has already begun to subside. The threat of the sun's warmth pushes people indoors, and they shuffle into the dark like tribes of Bedouin retreating beneath the protection of their tents, the blistering heat of the sun given free rein over the city for the next few hours. I adjust my hat, finally pulling out the pin and tossing the sad accessory onto the bed along with its companions.

Without ceremony, all the other pins holding my hair in place follow suit. My clothing is done away with, blouse and skirt soon draped over the back of the chair, sharing their space with the braces I've yet to part with. I lie on the bed, on top of the blankets that have served no other purpose except to add a much needed layer of padding to a mattress that sags beneath even my slight weight, and I close my eyes, count the fluttered beatings of my heart as my breathing begins to slow. I try not to move, even though the sweat builds on my bare skin, and my ears and nose are worried by a large fly.

At some point, I must have drifted off, because when I open my eyes, the light has changed directions, and the shadows cut across the floor at shallower angles. I pull my legs back, tucking them beneath me as I struggle to sit up. The heat has made my head thick, and my throat is sore.

Pushing damp strands of hair off my face, I reach out for the Bible that sits on the chair beside me. A nub of pencil is tucked between some of King David's Psalms, the closest thing to a bookmark at hand, and I flip through the pages for some minutes, absorbing nothing, but only feeling the weight of the paper, as thin as tissue, between my fingers.

So turgid are my thoughts at this moment, it takes some minutes for the knock at the door to rouse me. Not until the knock has taken on enough force to shake the dust out of the wall do I call out for a brief respite from the noise while I struggle to find the correct end of my skirt.

"A note for you," Mrs. Selwyn grumbles when I greet her at the door. My blouse still sticks to my skin as my fingers commence a short battle with the buttons. "Just delivered. I ought to charge you, you know, demand some sort of pecuniary reimbursement for all the trouble of trudging up here to bring this to you."

But she knows she'll receive no extra payment from me, so the wrinkled and folded slip of paper is thrust into my hand with a narrowed glance, as if her watery eyes will be able to see through me and into the room behind, on the lookout for some unholy ceremony her knock had interrupted. And all the while, her feline companion tangles with her ankles, his tail alone throwing a tuft of hair into the atmosphere with every pass. He protests once as Mrs. Selwyn backs away, her steps purposefully loud, an affectation meant to display all the energy she'll use to return downstairs and back into the depths of her chair. I've already closed the door on her before she's cleared the landing, and I glance at the note, reluctant to open it now that I've had an opportunity to read the poorly written direction.

One last minute of debate, and I tear at the shoddy seal, unfold the note and grimace at the still damp ink that transfers itself onto my fingers.

Dear Dorothea,

I pause for a moment, then blink as I realise those two words have been crossed out, with

another, much plainer salutation written below.

Dorothea,

The rest of the note barely suffices as a complete sentence. My eyes skim to the end of it, until they've fastened on the flowery signature that tells me more than the dozen other words managed to convey.

It takes a few minutes to dress and fix my hair, the last pin slipping into a hastily braided bun before I set my hat to my head, giving it a last futile nudge to keep it in place. Drawing in one more breath of stale air, I walk out of the room and down the stairs as fast as I can without alerting Mrs. Selwyn to my departure. But I feel her eyes on me as I walk toward the door, or rather, the eyes of her watchman, the grey cat, poised on a dusty shelf, so close to the exit I hear his purr in my ear as I duck my head and step out into the daylight.

Chapter Two

The juice trickles over Marta's plump fingers, settling beneath her fingernails as she tears off another strip of orange peel and quite unceremoniously tosses it over her shoulder.

"Are you sure you won't have some?"

I glance at the mangled fruit in her hands, the section of orange, squashed from her ministrations, dripping from her fingertips. But even with the unnatural heat of the sun beating down on the back of my neck, I'm not tempted by this morsel of refreshment.

"Never mind," she says, and pops the disassembled fruit into her mouth. A dribble of juice rolls down her chin, but it's gone in a second, a quick flick of her tongue lapping it up. "Oh, it is a right steam bath today, isn't it? Sure I can't get you something to drink?"

"I assure you, I am fine."

"Hmmph."

Another section of orange disappears, another chunk of peel thrown to the ground. All around us, the most stalwart of the city's pedestrians brave the midday sun. Men in swallow-tail coats and collars that refuse to wilt. Mothers leading herds of smartly dressed children from one shop to another. Pigeons fluttering around gutters that contain only the most distinguished forms of refuse. Even Marta shines in this part of the city, her shrewd eyes inspecting every hansom that rumbles past us, as if another business opportunity might be hidden away inside the noble equipage.

And look at how my dear Marta is dressed! I've never seen her broad shoulders decorated with such finery. Bronze silk trimmed with velvet, over a blouse edged with lace. It's a wonder she's not succumbed to the heat, wearing so many layers, but there's not a bead of perspiration on her upper lip that isn't wiped away with an embroidered handkerchief before the light has a chance to reflect off the moisture's surface.

"It's a shame," she says, once the fruit is demolished, a faint glistening at the corners of her mouth the only proof of its prior existence. "A real shame to see what's become of you."

She has seen me once in the last five weeks, and before that, it was a span of two years between meetings. I cannot but wonder which of my remembered selves she's taken to using as a comparison.

"You're wasting your youth, Thea, hiding away like you are."

"Ah." I look away from her in order to cover the subtle twitch at the corner of my mouth. "I wasn't aware matters had gone so far."

She pushes out her bottom lip and blows out a breath that bothers the dyed feathers poking out of her hat. "You're doing it right now, you know. Trying not to be seen. It's in the way you stand. I don't remember you standing like that when you were a girl." A dark look settles over her brow. "You need to go back to the stage, d'you hear?"

My fingers tangle together and break apart before she's able to read something more into my brief hesitation. "No," I say, at last. "I shouldn't have ever been there in the first place."

"Oh, really?" Her eyebrows, plucked into an unnaturally high arch, rise even further. "You were disposed enough towards it back then, or have I gotten it all mixed up in my head? Mind you, my memory isn't as reliable as it used to be."

Ah, the advantage of having someone like Marta among my acquaintance. I'm never without someone to remind me of my former mistakes.

"I was so young." And I wince at this poor excuse, as if every sin can be readily forgiven so long as it was committed well before the last of a person's molars have broken through. So I continue talking, offering up justifications that sound increasingly false to my ears. "It was different then. I thought it would help. I thought it would make me stronger. And it did, for a time."

"And I'm sure the money didn't hurt matters?"

A sigh escapes me, almost a scoff. She takes it as my reply.

"Two years you were in that bloody hospital," she says, leaping from subject to subject with all the skill of a seasoned acrobat. "You'd think there'd be an improvement of sorts. But look at you! Like you've not slept or eaten proper since Michaelmas."

There's something in her expression now, a flash of maternal concern. And then a blink, a turn of her head, and there, it's gone.

"How much money do you need?" Her voice is harsher now, a woman of business as her fingers delve into a discreet pocket between the voluminous folds of her skirt. I hear the clink of coins, and perhaps, if I turned my ear towards it, the rustle of a few bank-notes.

And now there is nothing left but for me to speak, and it's amazing how quickly I revert to the gestures of my childhood, my head lowered, something like complaisance tinged with shame shaping the words that seem to have stranded themselves in the vicinity of my throat.

"One month's rent, is all." Out of the corner of my eye, the glint of a sovereign. "I'll pay you back. You know I will."

"What about food?" She presses the coin into my hand, follows it with another. "You don't cook for yourself?" Her head shakes in answer to her own question. "You need to get a lining in your stomach before a good wind up and snatches you away.".

I've already stashed the coins out of sight before she passes a bank-note beneath my nose. Her grasp on the paper remains firm, and I make no move to possess it.

"In return," she says. "A favour."

My eyes follow the wrinkled note, until I feel like a cat stalking a frayed end of yarn. "I will do my best to oblige, Marta."

"I've a girl, older than you, but just starting out. She's taken to calling herself Lady Francesca. A load of tosh, really, but a few of my regulars have taken quite a liking to her."

She blinks down at me, her breath held. Unfortunately, I'm in no mood to give her the easy reply she desires.

"It's a wonder you can find enough customers in this day and age," I say, and allow my attention to drift to a vague spot located on the other side of the street. "I hardly thought communications with the afterlife were considered to be quite the fashionable thing anymore."

"Well, there's the thing, you see? All these ones being taken in for fraud, self-proclaimed psychics, Spiritualists, and all of them being charged with an assortment of criminal activities, it lends a dangerous air to the proceedings. Makes the old biddies and the fine gentlemen feel as if they're doing something they shouldn't. And you know as well as I, there's always a good living to be made in practices that make a person feel not more than a bit guilty after the fact."

She puts on a charming smirk, a sign of our old Marta, come out to play.

"You know," she says, gives my rib cage a nudge. "It would be a boon to her if you'd agree to attend one of her sittings."

"No." The word slips out, maybe too soon, as if I'd been waiting for the opportunity to use it.

"Not in a professional capacity, of course. I wouldn't dream of asking you to do anything more than sit in the background and enjoy the show. But your presence might be the recommendation she's been searching for."

A shake of my head. "Lady Francesca, you said?" I mutter, with a fine show of disbelief. The answer is still no.

Her gaze darts up to the sky. "She chose the name. Thought it might give her something more of a distinction among her peers, as it were."

"Makes her sound like a gipsy."

"Yes, well." Marta's bosom puffs outward, her chin rising as if to accommodate this change in proportion. "She can be a bit too eager sometimes. Dramatically, I mean."

I look up at her, and even now, after all the years gone by, I still feel small and timid in her presence. "But isn't that what you wanted from me? A more visible eagerness for the task at hand?"

"True. But even when you were being, well, how you could get sometimes—Lord, you know you were never an easy one to work with, don't you? But you had a quality none of these other girls are able to pick up on. You were..." Her painted mouth puckers as she searches for the missing word. "Genuine."

"Well, thank you."

"Now, that doesn't mean you couldn't have played to the audience a bit more..."

"Right. Of course."

"It's what they prefer now. People like to be dazzled, even if they know it's all for show. You know, I'm even pushing Franny towards starting out with a few card tricks. Quite a talent for it, she has."

The sun has reached its zenith now. The sheen of perspiration on the back of my neck begs to be wiped away, and on my upper lip, the salty moisture settles. Other pedestrians are seeking out the nearest shade, lingering indoors, clinging to the shadows cast by a building or even another person. But Marta strolls on, shoulders held erect as she nods in the direction of a red-faced gentleman who is too busy dabbing at his face with a handkerchief to return the salutation. And then she dives back into the conversation as if she'd never paused.

"But it's all for fun now, isn't it? Between you and me, our Lady Francesca couldn't make contact with a spirit if it gave her a right kick up the arse. I mean, no one believes in it anymore. But these coddled ladies and gents, they still get a thrill out of it every now and again, no matter what these scientific minds are spouting off. It's all entertainment in their eyes. The same as going out to the theatre, or whatever else it is that keeps them occupied these days."

"Daft fools," I mutter beneath my breath, though I've not yet decided to which group I've referred: the scientists, or the ones who abhor them.

"Now, see? That's the discernment I'm talking about! No suffering of fools from you, which means with your reputation and all, the only thing wanted of you is to give Franny a bit of a nod—a blessing, as it were—and folks will be more inclined to look towards her with something like respect. It's not as if I'm asking you to sign away your firstborn."

"At least, not yet."

"Oh, will you listen to this!" She cries out towards the heavens, to anyone who will listen, and a few people do turn their heads, but the attention is fleeting. "Smart words coming from you, but you've yet to understand something. It's all ending. To most people, you're nothing more than a curiosity, halfway to becoming a relic. Or even a criminal, when the mood suits." She pauses, and I feel her eyes on me at this moment, boring into me with a strength I believe could burn through a wall if given the opportunity. She swallows, so loud I can hear it, and down her throat go whatever words, whatever questions she's most desirous to ask me. "All I'm doing is offering you a bit of employment," she says finally, her voice quiet. "From the few who are still willing to pay for it."

If she expects this statement to trigger some sort of transformation in me, she's mistaken. That is, of course, if she even takes the time to measure my reaction before plodding ahead.

"Do you remember Lord Ryall? There he was, ready to toss money on you. Put you up in a nice house, give you all sorts of pretty things, but you weren't having none of it."

"If I remember correctly, Ryall's inclinations tended more towards the physical than the spiritual."

"Be that as it may," she says, pronouncing each word as if it's her first lesson in phonetics. "Chances like that aren't flowing as free as they used to. And what with this blasted heat, and all these other buggers waving their Bibles about, the pace isn't about to pick up anytime soon."

It's a struggle to match the length of my stride to her own, and as her temper increases, I'm left jogging two steps for every one of hers.

"But I've no worries about business picking up soon enough," she crows, a discreet look in my direction. A flick of her hand, brushing a feather off her forehead, and she's fully composed, the stream of pedestrians breaking around her as she halts in the middle of the pavement. "I've received more than a few inquiries about you, you know. People asking about your..." A small gesture, indicating my person from the waist upward. "Your gifts, and all. Now, not as many as I'd like, but after that business in Chelsea, well I'll say I've heard a distinct rise in interest about you. Just the other day in fact, there was a young man, quite determined to secure your services."

I can feel the frown on my face, pulling down the corners of my mouth until I think that left unchecked, the expression could drag me all the way down to the ground. "I am not going back," I say, and watch my words strike against her intentions with all the firepower of flower petals. "I won't return to the stage, and I won't have you hawking me off like a shopkeeper's wares."

She shrugs at this, but there is a glint in her eye, a thrill now that she realises I'm still as easy to goad as I ever was.

"So, shall I look forward to your presence at Lady Franny's next demonstration?"

A wonder, is our Marta Summerson. Never retiring a question until she's gifted with the reply she desires.

"I am sorry, Marta."

"Oh, I'm not asking you to put a single ounce of effort! Stand in the corner of the bloody room and glower at us, if that suits your fancy!" She wipes the back of her hand across her brow, the first display of irritation I've witnessed from her all afternoon. And now, I notice even her feathers have begun to lose some of their former buoyancy. "I won't have it, you know. I'll not leave you to waste away under old Selwyn's roof."

I blink rapidly, and the reaction is enough to award her this small triumph. For I know the lengths to which she'll reach in order to achieve a desired object.

"You'll do something to earn your keep," she says, her voice lower, the powdered lines of her face several inches closer to mine. "Even if it means I've got to haul you out by your stockings."

Such a rare occurrence, to hear her voice a threat, even one so mild as this. In the end, I'm forced to meet her halfway. I tell her, in words labouring under the strain of having been dragged out of me, that I will "think about it". And there, as simple as that, she's mollified. The eyes resume some of their previous sparkle, and the feathers—oh! The feathers!—begin to dance on an imaginary breeze.

"Very well," she says, as if I've still managed to disappoint her. Yet the shine doesn't depart from her gaze. And even more surprising, the folded bank-note finds its way into my hand, followed with the promise of two more once I've fulfilled my part of the agreement.

"I'll make no promise to you, Marta. You know how much I despise a séance."

But Marta will not allow her present happiness to be thwarted. "Oh, you'll come round." She beams, so brimming with confidence I'm almost inclined to believe her. "After all," she adds, and her smile broadens while her eyes retreat behind crinkled lids. "You have your price, just the same as all the rest of us."

Chapter Three

Mrs. Selwyn knocks on my bedroom door, three sharp raps followed by a pause the length of a breath before my privacy is snatched away from me.

"There's a man to see you, Miss Hawes." Her thin voice never fails to create an image of her larynx pinched between finger and thumb as she fills out her consonants. "Is this going to become a regular occurrence? I'll not have men running up and down these stairs all day and all night. Wear out all my carpets before the end of the year."

She blinks, tilts her head to one side until I think her cap might finally succumb to the pull of gravity, but the shapeless lump of fabric clings fast to her greasy curls, and ultimately, my eyes are drawn downward to the scrawny grey feline arching its back against Mrs. Selwyn's heels.

"Did he give his name?" I ask, and return this morning's bit of sewing to my lap. Only the edge of a handkerchief today—my last handkerchief—a repair to a small tear before the whole thing unravels to a mass of tangled thread in my hands.

Her dusty eyebrows pinch together. If the man gave a name, the information has already dribbled out of her ear during the arduous trip up the stairs. Nothing less than the flash of a coin would be capable of retrieving it at this point.

"He…" And here, her eyes narrow, suspicion deepening the wrinkles in her brow. "He says he knows you."

"Knows me?" I keep my breathing steady, even counting the seconds between one inhalation and the next.

"That's what he said, Miss. But, no." She catches herself, her gaze far away as she relives the conversation that must have transpired only moments before. "He said he knows *of* you."

And with the simple addition of a preposition, I'm back to grasping for needle and thread, tilting my work towards the light that filters through the window, my nose held in the air as if I've a pair of wire-rimmed spectacles perched on top of it.

"Is it away with him then? Because I'll be charging an extra shilling to your rent if you're going to start with bringing in visitors." The way she pronounces the last word, tainting it with enough revulsion to make me question the level of debate that even now must be underway inside her head. For which sort of immorality is worse in her estimation? Dabbling in the black arts, or welcoming gentlemen callers in the brash light of a Tuesday morning?

I glance up at her, but as my eyes leave my work, the needle pricks my skin, causing my next words to come out with more of an edge than I'd originally intended.

"No visitors, Mrs. Selwyn. From here on out, if someone calls for me, I would be much obliged if you could tell them I no longer reside here."

She sniffs, one corner of her mouth curling upward with the movement. Quickly, she wipes her hand across her nose before drying her moistened fingers on the back of her skirt. "Oh, of course, Miss. How silly of me to think you'd wish to be bothered, sittin' up here all day, every day." Her head lowers deferentially. "I'll be sending him on his way." One side of her mouth still quirked, she turns and walks out of the room, shutting the door behind her.

I must admit, I feel ashamed for having spoken so sharply. And when I hear her renewed tread on the stairs less than a minute later, I'm already rehearsing the beginnings of an apology under my breath. Better not to forget I paid her only yesterday for two weeks' rent, long overdue. And, what is even more important, that my tenure here depends entirely on keeping myself in her favour. However much of it there is to go around.

I look up, prepared for Mrs. Selwyn's knock. One, two, three, raps in all before I call out to her, my voice carrying a heavy enough note of contrition to be heard through the door and into the hall.

"Yes, Mrs. Selwyn? Is there something else?"

The door opens again, and the old woman's reedy voice pipes up from behind the great slab of warped wood.

"A Mister Chissick to see you," she announces, her watery eyes practically glistening in triumph, her fingers still toying with the coin that must have purchased Mister Chissick's passage to the upper storeys of the house.

And here I sit, not in any way prepared to welcome a visitor. Yesterday's stockings still lie on the floor, curled and crinkled like two intertwined snake skins. The uneaten end of a pasty sits in the midst of a ring of crumbs, more sustenance for the next mouse daring enough to venture into the room.

And there are other things. More than enough to showcase my lamentable housekeeping skills. An unmade bed, a stack of newspapers about to topple over, a floor in dire need of sweeping. But there's no time to put everything to rights, or to manage at least some semblance of tidiness, before there's a blur of skirts and dust as Mrs. Selwyn disappears, the grey cat letting out a shriek of irritation as she nearly tramps on his tail in her haste to remove herself from my line of sight.

Mister Chissick, however, does not disappear. Very near to the door he remains, hat in hand. A hat with a short brim that appears to have borne the worrying of his fingers on more than one occasion. Perhaps a bowler, in one of its finer days. The absence of a covering on his head allows me to study the man's features. Years of standing onstage, gazing out across a sea of darkened faces no doubt have trained me. Another blink, and I can even begin to count the individual lashes that frame his eyes.

He takes a single step forward and pauses. The light from the window crosses his face, setting fire to the tinge of red in his hair. A few strands cling to his forehead, darkened with sweat, and I'm reminded of the heat that adheres stubbornly to every corner of the room.

"Miss Hawes," he says, such a strength of certainty in those two syllables, and I'm nearly convinced the two of us are old acquaintances, the use of my surname a mere formality to be done away with once the offer of a chair is made.

"Mister Chissick?" I try out the name for the first time, pushing it towards the tip of my tongue, my jaw jutting forward with the exaggerated pronouncement.

"That's correct." A movement of his arm, and I suspect he stopped himself from offering his right hand in greeting. He glances around the room. I'm seated in the only chair, but despite the lack of furnishings, all of my forgotten manners come flooding back.

"Will you sit down?"

A slight hesitation before he commandeers the portmanteau with no small amount of grace, easing himself down in an attempt to mesh his own form with the hard lines of the makeshift seat. His hands find a resting place on his knees, his fingers drumming upon the hat now perched on his thigh. He clears his throat, or begins to, before he gives up on the endeavour halfway through.

A noise such as this fills me with an expectancy of a greater speech to come. But instead, long, tapered fingers reach into a coat pocket in order to retrieve a wallet, only to remove a folded slip of paper, yellowed with age. He unfolds it with such care that I half expect this mysterious note to bear the answer to some ancient riddle. And then he reaches out to slip the paper between my own fingertips, the battered page leaving a light layer of powdery residue on my skin, the evidence of its slow decay.

Mister Chissick nods to the document. "This is you?"

Even after all these years, the act of seeing my name in print still produces a twinge of surprise, centering itself in my abdomen before it spreads upwards—upwards and outwards—freezing my rib cage in place so my next breath will take some effort. It's a newspaper clipping I hold in my hands, the creases so worn that I wonder it didn't fall to pieces during the course of its journey from his hand to mine. It's impossible to locate any sign of a date, or even the identity of the paper in which this article must have appeared, but judging from the author's flattering tone, it cannot be less than seven or eight years old.

But it's the drawing at the top of the column that catches my eye, the black ink now faded to a dull grey. The young girl in the picture is so removed from my current self I'm ashamed to admit it takes a full minute to recognise my own portrait.

It's not a bad likeness, all told. Much younger, of course. See the softness in the lines of my jaw, my cheekbones barely visible? The hair is the same though: still pale, still thin. And the sharp point of my chin, forcing my face into the top-heavy shape of an inverted teardrop. In a fleeting moment of vanity, I consider folding up the paper and keeping it for myself.

"Miss Hawes?"

He reaches out for the fragile clipping, the sleeve of his coat climbing high on his wrist, revealing several inches of sun-deprived skin and light brown hair. With even more care than previously shown, he folds the paper in half, once more, and again. As it disappears into the recesses of his wallet, I can't help but wonder for how long my illustrated face has slumbered there.

"I had the pleasure of witnessing one of your demonstrations," he says, eyes down and fingers re-adjusting the folds of his coat. "Nine years ago."

"As did many others, I am sure." My gaze lingers round and about the area of his right breast pocket, but there's no outward sign of the portrait that resides inside. No doubt I should consider myself fortunate if I ever see it again.

"The papers always wrote very warmly of your particular talents, Miss Hawes. Some even heralded you as one of the leaders of the Spiritualist rebirth." His blue eyes widen slightly as he speaks, and when he leans forward the portmanteau creaks in sudden protest of his shift in weight.

And now, I find, a minute must pass before I'm able to locate my voice.

"Some papers did." One corner of my mouth twitches upward. "But not many. I was never theatrical enough to satisfy the tastes of most critics. And besides all that, Spiritualism is dead, Mister Chissick. Our countrymen have firmly embraced this new era of reason and logic. My time has passed, or weren't you aware?"

He says nothing to this. Only the same curious gaze that does little to lend my speech any strength.

"If that same paper were to write of me today, if they wouldn't consider it an utter waste of ink, I'd be painted as one of the greatest charlatans to have ever set foot in London. And that drawing wouldn't be half so flattering."

A hint of a smile from him, and I gain confidence he's listening. But whether or not he's bothered to truly absorb a single word I've said is a feat yet to be seen.

"I am no longer the same girl you saw—nine years ago, was it? People are too worldly to be moved by a few amateur parlour tricks performed by a slip of a girl in a white shift and bare feet. Unfortunately, perhaps, I am what the public makes me, and they've moved on."

The sun is moving steadily across the room, and my feet begin to feel the warmth from the shaft of light pouring in through the window. A soft rustle of fabric, and I've shifted several inches closer to the edge of my chair, this new angle casting young Mister Chissick's face in a warm-toned shadow.

Ah, I said "young", didn't I? And here's where a touch of my old superiority shines through. Any gambling man with a spare shilling would bet that Mister Chissick is my elder by no less than ten years. But still, I prefer to fancy myself as the most mature person in the room, the one most experienced in the ways of the world. Give me that satisfaction, will you? As slight a one as it is.

"And what about the spirits, Miss Hawes?"

I'm flustered momentarily by the realisation that the conversation seems to have progressed without my knowledge. "I beg your pardon?"

"Have they moved on? The spirits?"

When I still hesitate, he leans back, or rather shifts into a more rigid position that vaguely mimics my own.

"Mister Chissick." Strange how much I enjoy pronouncing his name, the feel of it on my tongue. "If you are even to trust in the existence of such phantoms, then yes, I believe they have moved on."

For me, it is no difficult thing to lie, but this one tests my limits. For another minute, I ramble on, speaking absolute nonsense, one word falling over the next as quickly as they enter my head. My guest listens with all the attention of an eager pupil, struggling to become the favourite of his teacher. But something else passes over his eyes, a hardening of sorts, and the brightness he carried into the room with his entrance fades as fast as he can blink.

"I see."

Two words are all he offers in the wake of my wandering speech. Without another sound, his hands return to his knees and he stands, the erstwhile bowler dangling from two crooked fingers as if he's forgotten about its presence. No farewell from him, no apology for this hasty departure, and he walks towards the door, one arm already extended, his hand curving around the smudged doorknob. When he turns around, I feel the oxygen pull into my lungs, and my chin rises. I use the movement as a distraction, so he won't notice the shudder that invades my chest under the weight of his gaze.

"Whatever you are, Miss Hawes," and he pauses, eyes narrowing. "Whether it was simply a few well-executed tricks performed for the entertainment of a gullible audience, or something else entirely, you do have a talent, and I'm sure it's one of which I'm in desperate need."

QUENBY OLSON

A long span of silence follows. For all of my skill at seeing what others do not, I stare up at him, my mind caught in the laborious chore of deciphering basic English into something I can understand.

"Desperate?"

He moves away from the door, his hat tapping out an irregular rhythm on his thigh. "I'm sorry, I didn't want to give you any cause for alarm." He sighs, and his pause serves to alarm me more effectively than anything else he's said until now. "I beg your pardon, but I was directed to a former associate of yours, and she informed me of your current whereabouts."

I nod my head once. "Marta Summerson."

"She said you wouldn't mind—"

"She says a great many things, I assure you."

He takes another step forward, the hat once more clenched between both hands, and the introductions have gone back to the beginning. "I feel a compulsion to be honest with you, Miss Hawes. I'm a man of God. Or it was once my intention, not so very long ago. I was to lead only a small congregation, but..." He spreads his hands, his arms, and I'm left to fill in the blank with whatever I can conjure.

"And you're compelled to tell me this because...?"

"Well, I think it would do much towards building a measure of... well, something of a trust, or a confidence between us, don't you agree?"

If I could make heads or tails of what he is trying to tell me, perhaps I could provide him with a more satisfactory reply. As it is, I can merely blink up at him for several seconds, while I wonder if his arrival here is nothing more than one of Marta's less successful attempts at a joke.

"Mister Chissick, I am afraid I don't quite understand your line of reasoning."

He takes this as an invitation to continue, and begins to pace from one end of the room to the other, seemingly oblivious to the mess that surrounds him on all sides. The moment he speaks, however, the pacing stops and his probing gaze finds its way back to my face.

"It's no secret how people of your *sort* are regarded by the church, Miss Hawes. Especially in these last months. But I assure you, I have never in my life shared the sentiments of those of my former acquaintance. It is one of the reasons why I was never given a congregation to lead, and also why I find myself standing here, asking for your help."

"So, I take it you've not come here to save my soul?"

There it is. That elusive smile, tight-lipped, bringing out a fine web of lines from the corners of his eyes.

"Mister Chissick?"

"Yes?" Still smiling, the poor man.

"What do you want?"

And now he is walking towards me, pushing his limp hair from his forehead as though to see me more clearly. He beats his hat against his leg, and I push down the urge to rescue it from his abusive possession before the wool is battered beyond repair.

"You will take no offense if I am blunt?"

"None whatsoever."

"It is a... delicate matter."

"I am afraid you'll find most things are delicate matters, but still we survive."

He clears his throat, nods twice, and returns to the portmanteau. For a moment, he sits forward, but this posture doesn't suit him, so he slides back, shoulders falling slightly as a long breath slides out of his lungs.

"There is a body." He hesitates there. But, no. It's not a brief intermission between statements, but rather a full stop, and it becomes my responsibility to carry the thread along.

"I assume you mean the body of one who is recently deceased?"

Another sigh. "Yes."

"Murdered?"

"That's how it appears."

QUENBY OLSON

"And you're here to request my help." Spoken without a hint of question in my voice.

An abrupt motion forward, and his elbows move to where the armrests would be, dipping a few inches when he realises none exist on this particular seat. "As much as you would be willing to give," he says, hiding his awkward movement with a straightening of his shoulders. "And, of course, there would be some remuneration."

Ah, so he *has* been speaking to Marta.

"Reverend." I shut my eyes, biting my lip at my mistake. "*Mister* Chissick, I am sure you're not unaware that our fair city has a veritable army of police at its service, detectives and whatnot, each and every one of them more than up to the task of pursuing the murder of yet another young woman. Mere sleight of hand is not enough to recommend me for this, or any task. I've no doubt a brief foray to Scotland Yard—"

"Miss Hawes?"

My hand fidgets with the edge of my cuff, tugging it down until I've worked at least a thread or two free from the weave. "Yes, what?"

He looks at me. It's a different expression on his face than before, and I sense he's studying me, his body quite still, his gaze fixed on mine. Finally, after a minute, or two minutes, or one hundred minutes, he opens his mouth to speak.

"I never said the body in question belonged to a young woman."

And this is when I'm undone. It was the ghost of a vision that leaked into my head while he spoke, the voices ringing to life and then dying as I pushed them out again. But because I was lax, because I failed to attend to all the details of our conversation, I lost track of which images were put into my head by his words, and which came of their own volition.

"I am... I am sorry." The stammering unnerves me, but I press on regardless. "It's this heat, I think. I can't..." The wave of a hand. A fluttering of eyelids. Nothing else, but it's enough to show that Mister Chissick is all concern.

32

"Shall I fetch you something? A glass of water, perhaps?"

"No, I am fine."

"Fresh air, then? I could open the window for you."

"Thank you, but, no." I neglect to mention that the window is well sealed with countless layers of paint and grime, aside from the amount of moisture in the air that has swollen the wood and distorted its shape so it may never be moved from its sill. But no matter, really, since I'm certain that should I ask him to reverse the flow of the Thames for me, he would not rest before finding a way to achieve it.

A moment of silence follows, as I strive for some level of composure. I tell myself not to raise my gaze from the level of my lap, but it's as if my sight has taken on a will of its own, and I'm soon studying the line of his jaw, the fine growth of stubble on his chin. "What you're asking me to do, I am not sure... I'd rather not..." At the look on his face, I close my mouth, rearrange my thoughts. "I've spent most of my career on stage. I am a performer, an actress. And not a very skilled one, at that. I don't think I am capable of providing you with the help you seek. In fact, I am quite certain I could not."

He is leaning forward again, always forward, until I think he'll abandon his seat entirely and drop to his knees in front of me.

"Please," he says. The only thing he says.

My eyes drop to the unfinished sewing in my lap, the neat stitches I'd been taught to do so well.

"You can walk away at any time. I wouldn't dream of forcing you into a situation that would cause you any sort of discomfort. But..." And now it's his turn to stammer, to hesitate, to flounder in the open sea of awkward pauses. And when he regains his voice, the words are softened, the edges buffed smooth during the time it took for him to line them up on his tongue. "One look, Miss Hawes. That's all I ask."

One look, he says. As if he has any idea what I might see.

Chapter Four

The street is shrouded in darkness, pushing out the glow from the various shop fronts until all that's left is a faint lightening to the gloom. Small half-circles and distorted rectangles of white and yellow edge the pavement, but the shadows rule this silent byway, hiding away all manner of humanity and leaving them to live and breathe the sharp tang of the city's underbelly—like toadstools taking up residence in the shadow of a rotted log.

A brief touch on my elbow, enough to make me flinch, and Chissick lowers his mouth until it is a few inches from my ear.

"Best stay close, Miss Hawes. Until we're in better company."

I look down at his hand, still hovering near the vicinity of my arm. After a moment, he takes it away, but the tension remains in his fingers, in the way he holds his wrist and elbow. And when I stumble over a large crack in the pavement, his reaction is instantaneous, one hand returning to my arm, the other on the small of my back, prepared to catch me should I fall.

"Thank you," I say, and he accepts my gratitude with a quick nod. His attention, however, has already returned to the darker shadows of the alley, his eyes narrowing as if to better identify an unsavoury figure that might be lurking in the dusk.

Though "unsavoury" might not be the best word to use here. "Suspicious" might be more precise, or perhaps I'm doing the inhabitants of this neighbourhood a disservice. There's nothing to distinguish these men and women from the people I pass every day— on broader avenues, streets well-lit by sun and flame and even a spark of electricity. It's the darkness that establishes their characters here, before they're given a chance to prove themselves as harmless individuals. I glance at a few of them now, sheltered in a doorway, their heads wreathed in a foul-smelling smoke that refuses to dissipate. Their shoulders are rounded forward, as if bending beneath the weight of this abominable darkness. All faces are turned away from the light, leaving me with nothing to examine but smudges and shadows, broken only by a blaze of flame when one of them strikes a match and cups the flickering fire between his hands.

And because my imagination is so prolific today, I look away from the man's features, exaggerated to those of a ghoul's by the sputtering light of his match. But curiosity emboldens me to take a second look, and this time, all the familiar traits of humanity are erased. Or perhaps the human face was a mask, and now that it's stripped away, I'm permitted a glimpse of the beast that resides beneath. But another blink, followed by a few puffs of smoke, and he's lost to the fog that hovers and dips below the eaves of the house.

"Through here, now," says Chissick, leading me towards an open doorway, indistinguishable from the dozen or so others in my line of sight.

"Stay close." His hand seeks out my wrist, but worse than that, I feel his thumb brush over the damaged strip of skin between my sleeve and the frayed edge of my glove. I move my arm, and momentarily thwarted, he settles for closing his hand around my fingertips. It's a gentle pressure, I notice, not pulling me along, but holding onto me, as if he fears I'll be snatched from his grasp the moment he lowers his guard.

A quick stumble as I put my foot down on the front step, and I glance down at the impediment, a man sprawled across the stoop, groaning at the unwelcome contact between my shoe and his rib cage. Any apology I could make is forgotten as Chissick steers me inside, through another door, and there's a brilliant light, so bright I'm forced to squint and shield my eyes with my hand. The noise is there, too. A regular cacophony of every tone and accent, squalling and laughing, every swear and curse imaginable, until I'm convinced there won't be this much sound until Judgement Day, when the trumpets sound and every soul congregates outside the gates of Heaven.

But I have every hope that Heaven will smell nothing like this.

It's a long, low room he's led me into, lit by a fire and streaming gas lamps that put out enough heat to fool me into believing I've stepped into a furnace. And there are the people, dozens of them, lounging along the walls, tapping out their pipes on the tops of narrow tables, tripping over benches as their balance deserts them. They talk, and they laugh, and they spit—yes, even spit—onto the floor, onto the walls, great gobs of dark brown tobacco juice shooting from their mouths with all the regularity of breathing. And so the walls are decorated with the effluvium of the room's inhabitants, spit and sweat and blood and piss and shit, a portrait of life in this part of the city, one I've only ever suffered the misfortune of visiting in my mind.

My guide takes great pains to shield most of this from my sight, his shoulders twisting around until his stride becomes something of a side-step, his narrow body acting as a screen that directs me towards yet another door, set into the wall at such an angle one would think it was added to the building's architecture as an afterthought. And maybe it was, judging from everything else I've seen up until now.

A glance over his shoulder, and he pulls the door open, not wide, but leaving enough space for a slender person to slip through into the darkness on the other side.

"I'll go first," he says, and I notice he still has a hold of my arm. He releases me for a second, his pale fingers beckoning.

I take a breath—for courage, I think—and immediately wish I hadn't. Another smell drifts in from this new opening, of mould and dust, but more than that. Mould and dust is the aromatic specialty at Mrs. Selwyn's, nothing new to shock my senses. But there's something else drifting upwards from the subterranean depths, something my senses revolt against. And then a sound reaches my ears. Footsteps, descending slowly, broken by a pause when Chissick must notice I'm not close behind him. Another breath drawn into my lungs, held for a moment, and it takes all of my resolve not to turn on my heel and run.

The first step whines in acceptance of my weight, accompanied by a small shudder that makes me thankful I'm unable to see how tentative a grasp the staircase might have on the wall. The next step is easier to take, now I know the depth of them, and by the third my hand has found the wall, my gloved fingertips soaking up all manner of effusion from the damp, cool stone.

"Careful on the last step," Chissick warns me, his voice devoid of echo or reverberation. Only dead noise falling out of his mouth.

On solid ground again, but already I'm losing my bearings. I feel a flutter of panic when the thought crosses my mind that I could turn around now and not be able to find my way back to the stairs. Closing my eyes, I breathe slowly, ignoring the musty smells that tickle my nostrils. In the distance, or maybe quite close, I hear a dripping noise. Not steady, but irritatingly erratic, and I imagine the pace of the falling water must match the irregular beatings inside my chest.

"How much farther?" I despise myself for asking it, but I need a destination on which to focus. The fear of treading through a dark maze of dank hallways while being assaulted by the odours of death and dying is simply too strong to bear in silence.

"Just along here," he says, and latching onto the sound of his voice, I follow.

Some part of myself must know what it is I'm about to see. I'm prepared for the soft glow of lamplight beyond the next doorway, for the pervasive odour that seems to adhere itself even to the fibres of my dress. The light has a warmth to it, incongruous in this chilly cellar, the damp rising up from beneath the soles of my shoes. It's the best place to store a dead body during this time of year, I think. And then Chissick steps aside, and I'm left to stare at the naked woman laid out on top of the rough, wooden table.

The scene is all so impersonal, isn't it? A corpse—and loath as I am to use a word with such gruesome connotations, there isn't a more fitting one in my mind—stretched out in front of us, naked as the day it came into the world. And fittingly so. The end like the beginning, ashes to ashes, dust to dust, and all the rest. But it could very well be a rag doll, or a lump of coal for all the attention we give it as a fellow member of the human race. The spirit is gone, and along with it, our ability to treat it with more reverence than our imaginings of this woman's former life can give to it.

Desperate to remove my gaze from the columns of white skin, stained underneath with the slow coagulation of blood, my eyes begin a careful search of the room, the arc widening with each pass, until I notice the open case of tools set out on a stool, an assortment of post-mortem weaponry displayed upon the case's red velvet lining. And my sight presses farther, and I can see the man standing on the other side of the table, sleeves rolled up to reveal thickset arms, just the meat and muscle of a forearm topped off with a blunt-fingered hand, and no significant narrowing of the wrist in between. These same chapped hands flex and run together as the man walks around the end of the table. And now the full width of his figure is on display, pushing and puffing through the room like the prow of a steamer. By the time he arrives in front of Chissick, he's puffed himself out, his broad chest rattling with the effort of this short exertion.

"Julian," the stranger says, punctuating the name by pressing his fingers to the right side of his nose and sending a blast of more than air whistling out of his nostrils. "Wondered where you'd gone off to. Began to think we wouldn't be seeing you again." Before he's finished speaking, his deep-set eyes, nearly black in this poor light, flick towards me. "A friend of yours?"

"U-um, Miss Hawes?" There's reluctance in Chissick's voice, as if he'd prefer to continue his role as a screen and keep me hidden from any other set of living eyes. "This is Trevor."

And there lies the end of the introductions. No clue as to whether "Trevor" is the man's Christian name or surname, but Trevor doesn't waste time with the delicacies of politeness, and leans towards Chissick, thick shoulder to thin.

"She's a better breed than I normally see you cavorting about with, but who can account for sudden changes in taste and temper, eh?"

A quick look of apology from Chissick, and he clears his throat, his single vocal protest to this discussion of my appearance. "How are you getting on?"

"Oh, it's slow business, Jules. Very slow when you're not given much to work with. Lookee here." The tilt of his perspiring head is meant for his friend, but I fall into step behind the two of them, bearing the large man's wary gaze with as much equanimity as I can muster.

"Here." He leans towards Chissick once more, but his eyes are very much pinned on me. "You don't think she'd be better off waiting outside?"

"She'll be fine," he replies, without a glance in my direction. His attention is now held by the girl laid out on the table, his gaze switching away from her before returning to the vicious wound at her throat.

No wonder he can't bring himself to look away for more than a few seconds, with the dark line of severed flesh at once as hideous and attractive as a monster's grin. And, in point of fact, it does resemble a grin. Follow the shallow curve of it, widening slightly at the center in its path from ear to ear. No other injury is visible, the girl's skin a papery white, contrasted by the dark auburn of her tangled hair, the bluish cast to her lips. And—oh—those lips carry a smile of their own, don't they? Very subtle it is, too. A smile of contentedness, of peaceful dreams, and… well, there's something else, but I can't quite identify it. Could it be pleasure? No, no, no. It's less intense than that. It's more like relief. There's relief in the faint upturn of those lips, and I feel a shudder at what could've put it there.

"It all looks fairly standard, don't it?" Trevor chatters away, pausing to sniff deeply before shaking loose the contents of his lungs with a harsh, wet cough. "One quick slash across the throat and she's done. But you see here? I thought something was iffy when there wasn't any blood on her. Not a single drop, you see? And here..." The rattle of metal against metal, and he produces a pair of tongs from the wooden case beside him. Giving his right sleeve another push to prevent it from sliding down past his elbow, he uses the tongs to pinch one side of the injured flesh at the girl's throat, rolling back the loose flap of skin until the wound is over an inch wide.

"See that?" he says. "It's like it's all been cooked, the flesh seared to nothing, right from one end to the other."

"Cauterized," I say, my voice cracking at the end of the word.

Trevor looks down at me from the other side of the body. "That's another word for it."

What might be in the man's gaze at this moment, I can't say. If hard pressed, I'd wager that he regards me as an intruder upon this conference between himself and his old friend Chissick. And so I leave them to talk. Or more accurately, for Trevor to babble about bruising and asphyxiation while I move to the opposite end of the table, so that the girl's legs are stretched out towards me. Her slender ankles are relaxed, allowing her small feet to fall into the delicate curve of a dancer's arch.

Along the legs now, and up to the hips. Narrow they are, and this trivial fact lends me some small portion of relief. For if the hips are still narrow, it follows that the young woman has never borne children, and if she's never borne children, there are no empty mouths left behind, crying out for their mother.

The fingers are elegant, as are the wrists, designed to bear the weight of various rings and bracelets, though no doubt any jewelry she may have had the misfortune to wear at the hour of her death was pinched long before her body had begun to cool.

Over the arms now, the dip of the waist, rising again into the chest. And upwards, past the fatal wound at her throat, up to the hard lines of the jaw, the enigmatic smile, the nose, slightly upturned. If her eyes were open, I know they would be dark. A warm, rich brown.

Skimming the eyebrows, across the flat plane of her forehead, and finally to the roots of her hair, deep brown but laced with a reddish tint, a warmth of colour augmented by the golden glow from the lamps.

It's Chissick's voice that jars me from my speculative silence. I look over at him not because he's speaking loud enough to overpower my thoughts, but because the words are softened, the last note drawn out on something close to a whisper.

"Could you give us a moment? Please?"

He says this to Trevor, who appears to recognise this particular tone of request. "I'll be upstairs, eh?" A sharp bow of the head, and the man rolls down his sleeves, delaying his departure long enough to mutter one last remark in Chissick's ear. "Next time you've got a girl tagging along with you, leave her on the pretty side of the door. In my experience, not many of them are too keen on all this grisly stuff."

Chissick lowers his eyes. "I'll keep that in mind."

The door closes behind Trevor, and I imagine him hoisting his great weight to the top of the steps. Lord willing, they'll still be intact when it comes our turn to depart.

"Are you all right, Miss Hawes?"

Chissick asks me this, I hope not because of any ill look on my face, but out of pure concern. No doubt brought about by the fact that I'm currently clutching the lower end of the table, the centrepiece of which happens to be a recently deceased young woman.

"If you need a few moments," he says, full of care. "A bit of fresh air…"

Where he thinks I'll be able to fetch a breath of clean air without first putting a distance of at least twenty miles between myself and London, I'm not entirely sure.

"No, no. I am fine." And to prove it, I release the rough edge of the unfinished wood, relying on my own balance as I walk around the table, my right hand flicking away a fly that worries the base of my throat.

"Do you need to touch her?"

The question strikes me with such force, that I have no choice but to turn around. "I beg your pardon?"

He gestures towards the body with a jerk of his finger that could be mistaken for a nervous tic. Now that Trevor has left us, I notice a significant loss of composure in Chissick's behaviour. Why, he can't even look at the dead girl for longer than it would take him to blink. "I wasn't... I'm not sure of your methods, and I was wondering if you needed to lay hands on the body, or communicate with it in some way."

"With the body?"

"Yes."

"Mister Chissick, that is nothing but dead tissue. I'd be likely to obtain a more shocking revelation from a corn husk."

This remark draws a wince of pain from him, but it's fleeting, there and gone before I can convince myself it ever occurred in the first place.

"I am sorry," I say, sensing the need to apologise. But he's already shaken it off, ruddy hair tumbling into his eyes as he removes his hat and rakes his fingers across his scalp, all the way from his forehead and down to the scruff of his neck.

"So, what happens now?"

A good question, one that echoes through my mind as I swat at the persistent fly and allow my gaze to rest on the dead woman's face. "I am not exactly sure. To be honest, I've never done this before."

His eyes narrow, two flecks of blue staring out from a fringe of brown lashes. "What about all the years you spent on the stage, telling people everything, secrets no one else could have known."

"On stage," I repeat after him. "But unfortunately, I never found myself much in the habit of visiting mortuaries and striking up a chat with the recent arrivals."

His gaze finds its way to the ceiling. "Then why are we even here?"

"Because you asked me to come."

No reply from him now. Maybe a sigh, a touch of resignation. Or maybe I'm beginning to cast a shadow of my own feelings onto those around me.

"Where did you find the body?" I ask after a moment's pause. And listen to my voice! So serious, as if I'm diving into the first stage of an interrogation.

"Oh, I didn't find her. It was..." He blinks several times as he arranges his reply. "Upstairs," he says. "Two floors up. By the time I'd arrived, they were about to carry her down here. I mean, it wouldn't do much for business to leave her stretched out for everyone to see," he finishes with some bitterness.

"No, I would imagine not."

A few more steps, and I'm at the other end of the table. Several strands of the girl's hair trail over the edge, and without a thought, I sweep them up and return them to the mass of tangled waves resting beneath her head. "She was found in the open?"

"Actually, she was... she was in bed."

If it hadn't been for the hesitation, I wouldn't have any reason to take anything unseemly from that statement. But I know very well what sort of an establishment I'm standing in, currently teeming with life only a few feet above my head. The maze of rooms fitted out with rows of beds, a few extra coins purchasing a mattress large enough for two.

"But what about during your demonstrations?" His sudden switch to our former subject drags my gaze back to his face. "What did you do, when you had to know something? When you had to discover some vital piece of information?"

"Nothing, really." And I can see the disappointment in him before I've even finished speaking. "I would wait. Not much more than that."

His eyes narrow, and the hand holding onto his hat brushes across his thigh. It's the most petulant movement I've seen him make since our arrival here. "Do you feel anything?"

Inside my ill-fitting gloves, my hands flex. "No more than usual." And there, I can't even look him in the eye.

"I see."

He begins to pace the length of the room, the shadows growing and relenting, almost opaque as he nears the wall. When he turns, the poorly defined shapes flicker into a thin, grey mist on the sweating stone. "The girl..." He glances at the table, but for no more than a second. "Her eyes were open when they found her. That's what they said. Wide open. And even by the time I arrived, I thought she might blink if I touched her. The curious thing... she was still warm. Dead for how long, and there was nothing about her to make you think her heart wasn't still pounding away inside her chest."

He's struggling with the particulars, not as they must have been recorded down for posterity, tucked away in files and left to collect the dust of years, but instead as he sees them in his mind, his senses still reeling from the memory of the dead girl sprawled across the bed, one arm flung out behind her, both knees bent as if she'd lowered herself in prayer, and then simply collapsed onto her side.

"You couldn't believe there wasn't more blood," I say at last, before I pull back, before the image takes on any more clarity. My eyes flutter open, the scene still imprinted onto the underside of my eyelids, as if I'd spent the last minute staring at the midday sun. I allow the rest of the details to fade, the mingled odours of sweat and lust, the high burst of laughter from the woman's throat, her head thrown back in ecstasy.

And now Chissick looks down at me, those cool eyes picking up the soft colour from the lamps. Slowly, he nods.

"The wound is so deep. She should've been soaked in it."

But there wasn't a drop, was there? I glance at her throat, at the faint crust of blood at the corners of her torn flesh, already dried to the colour of rust, the vibrant red of her spirit having long since evaporated into the air.

I move away from the table, stopping when the confusion of

images stirring inside my head makes it difficult to place one foot in front of the other.

"I've seen this type of death before." A flicker of pain, and I grit my teeth against it. "Some years ago. Four bodies, but all of them carried the same wound across their throat, the same burnt flesh."

And it's then my resolve slips, and I begin to feel what I had been fighting so hard to hold at bay from the first moment Chissick led me across the doorstep. The malevolence that resides here, pervasive in the way it envelops me, until I put out a hand, reaching out into space as a new pressure breaks down the barriers I took so much trouble to construct around my mind. A moment more, and cool fingers find mine, lacing between my knuckles as Chissick joins me in my new position, trembling on my knees, in the middle of the cellar's dirt floor.

"Miss Hawes, what's wrong?"

But I'm already on my feet, skirts swirling around my ankles as I walk out of the room, into the darkness of the hall, one hand extended, tracing the solid lines of the wall until I feel nothing against my glove but open air. By the time my foot lands on the bottom step, Chissick has drawn level with me, both of us vying for space as he follows me to the top of the stairs.

"It was the landlord that found her," he says, reaching out to open the door before we've even arrived on the landing. "Scared the poor man out of his wits, I'd say."

"I am sure he's seen worse."

Upstairs now, and the light from the fireplace dazzles my eyes. The common room is still bustling, exhibiting a strength of activity I suspect will continue at the same energetic pace until several hours past the first light of dawn. But I've no time to stare at the revellers, not with Chissick at my side, ready to shield me from this roomful of lodgers. And the ringing in my ears pushes me forward, with greater force than Chissick's hand at the small of my back. To the right now, and up a narrow flight of stairs, closed in on both sides so it feels as if I'm ascending to the next floor through a chute. Left at the top of the stairs, and the pounding of my feet on the dusty floorboards, the swish of my skirts along the walls sounds so familiar to me. But it isn't a memory, merely an echo of the visions flashing behind my eyes. The light along these musty corridors is feeble at best, but the entity clawing its way into the edges of my mind has taken these turnings before.

There are countless doors, doors that open onto rooms with only a single bed, others that open onto dormitories, low cots and mattresses lining the walls. Though at least half of the spaces are occupied, there's no complaint from any of the boarders as we barge into a room at the rear of the building's top floor. The space seems small at first, until I notice the partitions set up between each bed, six feet of wooden panelling from the floor up, leaving less than a foot of open space between the top of the screen and the ceiling.

"This way," I say, and the sounds, the smells drive me forward. Between the rows of beds, I catch glimpses of bodies, most of them in various stages of undress, those that even bother with the removal of clothes before getting down to business, as they say.

We've not gone ten paces into the room when Chissick makes a sound of protest, his hand on my arm, pulling me back towards the door. Suddenly, a female voice from the far end of the room cries out, followed by the sound of a man grunting between muttered curses. At this, Chissick breaks into a fit of forced coughing, filled out with words meant to discourage me from going any farther.

"Tomorrow," he says, still tugging at my sleeve. "Tomorrow, we'll come back, when there's not... this isn't... you shouldn't be..."

But none of his statements reach completion. A jerk of my arm pulls me away from him, and I move halfway down the line of beds, not having to count, but knowing when I've arrived at the right one.

The mattress is hardly long enough to accommodate a full-grown person, let alone two. Roughly square in shape, its lopsided appearance stirs to life a dark curiosity inside of me, and I take a moment to wonder how many bodies might have spent their time on this particular bed.

"Miss Hawes?"

The light in here is dim, most of it coming from a small lantern fixed to a hook on the opposite wall. I blink several times, giving my eyes a few seconds to adjust.

"Miss Hawes." Chissick is beside me now, close enough that I can feel his breath skirting across the edge of my hat, tickling the few loose hairs that have managed to work their way free of the pins. "What is it? What do you see?"

Such a complex question, one to which I could give any number of replies and not for one of them be called a liar. I straighten my shoulders, grimacing at the feel of sweat building across my upper back.

"She was with a man." The statement feels redundant the moment I say it, but I continue talking as I organize the stream of thoughts now flooding my mind. "But you don't know where he is, do you?"

"No one saw him leave, or if they did, they can't connect him to her." His face contorts at the arrival of an unexpected thought. "Did he kill her? Is that what you see?"

"No." I shake my head, my eyes squeezed shut until I see little white lights behind the lids. "No, he's innocent. At least as far her death is concerned."

"What do you mean?"

A small shrug is all I can give him, my arms stiffened against the throbbing pain that ebbs and flows inside my mind. "Well, he wasn't exactly paying his attentions to her over a cup of tea, was he?"

He considers me for a minute. It's now, I think, more than ever, that he begins to doubt his initial confidence in me. "So you don't know who...?"

"I think you're getting ahead of yourself, Mr. Chissick. Referring to our murderer as a person may be allowing it more credit than it deserves."

"But there are witnesses. People who saw her come in with a man, saw her go upstairs. There was no one else. There was *nothing* else."

But I'm shaking my head, despite the hoarse whisper of his continuing arguments. Both arms are crossed over my chest, my shoulders sloping forward, until I can turn my head and bury my chin into the limp border of my collar. Shuffling along the side of the bed, I move closer to the wall, my shadow shrinking from something grotesque and monstrous into a dark mimicry of my own shape as soon as I'm near enough to the boards to touch them. And I do touch them. Inside my gloves, the sweat is pricking my palms, settling into the fine creases that line my skin. Two fingers are all I use, and do you see that tremble? Just there? It runs all the way to my shoulder, but it's only visible in those two digits, slightly bent, stretching out and retreating in that last instant before they make contact with the wall.

One touch, and I've merged with the shadow, no sliver of light between us.

"So you've come back," I say, my voice the slightest of whispers to cross my lips. "All these years... And here I was beginning to think you were nothing more than a nightmare."

I pull my fingers away from the wall, but the connection isn't completely severed. Floating like a mist, the shadow follows the path traced by my hand. For several seconds it hovers, nothing more. And then a twitch of movement at its edges, almost a shudder, writhing now, contorting itself into ghastly shapes as it pushes out against some invisible boundary damaged by the touch of my two fingers. I hold my breath, afraid that the lightest flow of air from my mouth will disturb the obscure cloud. But the mist is already fading, nearly transparent now, and I'm left with nothing but a disagreeable odour on my fingertips.

I'm still rubbing the offending substance off my gloves when I turn around. Chissick is only a few feet away, but he didn't notice what happened. And so I'm left to wonder where I have seen it before, to probe at my memories for any encounter with a darkness that moved with all the stealth of smoke and water.

"I am sorry, Mister Chissick." I force out the words, even though an apology is the last thing he must wish to hear. "I am sorry, but I believe she was overtaken," I say, choosing that word instead of the one that jumped to the forefront of my thoughts. "She was overtaken by something within herself, something that had invaded her, corrupted her."

I hear him breathe, and I imagine that if I were to turn around, it would be to witness a reluctance on his part to acknowledge my poorly spoken insinuations.

"Are you saying she was possessed?"

And there it is, that word I had taken such care to avoid gifting with the sound of my voice.

"That is what I was trying not to say, yes." I look at him, the majority of his face obscured by the shadows that surround us. I feel a temptation to ask if he believes such a wild assertion, but I think I may be more bothered by how quickly he might take to agreeing with me than if he were to instead denounce me as a liar and a fraud.

"By what?" he asks, and I can imagine the tenor of his thoughts at this moment, at how swiftly we have delved into the realm of demons and assorted other night terrors.

"By her killer," I tell him, without a worry as to whether or not he will believe me. "And I am quite sorry to say that it has killed before."

Chapter Five

The pain builds with such skillful slowness, such cunning, that I'm scarcely aware of its presence before I've already succumbed. It's a simple exercise tracing it from its origin. I can mark the first twinges to Chissick's visit earlier in the day, the yellowed newspaper article passed from hand to hand, the sound of his breathing, the thrush-thrush of his fingers turning over the battered brim of his hat. Each moment so innocuous on its own, but they all seem to thrive off one another, until they've succeeded in tipping me over the edge. The remainder of the day's events were mere trappings, existing simply to lend more of a polish to the acute ache that now grazes my forehead.

It's a severe drain on what reserves of strength I possess, not only to fight the affliction that claws its way into my skull, but also to keep Chissick from bearing witness to its effect on me. With lips pressed together, nearly disappearing between my teeth, my hands curl into fists at my sides, the presence of my gloves enough to prevent my fingernails from gouging the flesh off my palms. But soon enough, the throbbing subsides and the voices inside my head quiet to a low hum. A lull before the next wave strikes. What better time to make my excuses to our Mister Chissick and decamp for Mrs. Selwyn's before I'm overtaken?

A few words of apology from me, and he takes the liberty of escorting me from the lodging house, of bundling me into the first respectable-looking cab to pass our way. A hand on my waist, helping me inside, and then we're jostling through the poorly lit streets. The lamplighters—those young boys, always appearing when day and night give way to the other—have become more lax in their duties as the houses slowly empty, more and more Londoners escaping to the rumored safety of the less populated counties.

I'm deposited outside Mrs. Selwyn's front door, an awkward farewell tossed over my shoulder in my haste to get inside. For a moment, I fear Chissick might try to follow me, but something in my voice must prevent him. A minute passes before I hear the muffled tramp of horse hooves from the other side of the door, the rumble of wheels over the uneven pavement. Another minute, and I let out a long-held breath through gritted teeth. He is gone.

But it doesn't follow that I should now find myself to be alone. I allow my eyes to adapt to the change in light, the dim yellow glow of a few candles tucked into various crannies around the low-ceilinged room, and I can make out Mrs. Selwyn's lumpy form, poured into the threadbare armchair by the dying fire. A soft snore emanates from her throat, her head thrown back in a position that will no doubt cause her neck and shoulders some pain in the morning. Her grey lips twitch in the thick shadow that falls across them, and from underneath an eyelid, a sliver of white, shining like silver in the candlelight that bathes her forehead.

One of the candles flickers in protest as I move towards it. I wrap my fingers around the base of it and slowly pry it loose from the ring of spilled wax securing it to the tabletop. I've no doubt she'll miss it in the morning, that it will be my door she'll approach first. I can imagine, even now, the suspicions that will run through her head, how I must have used the candle for some nefarious purpose, perhaps to call up one of Satan's minions to do my bidding. I want to smile at the thought, but a fresh wave of pain invades my sinuses and travels down, finally settling at the base of my skull.

One hand holds onto the wall for support as I make my way up the stairs. I take care to keep my feet close to the wall, away from the boards most likely to announce my presence with an ill-timed creak. From somewhere above me, I hear the familiar thump of Mrs. Selwyn's cat leaping down from whichever corner he had secreted himself for the evening. The animal makes his appearance less than a minute later, slinking around the corner to take up a position on the landing, one ear twitching before he licks his paw and swipes the dampened fur across the top of his head.

I'm outside my own door now, the cat circling around my feet, never near enough to brush against my skirts, but always moving closer, finally pressing his ears back as he sniffs at a clump of refuse that clings to my hem. I push him away as I step inside, shutting the door with a snap before he can slip in between my ankles.

"Oh, God."

Strange how it's always His name I utter in my darkest moments, the same moments He chooses to remain so stubbornly silent. I set the candle on the seat of the chair, the flame illuminating the fine, gold lettering on the cover of the Bible that still sits there.

But the circle of light doesn't extend far from the chair. It touches the side of the bed, leaving the rest of the room in shadow. It's within the candle's feeble glow I take up residence, my gaze fixed on the flame. I stare at it until I see it when I blink. In this way, I tell myself, I'm able to push away the darkness. The voices relent. The pain in my head recedes to a dull throbbing. I lower myself to my knees, my forehead pressed against the rough edge of the chair, grinding upon the wood until I feel nothing but its unfinished surface scraping at the topmost layer of my skin.

I slumber for an hour, maybe two. A gasp from my lips, and I'm rushed into wakefulness, my lungs drawing in tremendous draughts of air while I fight to separate myself from the last vestiges of sleep. The candle is out, knocked over, I presume, judging by the drops of hardened wax spilled across the seat of the chair. I stare at it for some minutes, somehow willing the wick to flame back to life without any intervention from my hands. But nothing changes, no disturbance in the dim light of the room.

It's no easy chore to return myself to an upright position, my lithesome days being long behind me. A hand on my knee, the other on the chair, and—oh!—how I wish for a third to knead the kinks from the small of my back. A few steps, and I've arrived at the window, my face only an inch from one of the grimy panes. The street below glows with a tenebrous illumination, but I wonder how much the filthy glass is to blame for the ominous look of the neighbourhood before me.

I scrabble through my pockets for a handkerchief—I've so few left of them now—and latch upon one wadded into a stiff ball I have to shake out several times before it resembles a slip of fabric once more. A single corner is enough, and soon I've cleared a small circle in the glass, enough to peer through, though it takes another moment or two until my eyes become accustomed to this sudden clarity of sight.

I see the details now. I see the soft rise of the curb, hidden beneath the refuse that hasn't been swept away for over a week. A few feet on, and there's the pothole that catches nearly every wheel on its path towards the river. One short skip over the marred cobblestones and there are the buildings across the way, shoddier than the one in which I currently reside, one sagging wall supported by a few well-placed boards propped against the crumbling façade.

The shadows are thin tonight, as if they're busy seeking their own dark recesses for shelter. It's in the midst of one of these shades I notice a lone figure lurking, so still that his edges lose definition to the murk that surrounds him.

And am I correct in assuming that the man trespassing through the shadows is, indeed, a man? Perhaps not. There are no clues to give him away. All I sense is his presence, and—further down, if I dare to prod the consciousness hovering on the other side of the street—a newly-found purpose, something of a goal, and a bit of impatience to set himself to the task now laid out before him.

I turn away from the window, feeling strong in the conviction that my own presence there has gone unnoticed. The candle is still on the floor, so I return it to the chair, to the already hardened circle of wax on the wooden seat. My movements are careful, and especially quiet, considering the lateness of the hour. By the time I leave my room, all of my weight is shifted onto the balls of my feet, the better to move down the stairs without alerting Mrs. Selwyn to my departure. It's only a moment of pause I allow myself when I arrive in the stifling atmosphere of the sitting room. A single glance towards the front entrance is enough before I change my mind, and retreat in the direction of the kitchen and the rear entrance that resides there.

**

I walk for hours. I've taken to following the same route nearly every night, always culminating in a brief pause near the river, my eyes lighting on Southwark Bridge but my feet never crossing it. I turn, keeping near to the factories, so many more of them now with each passing season. Most of them congregate near the water, and all of them puffing great columns of steam and soot and foul-smelling filth into the air. Boats trawl the river as well, putting loudly, their engines hiccoughing into silence before slope-shouldered sailors curse and spit and bring them back to sputtering life. Even last week, I saw a cab trundling through Drury Lane, and I imagined the clop-clop of horse's hooves replaced by the rhythmic chug of an engine, loud enough to send a clanging vibration through the carriage. And all around me the buildings rise, steadily concentrating the sounds, shutting them in so I stumble upon little pockets of noise that echo off the newly erected walls of wood and brick and stone.

It's across one of these walls that my gloved fingers brush, running through a sheen of moistened grime. The morning fog still clings to the tallest rooftops, but the silver haze of the humid sky shines above it, promising another searing day without relief. It used to be that I could take a stroll in the early morning hours and feel the chill of the previous night soaking into my bones. But last night, as so many that preceded it, there was no chill. Only the cloying heat that has lingered over the city since early spring. And all of those little pockets that hold onto the noise also hold onto the warmth, so that each night proves hotter than the last, the sweat that clings to the skin never given a chance to evaporate.

Remarkable that I'm not witness to more people disregarding the proprieties of our day. Here they all are, decked out in hats and gloves, their collars fastened like steel bands around their boiling necks. Their blotchy faces and stained underarms do little towards selling this particular brand of stubbornness, and so it is that every day finds a few more daring to abandon yet another rule of etiquette, sleeves rolled several inches higher, waistlines slack without the support of a corset to cinch them in.

And here's another reason to come out in the morning, when the day is at its coolest, for all of London seems intent on taking advantage of this slight reprieve: only an hour past dawn, and the streets are swollen with traffic, everyone rushing to conclude business before the worst of the heat sets in. Surrounded by such crowds, I weave my way here and there, using my elbows when necessary, apologies tumbling out of my mouth with all the timing of a reflex. I move without direction, making turns on instinct, and yet each switch eventually returns me to more familiar terrain. Not as clogged with bodies as the paths behind me, but still boasting its share of morning dawdlers, most of them keeping to the shade where it's still plentiful.

Loiterers, they are. Taking advantage of the residual coolness the sun's rays have yet to banish from the pavement. Not quite a chill, as I'm certain we've not had one of those for quite some time. Unfortunately, the lack of pedestrians lends no additional freshness to the atmosphere here. The effect is enhanced by the lopsided buildings that cling to each other for support, every crumbling brick and half-rotted slat of wood carrying a muted shade of grey—not quite black— as if everything is in need of a good wash.

It's beside one of these ramshackle buildings—my own building, I must add, complete with its faded placard done in green and white, boasting fine rooms for rent—that a familiar figure has taken up residence. Judging by the scattering of cigarettes at his feet, he's been there for some time, one shoulder braced against the corner of Mrs.

Selwyn's front doorway before a kind of fidgeting takes hold of him
and he falls into a round of pacing. A few rapid steps away from me,
and this could be my only chance to escape unseen. Behind me, and
only a few steps to the right is another alley into which I could easily
slip. A shortcut across an abandoned courtyard and I could walk into
Mrs. Selwyn's through the same rear entrance I used only a few hours
before. But the cowardly route is not as appealing as it was before the
appearance of the sun, and by the time he turns round again, I'm
thrown off balance by a quiet thrill that ripples through me at the sight
of his face.

He takes another two steps before he notices me, and then one
hand makes an instinctive grab for his hat, the other hand flinging
away a half-finished cigarette, the sparks bouncing and flaring out as
it rolls into the clogged gutter.

"Miss Hawes." Barely twelve hours since I last saw him, and yet
Chissick appears to have aged years. Dark shadows underline his
eyes, and his suit hangs loosely from shoulders that seem to have cast
off every overabundance of flesh in order to combat the heat.

I glance at the ground, at the streaks his footsteps have left in the
dry grime that dusts the curb. "Have you been waiting long?"

A peculiar kind of cruelty, I think, starting off with a question such
as this. And not even "such" as this. This exact question. Because I
feel safe in assuming it was Chissick I saw hovering in the shadows of
the pre-dawn hours.

"Not long," he says—he lies—the quick dart of his eyes giving him
away. He sniffs and his fingers twitch. No doubt he regrets having
tossed away that last cigarette with such haste. "I've spent the last
few minutes trying to knock up the courage to call on you, to ask..."
His grip tightens around his hat. "But I don't think your Mrs. Selwyn
likes having me on the premises. I keep seeing her cat skulking
around, and..." Another twitch, almost a shudder, and I realise that on
this certain feline, our feelings have reached something of an accord.

"I wouldn't take it personally," I say. My fingers flutter for a moment, scissoring the air before tugging at the absurdly long sleeves of my dress. "I am sure that if Mrs. Selwyn could manage a way of living without having to cross paths with another soul... That is, unless she derives too much pleasure from inflicting herself on others."

A look of surprise on his face, that I could make a joke after all we've seen together. He clears his throat and runs the back of his hand across his jaw, currently sporting a full day's growth of reddish stubble. "Um, are you well, Miss Hawes?"

Such a simple question, and yet it renders me unable to string more than a handful of words together. "Hmm, no. I mean, yes. Sorry, I am well. Reasonably."

Another nod, and his jaw moves, his teeth seeking out the soft flesh on the inside of his bottom lip. "I've come to apologise," he says, and hesitates there.

I say nothing to help him along.

"Last night, taking you to see... It was wrong of me, you know. Never should've presumed that it was any sort of place... Terribly sorry."

For a moment, I'm adrift in the broken cadence of his apology. And then I remember the young woman on the table. As naked as the day she was born, and bearing a wound that has haunted me with the same insistence as my own shadow.

"There's no need. I am fine." And to prove it, a small smile. "It certainly wasn't the most horrid thing I've ever come across."

I say it as an assurance that nothing he's done was capable of scaring me, but an odd look crosses his face, and I wonder if I've offended him. His eyes dart this way and that, his gaze seeking but never finding. When he looks at me again, a flicker, and it wouldn't take more than the gentlest prodding to let myself into his thoughts, his fears so near to the surface I can feel them pushing outward.

I take a breath and step back from him. The distance does little to help.

"Mister Chissick," I say, clinging to the formality his surname affords. The tightening of his fingers around the brim of his hat attracts my eye, and I notice the brushed black of his suit, a poor choice of colour in this weather, the cut of it alone advertising its design for a cooler season. But he wears it with the air of one resigned to doing his duty. Let the temperature climb to unbearable heights; he will not change into a less sombre shade of clothing.

And now I'm remembering him as he looked in the cellar of the lodging house, the odour of death in the air: an earthy smell, but imbued with a sharpness that would have soon coated the walls themselves. And there he stood at the head of the table, his gaze rarely leaving the young woman's pale face, while his own expression was well hidden behind a mask I assumed he'd cultivated over too many years of preaching the Word of the Lord and the never-ending battle for the souls of his prospective congregation. But I'd been too distracted to notice what is now so glaringly obvious.

"You knew her."

His Adam's apple bobs in his throat as he swallows. "I beg your pardon?"

I shut my eyes, my breath held until I feel an ache in my chest. "The woman, on the table." My gaze flicks towards his, before I'm back to scanning the discarded cigarettes on the pavement. "I am sorry. It's none of my concern."

He steps forward, still several paces away, but this simple movement acts as a confirmation, even before he opens his mouth to speak.

"She was..."

But whatever she was is lost as his mouth quivers into silence. It must be too soon, the memories too fresh to be brought up in conversation with a person he hardly knows. And perhaps he wonders if I already have access to these memories, and that the act of speaking them out loud would simply transfer them into a state of redundancy.

"I am sorry," I repeat the apology, this time for his loss, more than for any breach in conduct on my part.

An awkwardness springs up between us, neither one of us chancing a look at the other, the pavement, the pedestrians, the burnished sky itself all striving to hold onto our attention, until Chissick breaks the silence, his voice low at first, but gaining strength and resonance by the final word.

"Miss Hawes, I take it you've not eaten yet this morning?"

He must see the dumbfounded expression on my face, but he presses on, his obvious embarrassment cloaked by a torrent of words that will not cease, no matter how much his various shufflings and twitchings beg for silence. "I've not had anything since before we... and if you're not you're not otherwise engaged..." He looks up quickly, already wincing in anticipation of the rejection he knows must be on its way.

"Thank you," I say, and resist the mild temptation to refuse. "I'd be honoured."

Again, his fingers worry the worn edge of his hat, before he sighs and claps it on his head. When he holds out his arm for me, I falter.

"It's just a bit of a walk," he says. "I hope you don't mind."

Chapter Six

He holds his knife and fork at odd angles, as if he's afraid to smudge the cutlery with his fingerprints. The first bite disappears between his lips, barely given the softest of chews before it passes to the back of his mouth and down his throat. The second bite follows with almost the same swiftness of the first, but by the time the third forkful of sausage is raised to his lips, he pauses, suddenly conscious of my gaze upon him.

His shoulders are the first to react, shifting beneath the stiff lines of his coat. The movement continues down the length of his spine, until he has nothing left but to slide forward to the edge of his seat. One elbow leaves the tabletop, the other one suspended in the air beside him, retreating to his rib cage before he becomes aware of this new discomfort and it pushes out once more. Finally, the third bite is done away with, his jaw working slowly at first, his body settling into the awkward pose of one not accustomed to dining across from another person.

The dining house is small and sweltering, and the waitress weaves leisurely from box to box, carrying a meagre stack of plates, their steaming contents hidden beneath metal covers. I pick up my fork and chase a handful of peas along the rim of my plate, finally stabbing one of them before it rolls off the edge and leaves a greasy stain on the tablecloth. The custom is sparse at this time of day, but I would've expected more people to use the house as an escape from the heat. As if guessing my thoughts, Chissick sweeps his fork from side to side, a new potato glistening on the tines.

"It's a bit empty in here today." He takes a bite, chews thoughtfully, and washes it down with a swallow of ale and porter.

When he speaks again, his voice is considerably lower. "You'd think it would light a fire under their bottoms..."Another sweep of the fork—now empty—takes in the whole of the dining house's employ, most of them chatting quietly among themselves now that our meal has been delivered. "...not having as much custom to keep them occupied, but..." He stabs another potato, waits for the grease to drip from the crisp skin. "I'm not a man of business. Never had a head for it. Fortunately or unfortunately."

It's so quiet in the dining house, aside from the muttered conversation some tables away, that I almost feel as if we've trespassed in a private home.

"I wonder how long until there's no one left from here to Blackfriars," I say, and tease a parsnip with my knife.

So engrossed is he in slicing a large cut of lamb into pieces, it takes him a minute or two to acknowledge me.

"I'm sorry? What are you talking about?" He raises his arm to his mouth, ready to wipe a trail of gravy from his chin to his sleeve, but he sees me and so discreetly snags a corner of the tablecloth and uses that instead.

"Hmm, no matter."

And now I see my mistake, that I've succeeded in nothing more than garnering his interest. His eyes wide, he studies me with renewed curiosity.

"What is it, Miss Hawes?"

I blink and swallow a chunk of ham that had formerly lodged itself between my molars. "It's not so much of a secret, really. I suspect the papers are trying to keep it quiet, wise on their part as it would avoid stirring up any kind of panic. But it's not as if one can hide dozens, hundreds, maybe even thousands of people packing up and..." I stammer beneath his gaze as I search for the most fitting phrase. "High-tailing it out of London."

"How bad is it?"

Not a smidgen of doubt from him as to the veracity of my

statement, only the slightest hesitation, and even that might have been missed if I hadn't taken to watching for his reaction.

"It must be the heat," I say, and I'm fully aware of how well I've deflected his query with only the first words to come from my mouth. "It started soon after, I suppose. I noticed a few people here and there, the poorer classes mostly, packing up and simply walking away. But I see more of them, still not many, but they remind me of..." I draw in a breath, whether for fortification or to allow myself some time to think, I'm not precisely sure. I wrap my fingers around my fork and drag it through a mangled pile of summer cabbage. "They want to escape. As if London is a sinking barge and they want to be gone before the rest of us are submerged."

He leans forward, his elbows finding purchase on the tabletop. And if it weren't for the great slab of wood between us, I wonder how close he would be at this moment.

"And why are you still in London, Miss Hawes?"

The expression he presents is one that is all awkwardness with a touch of innocent curiosity. I've come to regard the directness of his gaze with some level of composure, though my preference is still to keep my audience at a distance.

"Because I am not the sort to run away. I fear I've become more of a harbinger, of sorts."

"A harbinger?" His mouth works around the word, tasting it, before a swallow sends it down for further digestion. "So you're not afraid?"

"Are you?"

"The people I see every day, I see fear in their eyes. And I think they may know something the rest of us do not." He lowers his chin first, and his eyes release mine, his lashes fluttering as he gnaws at the inside of his cheek. "I don't mean to imply that you don't know. I beg your pardon, Miss Hawes."

"Please, don't."

"I'm sorry?"

"Apologise, Mister Chissick." I rub the narrow ridge between my eyes with the side of my thumb. "You don't need to apologise. I appreciate your concern, but I am sure it would take a great deal for anything you say to cause me the slightest bit of offence."

His mouth moves, another apology already forming at the back of his throat, but he bites down on it, sends his eyes back to his own plate. And there sit the two of us, gazing into our platters as if we were both divining the future from an amalgam of gravy and lamb fricassee.

"Miss Hawes," he begins, so softly that I fleetingly wish he would begin every speech with the pronouncement of my name. "What did you mean last night? When you said that this entity of yours..." He shakes his head, as if attempting to knock loose the desired words from inside it. "Who else has died because of it?"

I set down my fork, clasp my hands in my lap. "If you've perused enough of the newspaper columns associated with myself, then I am sure you've seen mention of a certain tragedy in my past."

"A tragedy?" He shakes his head, but only a few seconds pass before I see his brow clear, his eyes widen slightly as they fix on my face. "Your family?" And before I can respond, he ploughs forward, leaving his previous question behind. "But the reports of what happened were so wildly varied, yet most of them agreed that there must have been an intruder—"

"There was no intruder. At least, none of the sort your imaginings can concoct."

"And you're sure it's the same?"

"Yes." And I pronounce the word just so, cutting down all further inquiries.

We both attend to our meals, eating with greater haste now that the food has cooled, taking what flavour we can before we're both scraping our forks across empty plates.

He remains seated at the table once his plate is removed, the set of his shoulders revealing no immediate intention to depart. Before him, his hands clasp and unclasp, and I wait for the words I can already sense a mere moment before they emerge from his mouth.

"That night," he begins, his chin lowering an inch as he speaks. "How did you...?" His eyes close for a moment, longer than a mere blink. "How is it you were unharmed?"

My own hands disappear beneath the edge of the tablecloth, my thumb sliding over the scars on my wrist until the movement takes on something of a ritual. A memory then, of a woman who briefly shared a room with me during my stay at the hospital in Chelsea. She was a Catholic, and even now, I can still hear the soft click of the beads they allowed her to keep, every attempt to remove them from her person only culminating in a violent outburst towards the nurses or her fellow patients. But the moment the beads returned to her grasp, the passion subsided, and she sank once more into a state of docility, her fingers working over the small wooden spheres while a subtle whisper from her lips accompanied the soft strike of the beads against one another.

Once more, my fingers sweep across the damaged skin of my arm, before I force myself to place my hands on the tabletop, my fingers splayed, my short, bitten nails visible.

"I don't know." It is a disappointment, I'm sure, to hear such a reply. For a moment, I wonder if I've lied to him without entirely realising it. And so I take a moment to remind myself, to assure myself that even a decade later, there is still a frightening void in my knowledge of what occurred after my mother guided me into the parlour that evening.

"Did you swoon, at the time? Perhaps you were rendered unconscious, perhaps you didn't see—"

"No," I say, my head shaking from side to side. I keep my gaze fixed on the backs of my hands, on the dry, damaged skin stretched taut between each tendon. "No, my senses were all in fine working order that night. I saw everything." I hear the faint murmur of voices around us, in the dining room, from the street on the other side of the wall, from the entire city, a great hum that threatens to rise to an unbearable pitch until I dampen it down.

"I'll take you home," Chissick says after another minute has passed. He wipes his mouth once more, his hat firmly settled on his head.

Together we leave the dining house, pausing for a moment on the edge of the pavement, both pairs of eyes watching the display of life that parades before us. Tattered and sagging, drooping beneath the humidity that swoops through the alleys, long lines of men, women, and children shamble. Women clutching parcels and children, men ducking their heads as they walk, hands raised to their hats, as if the subtle hunching of their neck and shoulders will be enough to combat the heat that pours down from above. And as if the city itself is in league with the abominable weather, the streets absorb the warmth, changing it into something of its own creation before returning it to the air, so that there's no escape from the heat, neither from above nor below.

He touches my elbow as we round the corner, a brief show of familiarity on this crowded street. Around us, everyone's eyes are already diverted, focused on the uneven pavement, on the perspiring backs that trudge along ahead of them. In front of Mrs. Selwyn's, we pause a second time, and I look down and notice the absence of used cigarettes littering the pavement, already swept away and replaced by a scattered mess of horse droppings.

I hesitate at the door, aware of what awaits me on the other side: Mrs. Selwyn, falling victim to the soporific effects of her darkened parlour, while a grey feline stalks from one corner to another, fixing its gleaming eyes on each new trespasser with a look that must make them aware of every misdeed committed since the last time they crossed the threshold.

No wonder I turn around, reluctant to reach this moment of farewell. Chissick hovers behind me, his weight resting on the balls of his feet, ready to move as soon as someone gives him the word. But it's something behind him that draws my eye, across the street, a man prostrate in the doorway of a public house.

I assure myself that he is not dead, but I cannot stop my gaze from leaping to the poor man's exposed throat, to the papery skin marked with grime, but still intact.

"Miss Hawes," he says, and at that precise moment, the sound of my name on his lips sparks to life a frisson of discomfort. But, no. It's something else, if I would only take the trouble to probe a bit deeper into the mire of my own querulous thoughts. "I've no doubt I've stepped into something beyond my level of expertise. But any assistance you might find yourself in need of, I offer it. As humble as it may be."

I feel the discomfort pass, and I raise my chin to meet his gaze. "Thank you."

His mouth quirks at this unanticipated response, and he runs a finger around the edge of his collar, separating the damp fabric from his skin. "Well, I'll leave you. But know that if you need to contact me, you can leave a note with—"

I place a hand on his arm, my fingers nearly hovering over the brushed wool of his jacket. My touch is so light, but it is enough to halt his words, his gaze seeking mine expectantly. "You wish to help me?"

"Of course," he says. "With anything, everything you may need."

I could almost smile, I think, at his eagerness. "I cannot ensure your safety. In fact, the more time you spend with me, I fear the greater risk you bring down upon yourself."

He shakes his head, his mouth already working, no doubt with assurances he has no fear for himself, only for my well-being. And so I tighten my grip on his sleeve, my fingers pressing into his coat, into the flesh of his arm, all of my strength going into that one movement until I see his jaw tighten and flinch at the pain of it.

"This is not human," I tell him, my fingers unrelenting. "All of the tales in your Bible, of monsters and demons, flames and hellfire raining down from above..." I remove my hand, my fingers flexing as the flow of blood returns to them with an unpleasant prickling sensation. "Do you understand?"

It is the faintest of tremors that passes through his arm, the same arm I returned to his keeping.

"There will be more deaths," I say, careful not to look away from him.

A sharp exhale escapes from his mouth, a breath I had not realised he had been holding. He nods, only once, but it is enough.

"If you're sure," I begin, and feel my spine stiffen inside my sweltering dress. "Would it trouble you to postpone our parting for a short while longer? If we're to do this properly, there's someone I need to see."

Another breath slides out of him, his gaze dropping to the pavement for the briefest of moments before his eyes return to meet mine from beneath the brim of his hat. "Anything you may need," he says, repeating his promise as he gestures with his elbow so I might simply reach out and slip my arm through his own.

Chapter Seven

Sissy sits on a wooden stool, the small seat rendered nearly invisible by her girth. One swollen hand reaches forward, floats over the tray of wooden tiles laid out across her lap, her fingers tapping out a melody I don't recognise. Her head bows down, the limp edge of her bonnet obscuring her face, before she raises her eyes again and fixes me with a pitiless stare.

"Still not sleeping well, hmm? Have you given laudanum a try?" A small smile, the pockets of fat in her cheeks folding upward.

"I am no stranger to the effects of laudanum," I tell her. "And, no, it doesn't help. In fact, it only makes matters worse."

Beside me, Chissick shifts from one foot to the other, his limbs taking on a restless quality now that the full heat of the day is upon us. "Miss Hawes," he begins, and is forced into repetition by my lack of attentiveness. "Miss Hawes, I don't mean to doubt you, but who is this?"

I turn my full gaze upon him, and he founders into silence. "Sissy is an old friend of mine, since before I ever set foot on the stage."

Sissy herself says nothing to this, only a muffled laugh seeping out between tightly sealed lips. The tiles slide and clatter about the edges of her tray as she leans to one side, her jaw working around a great wad of fluid she ejects from her mouth in a thick stream. I could be disgusted by such a performance, but the backdrop in which we find my old friend is no less unsavoury. The back of her head rests on a brick wall, stained with rivulets of a substance many times more putrid than the liquid that shoots from her mouth. As she rolls her head from side to side, I wonder if the transference of grime from the wall to her bonnet is equal to the amount of filth she gives in return.

And now that her mouth is empty, her tongue sweeps across her upper lip, clearing away the film of perspiration settled there.

"I'd invite you in, some place out of the way of the sun and all, but it's as hot under doors as without, so we'll stay round here, if you don't mind."

I nod in agreement with this garbled suggestion, though the sweat clings to my own back, and my head pounds beneath the sunlight. Seeking some portion of shade, Chissick moves closer to the wall, but not so near that any part of his suit brushes against it.

"You look less a lady than the last I saw of you," she remarks, her gaze travelling the length of me once more. Her right eye is cloudier than I remember, covered with a thin, milky substance that seems to swirl and settle as she tilts her head this way and that. And beneath the milkiness, small veins of blue, so I'm left with the disturbing sensation of being surveyed by a marble. "Smart, that is. Lesser attention drawn to yerself, the better. And with your history, I can't say that you'd be wantin' any uniforms drawn to the sight of someone like you wandering down here."

"I wasn't aware the police still bothered to come down this way," I say, with a glance that takes in the narrow alley behind me. Under the light of day, the rough men who lounge in doorways, the battered children screeching around corners exact no fear from me. Though there are shadows enough to make me pause, and I wonder how those shadows, those dark forms would react should I place my fingers upon them. Would they writhe and pull away from me? Would the smell of sulphur cling to my gloves for several hours afterward? Or would they remain fixed to the crumbling brick walls, only growing longer and spreading out, coating everything when the sun finally sinks behind the rooftops?

"Oh, we seen them from time to time. They don't like to make too great a show of it, but I know when they've taken to skulking round. Picked up Sally Bett's girl last week. You remember her, I'll wager?"

"Can't say that I do."

"Well, there never was much to recommend that one," she says with obvious distaste. "But here it's gotten to the point some of us can't make an honest living giving people what they been asking for."

I could venture to inquire as to her precise definition of the word "honest", but we've already trundled too far from the main point, and my mind aches with the realisation that as Chissick busies himself with an encore performance as my bodyguard, it will be my task to drive it back on course.

"Sissy, I've brought my friend here—"

"Oh, deigning to associate with the common folk, are we? But you're looking poorly of late, so perhaps I should say that this latest taste in company is something of an improvement, eh?" A wretched smile pushes up the corners of her mouth, and a leer—or something possibly interpreted as such—crinkles the corner of her working eye. "Just a friend, now? Not a husband or family or not?"

"A friend, Sissy. That is all."

She grumbles at this, because she knows she will win no more information from me, at least not anything she can achieve from something as plain as common conversation.

"So she's gone and taken up a friendship with you, hmm?" Her attention flits towards Chissick before the edge of her bonnet succumbs to the pull of gravity and flops down in front of her face, momentarily protecting the both of us from her unsettling gaze. "And what do you have to say about this heat, Sir?" She pronounces this last word with a hint of audible disdain. "Quite an unnatural occurrence, I'm sure you'd say. Perhaps it's the end of days upon us, eh? Of course, you'd know all about such apocalyptics and prophecies, what with your background."

I hear Chissick's slight intake of breath, but my hand on his arm prevents him from goading her further. "I don't need your party tricks, Sissy." My words bring her good eye back towards me, but the milky one remains fixed on some indefinable place beyond Chissick's shoulder. "And you can stop rooting around in his head, thank you very much. His thoughts belong to him and no one else."

This causes her to shut both of her eyes tight, and when she opens them, they're both directed towards me, pinning me in place. Beside me, Chissick steps forward, his left boot squelching in something that sends aloft an unsavoury odour. He looks down at Sissy, his gaze at once expectant and yet filled with censure.

"Out with it," Sissy says, pre-empting any speech either of us may have been about to make, while her swollen fingers hover over the tiles. "I've no patience for the niceties, all of that drawing room chatter you lot go and pride yourselves on."

Chissick's mouth opens and closes, his lungs unable to draw in a single breath of air. Clearing his throat, he glances at me, waits for my nod, and begins again. "Miss Hawes tells me you might be able to help us, that you have a gift," he says. "I assume not much unlike that of Miss Hawes."

A curse from her, but the laughter that rumbles through her chest dulls its blasphemous edge. "Very unlike that of our Miss Hawes here, and you'd be a wise un' to note the difference."

"Yes, well. We were wondering if you could... I mean, if you would..."

"Erghghm." That is the sound, at least, that erupts from Sissy's throat before she smacks her bosom with the flat of her hand. "I take it Our Miss Hawes hasn't been able to accomplish much thus far?" she finally warbles after a moment, her voice skipping over a few of the less important notes.

"On the contrary, she's been quite—"

"Quite, yes. I'd say that about sums her up." Leaning back, her bonnet flattens on the wall. Her right hand hovers over the tiles and her thumb taps on two letters in succession: R and Y.

"They blame us, you know," says the old woman, lowering her voice to a rasp that scrapes wetly along the back of her throat. And before either of us can ask as to which "they" she refers, she presses onward. "Accusing us of gettin' in, of corrupting the Queen, as if she ain't skilled at doing enough of that all by her own. And there's this weather, saying we've gone and made it hot, because anything hot must be doing with the devil." She shifts and spits, the thin legs of her stool creaking in protest. "I wonder what all they'd be chattering about if it had gone and stayed cold all summer. Ice and snow in July, hmm? Wonder what they'd be saying then."

Chissick takes this opportunity to lean quite close to me. There is a strong smell of sweat from him, and the air about us is so warm that when his breath touches my cheek, I feel no additional rise in temperature.

"Can we trust her?" he asks in a low whisper.

"No more or less than anyone else."

"Yes, but if she steers us wrong..."

"Ah, right. Of course." At once, I realise that my comment does little to alleviate his fears. And so I place a hand on his forearm, my touch gentle. "Don't worry. You can trust her, for the most part."

"Ay, you can trust ol' Sissy!" she barks, following it with a wet laugh that ends in a round of coughing. "Especially when this one doesn't have all the answers," she adds with a gesture towards myself. "Oh, Marta thought you could be stronger, always wanted to be pushing you, but... *tch*... you knew when to rein things in." Her milky eye swims before seeming to fix on me. "Better for all of us, that way."

Beside me, a brief movement. Chissick has returned to fidgeting, his collar now the victim of much smoothing and straightening. But the poor thing won't react to his ministrations, the heavy fabric too soaked with sweat to do more than take on an extra crease or two.

"You're not as close as you used to be," Sissy says, drawing my attention back to her. "Oh, your head used to be a thing. Couldn't breech it with a hammer and chisel, but no, you're not near as close as you used to be. You've gone and let something slip through. Careful, careful."

She taps another tile. Her thumb still pressed to it, she opens one eye, dull and milky in the shade of her bonnet, and peers down at the letter.

"A," she sighs, and wrinkles her nose. "Never much liked that one."

At moments such as this, I find no other option but to settle my heels into the ground. The woman is determined to take her time, to leech away one's patience, until her victim is left grasping at politeness, giving her the benefit of the doubt that these protracted visits are simply her crooked way of winning a few minutes of much sought-after companionship. I don't allow myself to assume that she enjoys this, that she is revelling in the power, the control she believes she is wielding. But all we need is a few clues, something I don't trust my own mind to provide.

"But it don't bother," she says, her jaw already working around the next batch of saliva. "I tell you, it don't bother, not one bit. Those lads from Scotland Yard come in here, waving their sticks about, acting like they're doing us a service, like I'm not the one paying to keep their collars starched, but it don't bother. A few more weeks, and there won't be any of us left to carry away. You seen the way people are leaving town? Well, I'd leave misself, if it wasn't for my..." Her feet wriggle out from beneath the stained hem of her dress, her ankles thick and swollen, flesh spilling out the tops of her ill-fitting boots. "...condition," she finishes, with a delicacy that deserves some credit.

Slowly, the various parts of her face shift into a more thoughtful expression, and I'm reminded of another time she wore such a look. Her eyes were clearer then, and both of those shining orbs graced me with an appraisal that seemed to see through all my layers of clothing, my skin, my flesh, all the way down to something I'm still not quite convinced can even be seen by the naked eye. And I'm convinced she saw it that night.

"But you'll stay here," she says. "The both of you, you will." And she says it again, nodding to herself, before her right hand turns a circle through the air and her meaty thumb alights twice on the next letter on the tray: L

"Oh, it's that, is it?" She pushes at her bonnet, wipes away the sweat gathered in her eyebrows and shakes the moisture off the tips of her fingers. "Ryall," she mutters, as if she's exercising her ability to speak for the very first time. Her good eye settles on me. "So it's a Lord that's gone and gotten hisself tangled up with this. He is a Lord, ain't he?"

I swallow over my next breath, currently lodged in my throat. "Yes. Yes, he is."

"Lord Ryall," she pronounces, her fleshy lips disappearing between her teeth before spreading into a grotesque smile. "Mmm, I remember him. Never met him. My sort didn't run in circuits with the likes of his, but you were up there for a turn, hmm? In the upper echelon, as they say?"

Chissick makes a move to speak, but a shake of my head, too slight to even worry the loose tendrils of hair plastered to my neck, and he releases his breath into the air.

In the ensuing silence, Sissy's hand returns to its place above the tiles, hovering for a full minute before the fingers pick up a rhythm she seems to pull out of the air. Her clear eye closes, and the clouded eye fixes on nothing as she strikes one tile after another, her movements lacking hesitation this time around.

"Ca-pal-di." She tests the word that her fingers spelled out. "Capaldi. Funny sounding thing, hmm? That ring any bells in your head?"

"I don't..." But I find I'm unable to finish the thought. I notice Chissick's fingers, frozen in place at his collar, his entire form rigid, but his eyes blinking rapidly—squinting, almost—before his gaze settles on something far away.

A push from me is all it takes. The lightest of touches, and there, in the back of his mind, teasing with the faintness of a childhood memory, I hear that word spoken above his head. And then I realise that it's not a word, but a name. And yet the memory continues to tease, to frustrate, until I'm forced to swear under my breath as the knowledge, just out of reach, fizzles and finally slips away.

"Oh, pret-ty words from you!" The old woman laughs, or wheezes, or makes an attempt at one before the weight from her chest presses her into the other. She coughs once more, wipes her mouth with the back of her hand and gasps out another chuckle. "Never thought I'd hear a lady say such things."

"I rather doubt there should be any comparison between my behaviour and that of a true lady, if indeed any such creature exists." I reach for one of the tiles. Small, flat, perhaps square at one time, but over the years the corners worn down to something not quite round. The letter is a simple mark, crudely gouged into the pale surface of the wood, filled in with black paint that chips away with a quick flick from my fingernail. "What about you?" I ask, purposely ignoring Chissick, while I turn the tile between finger and thumb. "Does that name mean anything to you?"

A twist of her mouth, and a sputtering sound that could be another shot of laughter. But, as if recalling her last show of merriment, she stifles the breath with a quick thwack of her fist against her chest. "Names don't mean a thing to me. Never have. And besides, it's not from out of my head. I'm only here untangling that mess you've got up there between your own ears."

She reaches up, tugs at her bonnet, and scrapes the back of her wrist across her nostrils. The fidgeting continues for another minute, but all the while, her gaze flutters back to the tiles, her eyes seeming to reflect each letter in the dark center of her pupil.

"I hear Marta's gone and nabbed herself a new girl. You seen her yet?"

I shake my head, then speak when I notice she's not looking at me. "No, I haven't had the pleasure."

"You should, you know. Check in on her, like. Make sure Marta knows what she's dealing with this time around. I'm always worryin' about her, wonderin' if she's gettin' herself mixed up in things that are too much for her." A meaningful glance in my direction. I bear it for as long as I can stand, finally turning my attention to the crumbling edge of the wall behind her.

"I've no doubt that Marta is quite capable of taking care of herself."

"Hmm, right. Quite capable." I look over to watch her nod, her chin disappearing into the ring of fat that hides most of her jaw from view. "You know, you look like hell, if you don't mind my saying." She chews at the corner of her mouth, her blackened teeth nearly indistinguishable from her rotten gums. "Is it still your head?"

Instinctively, I touch my forehead, my thumb burrowing into the ridge above my nose, grazing the abrasions left from the night before.

Her wiry eyebrows push upwards, nearly disappearing beneath the brim of her bonnet. "You've been having your pains again?"

At this, Chissick shakes himself from his trance and returns his full attention to me. "Pains, Miss Hawes? What does she mean? Are you all right?"

"Oh, don't you go worryin' yerself over her," Sissy tells him. "The Four Horsemen will come and go and she'll still be here, livin' and outlastin' all of us."

I try not to dwell on the bleak picture she paints with these words. I should be accustomed to it by now. The circuitous route her conversation takes, circling around the main topic with the same cunning a hunter uses to stalk his prey.

"Is it the voices, as well?" This spoken in such a bland, informal manner, as if she's about to pronounce her thoughts on the day's weather, or the state of this morning's porridge. "Have they come back?"

"I wasn't aware they'd ever left."

"Oh, well." She extends her hand over the tray, fingers rising and falling slightly, floating on a breeze that stirs nothing but those five plump digits. "You disappeared for a time, hmm? Heard Marta went and had you put away in one of them asylums, you know. The kind for folks who aren't sick in the body, but rather sick somewhere else." She grins and taps the side of her head with a greasy finger. "Only started to thinking maybe the spirits had gone and abandoned you, given you something of a reprieve, or the like. Either that, or I figured you'd up and tossed yourself off a bridge." She spits over her left shoulder. "One of the two."

I remove myself from the area around the miniature puddle she's produced, only to step in something else that slips beneath my heel. My adjustment allows me a moment to arrange what I want to say next. It's not an easy subject to broach, especially with Chissick so near, but after discarding several introductions, I take a deep breath and jump right in.

"Sissy, have you seen many bodies lately?"

"Bodies, hmm?" She closes one eye, leaves the milky one to its watery inspection of the ether. On her mouth is a small smile. Here's the main topic, finally arrived, after how many half-starts and diversions. "Not very specific, are we? Can't do much with that. Are we talkin' about what we see in our heads, or what's out there for the rest of the world?"

My fingers close around the small tile, turn it over, palm it again. "Dead bodies, Sissy. Real, dead bodies. Slashed across the throat. And the skin there, well... burned, I guess would be the best way of putting it."

She pulls a face, her lips stretching back in disgust. "That doesn't sound very nice."

Chissick clears his throat. "I assure you, it's not."

"Hmm, no. No, I ain't laid eyes on nothing like that." Her hand stills, but the fingers remain tense, poised even. "But there's something else, hmm? No, no, don't go shutting yerself up, trying to fill up all them chinks you've got forming in that head of yours. Just let me see it. Let me feel it. There's more to this you're not telling me."

"No." I take a step back. "You've done all you can. We've taken up more than enough of your time this morning."

I toss the tile back onto the tray. The strength of her glowering is potent as she picks up the small letter and sets it to rights with the others.

Her hesitation is nearly enough to undo me. Her eye, the good one, glazes over for a moment, maybe two. Her fingers stretch out, the skin pulled taut across her palm while her joints bend backwards as far as the various bones and ligatures will allow. Another moment, and her eyes find mine, both of them pinned to my face, and I find I cannot blink, I cannot even breathe beneath that merciless gaze.

"Then you should be off with yerself."

I swallow, a laborious movement that seems to sap every reserve of strength I possess. A few more seconds, and I can blink again, even turn my head away, but I'm too late. She has succeeded in breaking through, and she has seen inside of me, located that small kernel of darkness that only she bore witness to all those years ago.

She shifts her weight. Not to stand, for I doubt she's moved from the stool since before sunrise, but simply to turn her shoulders, her head tilted towards the alley, eyes narrowed, seeking each face that passes by for the prospect of a new customer.

It is during this moment of reprieve I reach for Chissick's arm, my fingers grasping a small fragment of his sleeve. But Sissy is already ahead of me, and her grasp on the tail of his coat is much stronger than my own.

"What about my payment?" she demands, the question directed at me while she holds Chissick as a hostage.

"Pardon me," Chissick begins, but I cut him off, reach into my pocket and retrieve a few coins, tossing them onto her tray before I can get a good look at them. His coat now released from her grasp, Chissick turns to leave. A glint catches my eye, and I realise that in my haste, I've gone and given away my last sovereign.

Sissy's lips twitch as she regards the money, and I fear she might spit on the ground near my feet, but she holds onto her overflow of saliva for the moment. Instead, she winks at me. Or perhaps it is merely a spasm of the muscles that frame her damaged eye. And then she does something that surprises me. She reaches out to touch me. But worse than that, she grabs my wrist, her fingers making quick work of pushing back my sleeve, exposing my scarred forearm to daylight.

"You've already tried to escape once, didn't you?" Her whisper is a contrast to the harsh pressure of her thumb, tracing the pale welts that slash across my wrist. "But it's not in your power to go dyin' whenever you like." She laughs, a thick sound that claws its way out of her throat. "You know, I'd go with thinking you being more afraid of death than you are." Her fingers slide, my wrist twists, and she releases my arm, lets it fall back to my side. Slowly, she shakes her head. "But you're not like us, hmm? Never was, I don't think. The things you hear, the things you know. I always told myself there was something a bit scary about you."

I have trouble keeping up with what she says, so I calm myself with the lie that it's all gibberish, every word of it. This is what I tell myself. That she's descended into a train of thought incomprehensible to anyone beyond herself, and yet I find I cannot look away. Not when that milky eye of hers fixes on my face with such a forward glare, as if that one eye, clouded and swirling, leaking fluid that dries to a crust on her eyelashes, has the ability to commune with the entities fighting to be heard inside my head.

"Oh, it's no doing, struggling like you are." She exhales and her head sinks back onto the brick wall, the strings of her bonnet disappearing among the ripples of flesh beneath her chin. "It goes and turns them angry against you, makes the spirits try all the harder to have a go at you."

A glance over my shoulder to make sure that Chissick is a safe distance away, and I pull at my sleeve, rearranging the cuff until my arm is hidden. "What would you have me do? I can't let go. I am the only thing holding them back."

She snickers softly. "Oh, you think you're such a smart one, hmm?

Such a clever one." She taps her bosom, where the bag of tiles is still secreted. "I don't need these to tell me things. And I know you can't hold them off for all and forever, not with them always having such an interest in you. And you've already slipped up once, haven't you?" Her eyes fix on my wrists, on the poorly healed wounds hidden from her view. "You're not as strong as you'd like, and they'll find a way to break you down, if the one attemptin' to have the run of them has anything to do with it."

I feel my spine snap straight at her words. "You know who it is? Who's behind this?"

But already, her head shakes. "They're all cloaked, like. I can't see a thing of them, not with either of my eyes."

"Is it Ryall?" I dare to ask, my voice as low as I can make it while still keeping it audible to her ears. But it's my turn to shake my head, for I know Ryall's sort too well. He's the sort to dip his toe into the edge of mischief, but he would never wade in as far as this.

"They're a cunning sort, that's all I can say." Her voice is a rush of air, nearly as low as my own. "And they'll bring this entire city down on our heads if you're not careful."

I close my eyes, the better to avoid the fleeting look of sorrow that crosses her face. "I'll be fine."

"Then go home," she says. "And take a look in on Marta when you get a chance. She'll be mirin' herself into some trouble yet. I tell her that, but does she listen? Nah, she's near as bad as you. But don't you be worryin' about me," she adds with a wink. "I can take care of my own self."

And there it ends. I drop another coin onto the edge of the tray, onto the pile of coins she makes a great show of ignoring until I've turned and taken several steps away from her. I look back in time to see her fingers dart out with the speed of a basilisk, the money gone, most likely already hidden away in some secret pocket of her dress.

Go home.

Her instruction repeats itself over and over, until I'm forced to obey by the simple desire to put an end to the iteration. It takes only a few hurried strides to catch up with Chissick, and soon we have made our way into another dilapidated alley, Sissy and her burdened stool out of sight.

Chissick says little, only being polite, giving me ample time to gather my thoughts and form my next speech. When I finally put voice to my thoughts, I'm incapable of looking him in the eye.

"She gave us some help." My bottom lip threatens to tremble, and I grasp it between my teeth until it goes still. "I don't know how much, but there's always something in everything she has to say."

Chissick nods, though I'm not sure he understands. He takes my arm and easily steers me around a pile of rotting vegetables thrown out into the street. I feel his gaze upon me, searching, but I will not bite.

"Take me home. I think I need some rest before tonight."

"Tonight?"

I manage a small smile, pained, but there all the same. "I owe Marta a favour. Nothing important."

"Ah."

A single syllable, containing every question fighting to flow from his mouth and spill themselves at my feet. But it is the last and only sound out of his mouth before he lowers his head and returns me to the uneven frame of Mrs. Selwyn's front door.

Chapter Eight

Mrs. Damant's parlour is decorated in a singular style I've come to expect from every wife presently languishing between middle class and proper respectability. The entire room gives off an air of calculated antiquity. Nothing is too new, to begin with. New furniture might beg the question of the age of the money that purchased it. But neither is anything too old, as the tale of a chest of drawers passed down from a vague set of Tudor ancestors might be greeted as a fair bit of overreaching, as far as believability is concerned. Every colour is muted, every cushion is firm. There's not a trace of ease or comfort to be found here. Leave that for the next generation, when Henrietta Damant's existence as a coster's daughter and her husband's humble beginnings as a draper are long lost to the haze of good credit and poor memories.

It's here, in this very same parlour, I'm introduced to Lady Francesca.

Offering up her right hand, she fixes me with a stare that crinkles the smooth skin between her eyes. Her other arm is held behind her back, as if she's attempting to prove that she could turn away from me at any moment and thoroughly sweep her memories of me in the next. But the rest of her stance betrays her, and I know that she'd much prefer to stay right where she is.

Her eyes flicker, and I catch a glimpse of red creeping in from the corners, tiny veins as thin as threads. I'm graced with a slow nod as I grasp her fingers—long and tapered, boasting a ring or two on every one—and I can't help but assume that at this particular moment, she regards me as a threat to her newly acquired livelihood.

She asks after my health, and follows this with a few other

inquiries, all perfunctory. And at the end of this miniature interrogation, she raises a plucked eyebrow.

"I have to say, you're the exact picture of what Marta described to me."

I could spend a lifetime musing over such a statement as this. My curiosity is piqued not only by the description that Marta must have composed, but also by the fact that I appear to match this portrait after the trade of a few pleasantries. And I'm aware of my current state, of the shadows of exhaustion that must linger in the dips and hollows of my face, of my hastily dressed hair, of the odours of sweat and refuse and the lingering scent of dead bodies that no cheap perfume can fully eradicate.

But I waste no time attempting to piece together the dialogue that must have occurred between Marta and her newest protégée, because I'm currently distracted by this shining example of the former's marketing skills.

A young gipsy she is, complete with dark eyes and hair, beads and fringes and bracelets that clink against each other with every movement. And I could almost bring myself to believe in the authenticity of our Lady Franny, if it wasn't for the soft hint of Yorkshire still clinging to her vowels.

"I hear you've taken to hiding away," Lady Francesca says, smiling politely. "But it's a difficult life for the likes of you and me. It's only a shame that some of us are more..." She twirls a sparkling hand through the air, her fingers trawling for the desired word. "Equipped to deal with the trials involved."

Her voice grates along the inside of my ears, setting my teeth on edge. I study the unlined planes of her face, no hint of shadow or strain but for those vivid red veins, staining the whites of her eyes. A step towards me, and that could be gin on her breath. If she's ever been in contact with a spirit, it's never been more frightening than one she could mix into her afternoon tea.

"I'm glad you've accepted Marta's invitation." Her bracelets tinkle as she secures a curled lock of hair behind her ear. "She was so determined to have you as one of this evening's sitters."

If it is sincerity I'm searching for, I will be hard pressed to find any here. Lady Francesca's expression is too calculated, the mouth boasting a tepid smile that never completes the journey to her eyes. She tilts her head to one side, as if turning to hear me better. I raise my smile to match her own, and speak in a clear, concise voice that bears no hints of any latent mysticism.

"Yes, well. As Marta has often said, everyone has their price. And it just so happens that she's in a position to meet mine."

Lady Francesca blinks at my candour, her jaw slack enough to allow me a glimpse of all her bottom teeth. From several feet away, Marta must notice this change in her charge's expression, and so she puffs her way in our direction, brooding over us like a mother hen about to scold her fledgling chicks. As she steps up beside Francesca, her elbow makes solid contact with the younger woman's rib cage.

"Here, Franny. Why don't you go on over to Mr. Whorley and have a nice chat with him. And be sure to flourish it up like you do. Go on, now."

Charged with this task, Lady Francesca turns to leave. But before she can take more than two steps, I reach out for her arm, my grip firmer than I intended it to be.

"Tell him," I begin to speak, and I nearly lose my concentration as her eyes fasten on mine. But the ringing in my ears pulls me back on course, and the next words out of my mouth are sounded and lost before I can spend a moment to ponder their meaning. "Tell him that you're sorry for his loss. Tell him that, and mean it."

The expression on her face is not what I would've expected to see. There's irritation tugging at the corners of her mouth, but underneath, I would swear that I recognise fear.

"Just go," Marta says from behind me, and Lady Franny doesn't bother to hide her relief at being so neatly dismissed.

I stare after her for several seconds. Minutes, maybe. It feels as if

84

time slows down while I wait for whatever Marta is about to whisper in my ear.

"I have to say, I liked that. Very nicely done and all. You keep giving her little hints like that, and there'll be no stopping her."

I watch Francesca bow her head as she says something in a low voice to Mr. Whorley. "It was only a flash," I say. "Hardly defined. More a feeling, than anything. Something reaching out to him."

She gestures towards the two people deep in whispered conversation on the other side of the room. "Mr. Whorley," she says, in her own rough approximation of a whisper. "Who died?"

"His mother." I shut my eyes and look away.

Marta nods, as if she should've known. "And when did she pass on? That is, if this little feeling of yours has made you privy to such particulars."

"Not more than a few minutes ago, at the most. Three or four, maybe. Or she could be about to die. It's... It's very close." I shake my head, eyes shuttered as the truth becomes clear. "No, she's gone. She's dead."

The final word casts a dismal pallor on our conversation. Neither of us looks at the other, Marta taking the time to examine a dull painting of hunting dogs that decorates the wall, while I attempt to clear my head, to reclaim power over my own thoughts. A few feet away, Lady Francesca is still in conference with Mr. Whorley, her expression a carefully constructed portrayal of the deepest sympathy. Franny's attempt at flourishing it up, no doubt.

"Any other insights you'd care to share with us?" Marta asks, after a suitable amount of time has passed. "If you could come up with something for Mrs. Damant herself, it would be a boon, a real boon. Always good to include the host in these things, you know. Makes 'em feel important, singled out, as it were."

"I'll let you know," I tell her. But already, my barrier is slipping away, and other details, concerning Mr. Whorley, concerning everyone present, begin to come through. I could tell Mrs. Damant about her dreams of the last week, about what will inhabit her nightmares for the months to come. And there's Mr. Jones, who lost his wife, Annie, two months ago. His wife, who shot herself in the head rather than bear another minute married to him.

"And what about the séance itself, eh?" Marta says, pulling me back into the room, forcing my attention onto her and, thankfully, her alone. "What have you planned? Nothing too flashy, you know. But—"

"No," I interrupt her. "I plan to be nothing more than an observer. You knew that very well when you asked me to be here tonight."

"All right, all right," she sighs, momentarily defeated. "But I'm not too worried. I've never seen you sit at a circle where something not half unusual failed to occur."

"Well, here's hoping tonight will prove a break with tradition."

Marta does little to hide her disagreement. A slight tilt to the upper lip, a deep fissure in the skin above her nose, and any words she might have to say are made redundant. But she doesn't speak, only reaches into her hidden pocket, so skillfully sewn into the folds of her skirt that I blink at the near illusion the disappearance of her hand produces.

"I'll get this out of the way now," she says, without looking at me, her attention fixed on the small roll of bank-notes she slides between her fingers. "You met your end of things, showing up here, so..."

I try not to count as she peels them, one by one, off the roll. As she presses them into my hand, I'm tempted—oh, so tempted—to press them back. Sever my ties with her, as it were. But instead, I fold the notes into my palm, allow the filth of them, the dirt from a thousand other hands, to mingle with my own.

"There's something else," I say before I tuck the notes away, folded and out of sight before any eyes from another part of the room are drawn towards me. "Something else I want for coming here this evening."

Marta waves her hand, flicks my words away with a sweep of her fingers. "Well, you'll not be getting another penny from me, so you know what you can do with that request."

"It's not money. It's your help I find myself in need of."

"I wasn't aware the two could be separated."

I pull at the ragged lace that edges my sleeve. "Are you still on speaking terms with Lord Ryall?"

"With Ryall? Lord, I thought you were long finished with him."

"And it's not an acquaintance I am eager to renew. But there are circumstances…"

"Ah, I see!" A clipped laugh, her chin raised an inch. The unabashed superiority ripples upward along her spine. Before I can explain, if that was ever my intention, she holds up her hands, barricading herself against any paltry argument I might feel inclined to make. "We don't exactly take our turns in the same circles, times not being what they once were, but I could put in a word or three, depending on what it is that's brought about this newfound respect for the man."

"I never said I respected him. I only want to see him."

"A private audience, then?"

"No." I cough and lower my voice as soon as I realise that our conversation has piqued the curiosity of one of Mrs. Damant's guests. "Something less personal. I'd also prefer access to his home, if you'd be capable of procuring such a thing. With some amount of freedom in which to move around."

Her eyes narrow. It's hard work to prevent my knees from buckling beneath such a stare.

"Is that all?"

"No. I'd also like the invitation to include an acquaintance of mine."

"An acquaintance." Marta's voice loads those three syllables with a heavy measure of suspicion. "And would I be familiar with this acquaintance of yours?"

"I don't believe that much is pertinent to my request."

Stymied, it seems, she puts on an air of taking my request with a reasonable amount of seriousness. "Would you care to tell me what will happen if I don't agree to your terms?"

"Then I declare to everyone within earshot that your Franny is a fraud, I walk out the door, and I take your crisp bank-notes along with me."

Now I must wait as she deliberates, weighing every option, attempting to out-manoeuvre me and still come out with the much coveted upper hand. Finally, her nose wrinkles, and she blows out of the corner of her mouth. "All right." She nods, and repeats the phrase. "I'll do everything I can. But I'd like to know what's changed with you, how you've come to be so bloody hard."

I hope that these are rhetorical musings, and nothing to which she expects a reply. I can hardly tell her where I spent the previous evening, or that my company included a deceased prostitute and a man who absconded from his chosen career in the church under circumstances that I suspect are less than savoury. But time, it seems, has saved me. For here comes Mrs. Damant, nothing more than a whisper of silk and bated breath to announce her appearance at Marta's side.

"The room is ready," Mrs. Damant tells her, this comment punctuated by a slow smile from Marta.

"Then so is Lady Francesca," she replies. And with a sideways glance at me, she goes off to fetch her darling protégée.

Chapter Nine

The table is round and sturdily built, the carved claw feet displaying scuff marks and several years' worth of battering from a maid's broom. Constructed from a dark wood I'm unable to identify at first sight, the piece stands as an incongruity against the room's decor. But it's the cabinet that continually draws my eye. The size of a small wardrobe and tucked into the corner of the room, it seems to lure the shadows towards it, absorbing the faint light from the recently filled lamps.

At Marta's instruction, the shades are drawn, the lamps turned down, and everything is cast into semi-darkness, an artificial twilight that vies with the street lamps shining brightly outside. Behind us, one of the servants closes the door, and now even the air loses its freshness, completely shut in as we are.

A lack of noise seems to pulse outward from the center of our little group, until I suspect it could gain enough strength to push over whatever solid objects had the misfortune of standing in its way. Lady Francesca makes a small sound in her throat, but this prelude to speech merely puts a slight dent in the oppressive silence instead of breaking through it. So she tries again, this time managing to catch the attention of the other sitters, before she raises her face towards the ceiling and begins.

"And it shall come to pass afterward, that I will pour out my spirit upon all flesh, and your sons and daughters shall prophesy, your old men shall dream dreams, your young men shall see visions. And also upon the servants and upon the handmaids in those days will I pour out my spirit."

Her voice fades and her chin lowers to her chest, her mouth

murmuring a final word I discern more from the movement of her lips than from any sound that reaches my ears.

"Amen."

And with that, she sits down. The rest of us quickly follow suit, our change of positions accompanied by a chorus of shufflings, half-muttered apologies, and the muffled scrape of chair legs on the rug as we struggle to fit a dozen bodies around a table that appears to have been designed for eight.

"Now," Lady Francesca says, and says it again as if she's attempting to free something that has lodged itself on the back of her tongue. Slowly, she unfurls her fingers, her oval nails shining dully in the soft light from the nearest lamp. Her rings and bracelets clatter as she lays her palms flat on the surface of the table, and there's a nod to her partners before everyone moves to do the same.

The wood is cold against my skin, an unusual pleasure as the air behind us grows steadily warmer. The man to my right perches on the edge of his seat, his back straight but for the slight forward slouch of his shoulders. He glances at me out of the corner of his eye and gives me a benign smile.

Finally, Lady Francesca summons the full strength of her voice, but skimming beneath every word, I hear Marta's tutelage, shaping each syllable, drawing out every breath so there's something of a rhythm to her speech pattern. Almost a chant, and I realise that in all my years of speaking in front of others, I was never able to manage quite so well as this. In fact, her voice has such a hypnotic effect on me that I fail to attend to what she's saying, instead taking this chance to study the other people seated around the table.

There are no neophytes here, that much is plain. The older ladies know how to sit, their faces taking on the look of someone about to slip into a trance. I've no doubt they have all dabbled in the privacy of their own homes, invited neighbours over for an evening of rapping on the furniture, or perhaps shut themselves away for an hour or so while allowing the spirits to communicate with them though pen and paper. I sense the thinness of the barrier around some of them, and I wonder if it's my place to warn them away from experimenting any further.

Maybe it's because my mind is distracted by these thoughts that it takes a moment to notice the sudden drop in temperature, the cold that brushes over my knuckles as it pushes towards the outer edge of the table, but doesn't move beyond it. The other sitters have already reacted, and I'm conscious of them stirring in their chairs, their breath quickening as they take more air into their lungs than they seem to release. I look at Marta, ready to convey my astonishment at her protégée's abilities. But her neck is corded with tension, and as the first prickling of dread places its pressure on the back of my own neck, I realise this is not part of the prearranged program.

But Marta's opinion on this turn of events is insignificant, as Francesca raises her chin, rolls back her slender shoulders and slides her hands forward until her elbows are locked straight. This is her moment, and the pleasure of the other sitters at this physical sign of an unknown presence in the room only serves to raise her self-assurance to undiscovered heights. Here is Lady Francesca, communer with the dead. Despite the departure from their well-rehearsed performance, Marta has to know what a stroke of good fortune this is for her current star.

"Please," Francesca entreats. "We must concentrate. Clear our minds of all troubling thoughts. Please," she says again, but this time, it's not to those of us seated around the table. "Is someone there?"

Beside me, the man with the benign smile twitches in his rounded shoulders. I close my eyes, my hands pressing down upon the tabletop as I search for some way to control the throbbing sensation that pushes up from beneath the heavily varnished surface. And while I do this, eleven others are opening their minds, begging the spirits to come through. I take no account of the odds against me, but focus on the force near the center of the table, probing it for a weakness, for anything that rings of familiarity. At this, the voices prowling at the edges of my conscious begin a round of jeering, but it's merely a distraction. The real menace is in front of me, putting pressure on the top of my head, on my chest, until it becomes too difficult to snatch more than a shallow breath to keep from passing out.

"Are you looking for someone? Is there someone here that you know, that you wish to contact?"

The tone of the questions puts Francesca's lingering immaturity on display. Until today, this has only been a farce, a well-calculated one, but nothing beyond the limits of what she or Marta could control. When the table shudders, rising a few inches before slamming back down to the floor, I know that something like this was already scripted to happen, but the timing is wrong. Again, I look at Marta, and the question is written across her face.

Are you doing this?

Oh, how I wish I could say yes. To claim control over all of this, and to have the power to bring it to an end whenever I would wish is a thought too tremendous to imagine. But even as I struggle to send a reply to Marta from the other side of the table, I notice that the terrible cold has dissipated, replaced by a strange, sultry warmth that may be nothing more than the mingling of our long-held breath hovering inches above the tabletop.

And here seems to be the end of it. I could almost feel disappointed if my personality tended in that direction. The table, great and monstrous thing that it was only moments ago, has transformed back into its more innocuous state, simply another piece of furniture resting beneath our splayed fingers. And there's my regret at having applied the word 'rest' to this carved block of wood, with that single syllable instilling a life into its grain, one I'd rather wish it didn't possess. Now the light regains some of its former brilliancy, the most opaque shadows banished to the room's farthest reaches, shivering near the drapes and behind Mrs. Damant's chaise lounge. The tension that held us all in thrall releases us, its grip loosening with such slowness I can still sense its touch, the lightest of tingles between my shoulders.

That it doesn't disappear entirely is what feeds the belief that this isn't an ending at all. Oh, nothing so blessed as that. This is but a pause, a brief intermission before the commencement of this evening's second act. But, as if working contrary to my suspicions, lines dissipate from the others' foreheads, and shoulders begin to droop. Now that the unnatural cold has left us, everything wilts, starched collars and pinned curls flattening before my eyes. In the middle of this relaxed atmosphere, Marta chances a smile brimming with relief, and Lady Francesca takes the lead once more.

She speaks, but I don't attend to her voice. Her words fall out of her mouth as if they were learned by rote, sounding stilted and self-conscious after the jolt of spontaneity that carried us this far. The scrape of chair legs marks her rise from the table, and now the performance has fully resumed as we move swiftly forward to the next scene.

Francesca preens for a moment, her motions slow and methodical, an attempt to convey the calm we should all be feeling, before she moves towards the free-standing cabinet in the corner of the room. She enters by herself, opening the unmarked door and stepping inside. On cue, Marta rises to her feet and makes a quick round of the room, turning down the lamps again until the only light is a few thin seams of yellow from the edges of the covered windows.

It's awe-inspiring, how rapidly we shift back into something not far removed from the most banal of routines. I've seen all of this before. Not from Francesca, but from the dozens, the hundreds of others like her that used to exist. I wonder that Marta can settle for staging a show that follows such a rigid set of guidelines, but this is where I suffer from my ignorance for what the public truly desires. No real truth, no answers that delve into anything more revealing than the vaguest of details. And it's all these years later that Marta's instructions come back to me, like a lesson memorised from the pages of a children's primer.

Give them a show. It's the tension they want. The suspense.

Minutes pass while my eyes adapt to the light, or the lack thereof. And then a soft rapping sound comes from inside the cabinet. Marta beckons to one of the gentlemen at the table, and per her instructions, he walks to the cabinet and opens the door.

There sits our Lady Franny, her ankles and wrists bound to a straight-backed chair. The man examines Francesca's bonds, tests each of the knots along the pale stretch of rope used to fasten her down. And while the young man is so engaged, I slip out of my chair and move to Marta's side, barely a rustle from my skirts as I rise onto the balls of my feet and whisper in her ear.

"You should stop this."

Her head whips around, the feathers that adorn her shoulders tickling my chin as she searches my face in the dim light.

"Are you out of your bloody head?" The words are clipped short, the touch of her tongue to the roof of her mouth producing more sound than her low voice.

"There's something here," I say, feeling foolish all of a sudden, like a child reporting the presence of a ghoul beneath her bed. "The table, Marta. I know your tricks, and that wasn't one of them."

"No." The whites of her eyes glint in the dark. "I assumed it was one of yours."

"I don't..." *have any tricks*, I want to point out, but I'm beyond wasting my breath in my own defense. "Call her out of the cabinet."

"In a minute." She turns as if to brush me off, but I realise it's only to step aside and treat me to a full view of whatever is about to transpire.

"Marta."

"Do you want your time with Ryall or not?" She holds up her index finger. "One minute."

I retreat to my chair, but instead of sitting, I stand behind it, gripping the back until I lose all feeling in the tips of my fingers. The man announces the knots to be genuine, the wood of the cabinet solid. Again, the door swings shut and we're left to watch the blot of shadow that hides Francesca from view.

One minute.

I stare at the center of the cabinet's door, my pulse ticking twice for every second that slips away. So consumed am I in the task of counting out such small measures of time I hardly notice the glimmer of white that appears at eye level with those seated around the table. After some hesitation, the faint oval shudders, and I notice it's rather far back, and only now begins to move forward.

The eyes are the first discernible things to greet us, cold as marbles, fixed and glassy. The entire head is swathed in shreds of white fabric, but not a thread shifts out of place, and I imagine they would stay that way if buffeted by the winds of a hurricane. There's no body to accompany the mask-like face, speckled and eerily translucent around the edges, as if I'm staring at the image of someone who dared to move while their portrait was being taken. I must admit, it looks very much like the disembodied head of a ghost, or at least, very much like the form that most people believe ghosts to take. Add the rough drag of a few chains, the mournful whistle of air pushing through a gap in the casement, and the scene would be complete.

But there isn't any noise to attend the materialization. There's the soft sound of breathing from those around me, and behind that, the tickings and creakings that every house produces when all conversations cease. And behind that, the whole of London, no doubt. But in here, the loudest thing is the rush of blood ringing in my ears. And the voices, always the voices, their tone taking on an urgency now, an excitement that begs me to spare some paltry show of attention for them.

It's these voices, my ever-present companions, that present enough of a distraction to draw my eyes away from the death-like face still lingering in front of the cabinet. Before me, the smudge of darkness that is the cabinet seems to grow and change shape, until I realise that it's the shadows, all of the darkness in the room shifting at once, pulling inward, converging on the large piece of furniture that stands there.

I make to run forward, but the pressure is already there, on my throat and my upper chest, and when I open my mouth to breathe, I feel the darkness clawing at the edges of my parted lips. A moment of panic overtakes me, because I recognise the malevolency behind these shadows, the same force that stripped me of my family so many years before. Behind me, Marta springs into action, but not as Francesca's rescuer. Instead, it's my arm she grabs, and in the middle of the tussle, the pale mask flickers once, twice, and goes out.

The moment the face disappears, everything changes. Cries shatter the silence that had enveloped us, and an insistent knocking that soon gives way to a dry scraping reaches our ears. A single tug pulls me free of Marta's grasp, and I shut my eyes as I stumble forward, wincing at the burning cold fingers that find their way around my throat. I fumble for the latch on the cabinet door, all the while holding my breath, the darkness right there, teasing my nostrils, settling into the lines at the corners of my squinted eyes. As soon as I feel the chill of the metal handle, I pull, my fingers slipping as I struggle with a single panel of wood that's suddenly infused with enough weight to frustrate the efforts of a dozen grown men.

"Let her go."

Listen to how soft my request is, the low note of supplication in my voice. I doubt that any of the sitters still loitering behind me took any notice of it, but it wasn't for them to hear.

I shiver as a new sensation takes hold. In front of me, all around me, the darkness condenses until I can't see even with my eyes wide open. A shudder ripples through the malignant cloud before it pulls back, retreating to the edges of the room with such speed that the return of the dim light nearly blinds me.

Tightening my grip on the latch, I wrench the door open, expecting to find Francesca still bound to her chair. But her body is wedged between the chair and the dusty floor of the cabinet, one of her arms raised up as if it were a shield.

And now Marta is beside me, the both of us scrabbling to reach inside, Marta occupied with shifting the chair out of the way while I clumsily reach an arm around Francesca's limp form and drag her out onto the parlour floor. It isn't until I'm on my knees, her body sprawled across my lap, that I finally gaze down into her eyes.

She is dead, I think. The first thought to enter my head, but I won't accept it. Even now, as my hands search her throat for any sign of life, I can feel the tenuous connection that keeps her here in this world. Brushing her dark hair away from her face, I stare down into her eyes, at the tiny red veins reaching towards the irises.

"Don't let them take you."

I lick my lips, a nervous reaction more than anything. There isn't enough saliva in my mouth to chance a swallow without choking.

"Come back," I say, the words gasping out of my lungs. "Come back. This isn't..." I shake my head. "Not yet. Not yet."

A moment passes. A tight circle of onlookers has taken shape around us, so close that if I were to suddenly straighten up, I would smack the back of my head squarely against Mrs. Damant's hip. The seconds turn into a minute, and both of my hands frame Francesca's face, my thumbs resting on the sharp slant of her cheekbones.

The sound begins in her chest, something like a gurgle, before her back arches away from me and a rattling breath floods her lungs. Then the coughing begins, and she reaches for her throat, her fingers flexing and curling like talons as her fingernails dig into her skin.

"It's all right." Like a mother, I sound, speaking to a child recently woken up from a nightmare. Still smoothing the hair away from her damp forehead, I cradle her in my arms as she rocks back and forth, her motions bringing her closer and closer until she presses her face into my shoulder and begins to sob.

"I'm sorry," I hear her say. Again and again into the crook of my neck. But it is not to me she speaks, and I cannot help but wonder to whom she owes such a litany of apologies.

The sobs quickly turn into violent shakes that rattle her from head to toe, and someone thrusts out a handkerchief as Marta walks around and leans over the two of us. When my eyes meet hers, I don't disguise the rage that overwhelms me.

"I gave you your minute."

She winces at this, but doesn't say a word.

"Our bargain?"

Slowly, she extends a trembling hand and applies the lightest of touches to Francesca's shoulder.

"Ryall is yours," she says, her usually strong voice faltering, stumbling over the words. "I'll get you your audience with him. And anything else you may want of me."

Chapter Ten

Marta puts forward the suggestion that I return home with her, to spend the night in my old room. I know that her real intention is for me to keep an eye on Lady Francesca—as if my proximity hadn't already caused the girl enough suffering—so I refuse her offer with as much delicacy as I can summon after such an experience, lowering my voice, bowing my head, promising to pay a visit after a full night's rest has wielded its restorative powers on the both of them.

To sate my own need of restoration, I decide to walk home, my hands wishing for pockets my shabby skirt does not provide. Though the moon is large, its pallid glow doesn't reach far below the rooftops, and I'm left to slog through the darkness that clings to the uneven cobblestones. I travel far enough that the urbane snobbery of Mrs. Damant's neighbourhood is left behind, my slow stride now carrying me onto more dusty roadways, flanked by houses that grow closer and closer together until one is nearly grafted onto the next.

An unnerving lack of sound greets me here, the hubbub of the livelier streets pushed back until it can be mistaken for nothing more than a dull ringing of the ears. It is embarrassment, I think, that creates such an absence of noise, for the buildings here are still large, their patched walls carrying a history that climbs towards three figures, but their rooms no longer housing the same genteel respectability for which they were erected so many years before.

Nearly every trade imaginable is hidden from view, shirts being sewn in this basement, nails pounded into the heels of already broken-down shoes in that attic over there. Some of the street's inhabitants have thrown off all attempts at retaining decency and simply hang up their wares for everyone to see. Even now, through a cracked pane of glass, I glimpse a bald man rearranging his shop's window display to be ready for the next day's business, the items for sale nothing more than bits of rag and useless military equipment, the latter better returned to the foundry from which it came.

There is no pause in my movements as I pass the grime-encrusted window. The man raises his eyes for a moment, perhaps to gauge my interest in his offerings, but I quickly look away, move on, away from the display, away from the gaze that remains pinned to my back until I've ducked around the next corner.

Odd that I should still feel as if I'm being watched. Like a small irritation, buzzing and retreating from the nape of my neck before I can swat it away with my gloved hand. I look round, to the left and the right, but it's only dusky shadows on all sides, occasionally broken by the glow of a lamp through a neglected back window.

It takes less than a minute for the paranoia to burrow in, not quite beneath my skin, but deep enough to lend a burst of speed to my wandering pace. At the same time, I try not to draw any additional attention to myself. But my body and my mind, always at odds with one another, are having a difficult time finding a state on which to agree. Without making something of a spectacle of myself, I walk faster for several paces, head down, elbows poised and ready to drive against any impediment to come my way.

Ahead of me, thirty feet or so, a huddle of persons—Three, I think? In the gloom it's difficult to say—are occupied in taking up a good portion of the narrow roadway. Though "huddle" could be the paranoia speaking, for they're not huddled at all, but standing in the most casual of groupings. And as I approach, I hear their voices, one of them boasting an accent that is strange but not unfamiliar.

I stand still, listening. A small amount of time has passed, enough that my stillness has begun a slight swelling in my feet, the blood pooled below my ankles until my toes press against the inside of my shoes. I know that I must move, and so I take a step, wriggle my foot beneath the hem of my skirt and wait for the prickling sensation that is a mark of my slumbering limb's return to life.

Another step now, and I'm near enough to a woman and her two companions to hear what they're saying. I don't know what I expect to overhear, some great conspiracy or plot, no doubt. Dark dealings of the vilest sort. And here I would be, a witness to their nascent plan.

But, no. It's nothing as interesting as that. There are a few remarks on the weather—the most shopworn topics of conversation to be had nowadays—and a query as to the health of a certain Miss Crowden, and that is all. Before I'm aware of it, the three are already making their farewells, proving it to be only chance that brought them all together on this particular occasion.

I stare after them, dazzled. Having come upon them in a group, I find it difficult to watch them move their separate ways. The two men remain together for a few steps, but soon break apart before passing out of sight. The woman, however, hangs back for a moment, fixes her bonnet, tucks a brown sprig of hair behind her ear. A rustle of fabric, the scuff of a slipper on the pavement, and she, too, takes her leave of the place.

It's nothing more than a reflex that sets my feet into motion behind her. The rest of my surroundings are static, so why should I not anchor myself to this elegant creature, all thrush and whisper as she glides before me?

Some part of me feels a covetousness as I trail in her wake, for her beauty—undeniable, truly—seems to cast a wider net of shadow all around her, so that every other figure, every other face—my own included, I'm humble enough to admit—are unable to garner even the smallest measure of attention necessary to be forgotten. But here is the benefit to my lowly status, for as she makes her way from one street to the next, I close the distance between us, until I'm near enough to hear the soft strike of her heels on the roadway, the soles too thin and too delicate for such a walk as she's chosen to undertake this evening.

Indeed, I'm left to wonder what has brought her to this

neighbourhood, alone, and with all respectable business hours long passed. The obvious conclusion the mind leaps to is also one of the most base: She is a prostitute. The two gentlemen—if such a complimentary title should be applied to them—her customers. But after such hasty labelling, one is forced to look closer. Yes, she is beautiful. But should that be enough to condemn her? Her dress is bold, every woven inch designed to allure, and yet there is nothing in the woman's posture that says what lies beneath the clinging fabric is for sale.

Most remarkable of all is her confidence. Shoulders held back, chin high, eyes disregarding whatever demons may hide in the darkness, she shows not a single ounce of fear as she navigates the deserted streets. And another truth soon becomes clear: she's travelled this way before.

It takes less than a minute to remember where I am, about twenty minutes' brisk walk from Waterloo Bridge. Too far yet to hear the ships, but the stench is enough to mark my approach, stronger each day as the water recedes. For it's the water that evaporates, leaving the muck, the filth, and the garbage, until I wonder if the Thames will soon be nothing more than a ribbon of rotting sewage and stranded tugs.

And there is the woman, not fifteen paces ahead, an aberration in this dismal place. I watch as her fingers—long, tapered, the drudgery of menial housekeeping tasks apparently unknown to her skin—flutter for a moment after she removes a soft brown glove. Those same fingers curl into a small fist, two knuckles pushed out beyond the rest to sharpen the sound produced as she knocks on a plain wooden door.

I wait with her, though with enough distance between us to allow me the freedom of breathing, of dabbing the perspiration from my eyelids, without being seen. She maintains her perfect posture as she stands before the closed door, her spine drawing a line that would make the strictest schoolmistress proud. Her hands find themselves in front of her waist, one gloved, and the other bare, her fingers laced together so that the contrast between pale skin and dark glove brings to mind the stripes of a zebra.

A minute slips away, followed by another. My thoughts toy with several possible futures. She will knock again. She will break the door down. She will turn and walk away. Will I follow her if she does?

But before I'm allowed to ponder my own question, a shuffling noise, a loud click, and the door swings free.

Another woman looks out onto the street; barely a woman, her soft face still carrying the roundness of an easy youth. Her mouth catches my attention as she smiles, a splendidly full bottom lip curving downward as her cheekbones gain prominence. A broad smile for her unexpected visitor. The two women embrace before stepping apart again, hands still clasped, smiles unfaltering. The second woman is backlit by a grainy yellow light, and I blink as the light seems to shift and change before my eyes. And then she steps aside to allow her visitor to enter, and I see an oil lamp on a table, its poorly trimmed wick sending a profusion of swirling smoke into the air.

The door closes softly after them, and with their exit from the scene, I'm once again left with my former question. Will I follow her?

It is the closed door, of course, that gives me my answer. Alone again, I feel a familiar tiredness leech into my bones, an exhaustion I doubt any amount of sleep will fully dispel.

I want to rub my eyes, my forehead, and I raise my hand to do just that, gloved fingers brushing loose tendrils of hair from my face, sliding back until they've grazed the vicious knot of muscles at the nape of my neck. A fleeting desire takes hold of me, to return to Mrs. Selwyn's, to return to my room, undress, lay across my mildewed bed. Not to attain any kind of rest, but only to cease wandering, for a time.

Move along, the old voice reminds me.

And I nod in agreement with such sound advice. "Move along," my voice cracks. "Nothing more to see."

***

It is still night when the message arrives. Indeed, the faint light of dawn is only beginning to illuminate the crooked square of my window when I hear a soft tread on the stairs, and a creak of floorboards, before a whisper of sound—no, hardly even that—and a slip of paper is pushed through the narrow space beneath my door.

I feel no inclination to move from my bed, at first because I've no wish to begin an audience with another person at such an early hour, and also because the burgeoning day has finally allowed me a chance of rest. But it takes only a minute for my curiosity to send my feet skimming over the floor, one hand pushed out at my side for balance as I bend down and pick the small square of paper from the floor.

Marta's handwriting is unmistakable. There is no salutation, nor even the evidence of one begun and as swiftly abandoned. One line is all she has bothered to communicate, the ink smeared in her apparent haste to have the correspondence delivered to my hands.

Thurs. night, Ryall's house in Grosvenor. He'll expect you, and your friend.

Not ten hours have passed since I first spoke my request in Marta's ear, and here, scrawled across this sheet of paper, is the culmination of what must have been a great deal of contrivance on her part.

He'll expect you.

I fold the note in half before tossing it onto the end of the bed. My gaze skips from one corner of the room to the other, this single sweep taking in all of my earthly belongings where they lay, draped across a few meagre pieces of furniture or left to moulder in damp heaps along the wall. The starkness of these surroundings serves as a reminder of all I will need before I can make any attempt to turn up on Ryall's well-swept doorstep. A fine dress, I think. And gloves. Proper gloves that show no evidence of having been repaired with such regularity they no longer carry any resemblance to their original form.

And, of course, my friend. A friend who will need to be informed of his intention to escort me to the home of Lord Geoffrey Ryall in less than three days' time.

Chapter Eleven

The house stares down at us, a motley collection of building materials stacked one on top of another—bricks, mortar, bits of wood, chiselled stone—all of them shaped into something that could stand as a monument to confusion. Every architectural style of the last century is displayed on the face of the three-story house. A bit of Greek Revival around the front door, a touch of Gothic marking the cornices that edge the roof, and there, overwhelming half of the building's public side, a multi-storied window that catches the glow from the streetlights, reflecting it, and creating a pool of golden light on the pavement below.

We are not the first guests to arrive, Chissick and I. A line of carriages precedes us, the stamping of hooves, the groan of slowing wheels an overture to our humble approach. There is no sleek cab to deposit us at the door, no coachman leaping down to lower the step. We are on foot, near enough to touch each other, but when Chissick offers his hand to help me up the building's front steps, it soon returns to his side, unused.

It's not my intention to offend him. A simple attack of nerves has made me forgetful of my better manners, but by the time we arrive at the top of the stairs, with Lord Ryall's man staring down at us like a hawk on his perch, I summon up enough confidence to clear my throat in anticipation of any speech I may have to make.

The man—is he a butler? I'm not familiar enough with such amenities to recognise the various members of a house's staff on sight —renews his glare, in fact, seems to draw upon some hidden reserve of energy that only narrows his eyes to two dark slashes beneath his creased brow. I produce a small card, the hard-won invitation delivered from Marta only a few hours before, and the severity of the slashes begins to relent. A bit.

The man only glances at it. He will not reach for it, as if touching the document may sully his pristine white gloves. But I can feel an urge radiating from him, the strongest desire to rip the invitation from my grasp, to examine it, hold it up to the light as if searching for a telltale watermark. But the aforementioned glance, followed by a nod, is all we receive. The way is now clear before us. Chissick touches my elbow, and we move inside.

The front hall is an obstacle course of people, all of them bedecked and bejewelled in every sort of finery. Even in my new gown—more than a month's rent exhausted on its acquisition—I'm out of place, and Chissick beside me, with his face neatly shaved, his suit brushed and his shoes buffed to a shine that would render any available mirror obsolete, only barely brings us to rank above the average philistine. But if it is a fear of being discovered as an imposter among London's lesser members of the peerage, I've little to worry about. For by the time we make our arrival, the first round of glasses has already been emptied, the second only half-full. Chissick nods at a man dressed in a suit nicer than his own, a silver tray of crystal cups balanced on the tips of all five fingers, but turns down the proffered refreshment.

From somewhere, I hear music trickling out, the sound for a moment pushed back by a sudden swell of conversation, and louder again as a break in the press of bodies allows the melody to drift through. Some piano, I think, and something else. A cello, perhaps. Or it could be a violin, considering the paucity of musical knowledge contained inside my head.

Chissick remains attached to my side as we struggle to make progress through the house.

"Ryall always enjoyed a crowd," I tell him, raising my voice to be heard over a raucous peal of laughter so close to my ear that I wince at the spray of warm saliva that lands across the back of my neck.

But even this, I must admit, is nearer to Bedlam than an evening out with London society. The amount of bodies, the heat that must at this very moment be accumulating above our heads; a mingling of exhaled breath, of hundreds of limbs politely wrestling for space, of too much light offering little more purpose than to highlight the perspiration decorating the forehead of every person too slow to reach for his handkerchief; all of it mixing together, a slurry of breath and perfume and silk, and I think—I find I must hope—that even Ryall cannot derive any pleasure from this.

"Miss Hawes."

I start at this pronouncement of my name, not because I had forgotten Chissick's presence—how could I have? As he's once again taken on the unspoken role of bodyguard since our departing Mrs. Selwyn's together—nor because of his proximity, for I doubt he will allow more than an arm's length of distance to pass between us until he's seen me safely deposited on said doorstep once again, but simply because I had allowed my mind to wander.

"Miss Hawes," he says again, softer this time. "What is it?"

"Hmm?" I turn to look at him, all the while curious as to the expression that must have decorated my face for him to ask such a question. "Oh, it's nothing. I've been here before." I hope he will not require a more detailed explanation, but he gives me a nod of the head as if he must understand.

There are memories here, I cannot deny it. I want to think back to the last time my heels scuffed across this parquet. The walls are a different colour now. And the staircase... I don't recall such a dark wood for the railing. Less furniture over here, a more vivid brocade beyond that door, but it is the play of sound off the ceiling, off those subtly altered walls that lingers. Ryall's house always had a gift for sound, for capturing it, seeming to amplify certain noises while dampening others into silence. I glance towards the stairs again, and I feel a pull of sorts, as if something beckons me to the upper levels of the house.

I reach out to grasp the edge of Chissick's sleeve, finger and thumb poised to pinch the heavy fabric and gently steer him through the crowd, but a voice calls out to me, stalling my progress before I've even begun. This particular voice doesn't sound from the chorus inside my head, nor does it have its roots in the ether. It comes from a body of flesh and blood, a body that moves towards me with great haste, while all the other figures in the room show hardly a ripple as they break before him.

"My dear, dear Thea."

Ryall has aged little since I saw him last, a few additional lines flanking his mouth, a bit more plumpness rather skillfully hidden beneath a starched collar. His eyes are the same, still little more than shards of blue ice beneath dark brows. Yet all of the chill melts away as he grasps my hands, cupping both of them within his own.

I wait for the smile I'm certain will appear. A softening at the corners of his mouth, and his eyes narrow as his cheekbones push upwards. The smile does indeed make a fair showing, but there is something else, a kind of eagerness fueling it from within. But I read more than a desire to voice the welcome due to me. I feel a most overwhelming want to watch the back of me leave his home once and for all.

For a moment, his head seems to bob on his neck, and I fear he may be about to brush a kiss across my cheek. But he checks himself in time. So the smile grows tighter, the light behind his eyes darkening as he gropes for better control of the situation I've presented to him.

"You're looking well," he says, his hands still encircled round my own. "Ah, so very well! But how impolite of me to stand here without a single word of acknowledgement for your companion?" A glance at Chissick before his gaze returns to me. And with the return of his attention, I'm struck with the sensation that he and I are two actors in a play, that the lines already spoken were taken from a script, and now the burden of the spotlight has suddenly shifted onto me.

"Mister Julian Chissick," I say, a turn of my hand presenting the one man to the other. "This is Lord Geoffrey Ryall. A very... Well, I've known him for some years, at least."

This introduction spurs Ryall into releasing my hands, only to tuck his fingers into the crook of my arm. I wonder if Chissick notices the possessive hand now pressing on my elbow, but I fear he's too overwhelmed by his surroundings to witness such a small movement.

"Pleased to meet you, Sir." Chissick nods once. And, no. He does not see Ryall's hand, does not know how the man's fingernails dig into the paltry amount of flesh I possess.

"Ah, any friend of Thea's is more than welcome—most welcome here!" There is something to Ryall's tone, a thickness he lends to the word "friend" that does not agree with me. Or perhaps I'm too glutted with suspicion to take anything from his mouth at face value. "Have you had something to drink? Some punch? No! Ah, it cannot stand for another minute!"

Before either Chissick or I can speak, three glasses are procured. Chissick holds onto his as if the liquid contained inside might have been ladled from one of the Thames' more questionable tributaries, while I take a perfunctory sip, enough to wet my lips, and enough to know that I will not want a second dose.

Ryall finally releases my arm, drains half of his glass in one swallow and lets out an exhalation I could almost mistake for a laugh. "So, Mister Chissick, is it? How long, may I ask, have you been an admirer of Thea's extraordinary work?"

"How long?" Chissick's eyelids lower as he ponders this question. "Years. Nearly a decade, if my memory hasn't failed me."

"Ah! So you were a witness to our young Thea, when she was the Spiritualist prodigy, all rosy cheeks and hardly grown out of her nursery dress!"

I could take this moment to point out that never in my short life have my cheeks carried more colour than was necessary to assure passersby I was still among the living, but Ryall's voice cuts across mine before I can push a single word off my tongue.

"And what about tonight, Thea? I'm sure—I'm absolutely certain

I'm about to overstep all forms of etiquette speaking as host to guest, but would it be too much to ask for a small—really, I've nothing extravagant in mind!—a small demonstration? For the guests?"

"No, I'd rather not."

"Or you could do something with each person one at a time! I read an absolutely fascinating article about a woman—very much of your profession—who spent an entire evening seated behind a curtain, or shade, or... Anyhow, she would tell them secrets about their lives, without ever laying eyes on them! I could have my man set up a screen in the library—it's quite out of the way in there—and then we could have a sort of raffle out here to decide who would be allowed to take the first turn with you, and—"

"Ryall," I say, and whether because of my harsh tone, or because of the lack of title connected to his name, he falters into silence. "I apologise, but I did not come here tonight in any professional capacity. I don't know what Marta may have told you, but I don't do that anymore."

He watches me with an anxious curiosity. Again, his hand returns to my elbow, and he takes a step nearer to me, his posture a blatant attempt to prevent Chissick from coming to my aid, should I need it.

"Perhaps you would grace me with a private audience, Thea. I've carried something on my mind, of late. And with your help..."

The hand tightens.

"I'll give you five minutes," I say. To show his agreement, he releases my arm, presents me with a smile.

"In the library. I trust you remember where it is."

I wait until he is gone, until the crowd of guests close behind him like a curtain swinging into place, and I turn to Chissick. Poor man, he's still clutching his untouched glass of punch.

"You'll have to wait out here for me," I tell him, my hands at my sleeves, adjusting the crimson puffs that seem to hover over and around my shoulders, like satin meringues. "I told him he could have five minutes, but what he'll have to say to me shouldn't take even that much time."

"You're going to speak to him? Alone?" His tone is incredulous. No, not incredulous. Disapproving.

"I've known him for many years."

"And? That's no proof of the man's character."

I close my eyes. "You're right, but I assure you, no harm will come to me."

Oh, the expression that crosses his face upon my saying those words. He doesn't believe me. But not only that. He is prepared to fight, should it come to that.

"Chissick." I could touch his arm. My fingers are near enough they would only have to unfurl a bit in order to brush his sleeve, but I hesitate—only for a second—and all of my courage drains away. "If it will give you some comfort, come along and stand outside the library door. You'll only be a few feet away."

He wants to protest. The slight rise of his shoulders, the cords in his neck showing themselves for a moment before disappearing again. His left foot scuffs across the floor as one of his hands takes hold of the other. At first, I'm mystified, and then I notice he's done it only to halt whatever fidgeting had been about to overtake his arms.

"I don't like it," he admits, so low that I can only decipher the words by reading his lips.

"Neither do I," I say, before I turn and walk away from him.

Chapter Twelve

Ryall's first action is to offer me a glass of wine. His second, once I've declined the drink, is to remove a stack of books from a chair in order that I might take a seat. When I shake my head at the vacated cushion, the last of his etiquette fails him. He removes his jacket. He loosens his collar, wearing down the work of the starch with a few brief tugs. He is about to sit down himself when he glances in my direction. He must not want to sit, must not wish to put himself at any kind of disadvantage while I'm still on my feet, poised as I am so near to the door. A swear under his breath, followed by another loud enough for me to hear, and he faces me, any hint of his previous aplomb neatly wiped from his face.

"What is it that you need? Money?" He reaches into a pocket and withdraws an impressive wad of bank-notes. One, two, three of them are counted off the roll. And there they are, clasped between his fingers, at arm's length, mine for the taking, if I will simply cross the distance between us and claim them. My own fingers twitch as I imagine the freedom that will come with those simple pieces of paper. The amount that he's offering me, before we've even begun to bargain, and I wouldn't need to beg from Marta for well over a year.

"I assure you, Ryall. I don't want it."

A smile from him, but the notes remain out in the open. "Still unwilling to take any help from others? I would've thought you'd grown out of that by now."

"I've had more than my fair portion of charity from you over the years."

He blinks, thrown off of the course he'd set for the conversation. "I'm sorry if I've offended you. Believe me, it was never my intention."

This, I understand, is my opportunity to apologise. I could lower my chin, mumble a few soft-spoken words that would return him to his former state of ease. Instead, I bite my lip. The silence lingers.

"Forgive me for not inquiring sooner," he says, after a sufficient pause. "How is your health?"

"I am well enough." If he expects a more lengthy description of my current spate of ailments, his disappointment will be a keen one.

"You can't imagine how often you've been in my thoughts. I made certain to receive regular reports of your progress from the doctors, and when I heard that they were considering you for release, how worried I was that you would be too fragile for such a great step forward. And when I tried to make inquiries as to your whereabouts, it was to find that you'd just disappeared."

"As you can see, I am alive and unscathed. For the most part." I move one step farther into the room, remaining near enough to the door that Chissick will still be able to hear all that I say, should curiosity drive him to press his ear to the door. Fortunately or unfortunately, I don't believe he's devious enough for such a thought to even skirt through his mind for consideration.

"Ah, Thea." He takes a step to match my own. I notice the bank-notes still pinched between his fingers, though his arm now rests at his side. "You've no idea how surprised I was when Marta contacted me the other day. And to think that after all this time, you were once again the main topic of our conversation."

"Should I be flattered?"

I watch as some of the colour goes out of his face, and his mouth —or, more accurately, his bottom lip— hangs lifeless, before he's able to regain some of his lost composure. The change in expression lasts only a moment. Had I been less observant, I might not have caught it at all. But that single moment is enough. It tells me more than I could have hoped to discover over an hour's laborious conversation.

"I wonder," I say, my words chosen with care. "What do you think has brought me here tonight?"

"Marta said—"

"No, not Marta." I take another step forward, all the while praying that the movement will be enough to distract him from the tremor in my voice. Ryall holds his ground, but I notice the shifting of his weight, a physical demonstration of the indecision that must be now plaguing his thoughts. For I must seem a bold thing to him, no longer the quailing and innocent girl of old.

"I think," he begins, before a shake of his head changes his tense. "I thought that you had come to see me." He twitches, and I sense a new agitation overtaking his limbs. "Perhaps you would care to tell me about that friend of yours, hmm? I don't know what you're doing with the likes of him. Looks about as well dressed as a grocer."

He's almost sullen now, is our Ryall. And with another glint of his eyes turned towards my face, I see the hurt etched across his brow. Could it be a streak of jealousy that is driving Ryall's behaviour this evening? I touch my arm, the flesh still smarting from where his fingers had squeezed my poor elbow. And I think back to how possessive that grasp was, as if he feared Chissick had been about to spirit me away forever.

Breathing out, I spread my fingers and smooth down the front of my skirt.

"Julian Chissick came to me for help."

"Help?" Ryall echoes, one brow arching.

"The kind of help he assumed someone with my history could give."

Immediately, his face brightens. In his mind, Chissick has been demoted from rival status to something lesser and much more insignificant. "So, Marta was wrong?"

"Wrong about...?"

He claps his hands together, palms gliding across each other for a few seconds, back and forth, back and forth, until I think he might be attempting to create a spark between his fingers. "She said something about you having given it all up, your demonstrations and such. And after your attack, I really can't blame her for thinking such a thing."

Ah, yes. My attack. I must say, I have to commend him for his phrasing. Quoted in front of any polite society, and they would be left to believe my worst affliction nothing more than a tendency to faint at inopportune moments.

"And you," I say, with a small gesture in his direction. "No doubt, were of much the same belief as Marta."

He bows his head. "How could I not be? I worried about you, Thea. I worried for your very life. You were such a beautiful creature, and to be struck down in such a way, to be tormented..."

"Yes, of course."

"...horrible to witness..."

"I am sure."

"...I only wished to help you..."

"I know."

"...in some small way."

A beat of silence between us, and I hear Ryall release the last of what must have been a long-held breath. I don't wish him to speak anymore. It's not that they're lies spilling out of his mouth. Indeed, I think he places more stock in his sincerity than any man could. But every time his mouth opens, every time his voice arrives at my ear, I'm overwhelmed by his longing, his want. It shrieks through my head at such a pitch, until I feel as if I've already committed every act brought to life by his imagination.

When he raises his eyes again, it's not to look at me, but to study the few slips of paper clutched in his hand. I read the confusion on his face before he recognises the bank-notes, their crispness lost to several minutes' worth of perspiration from his palm. A glance to me, but I shake my head. As he returns the money to his pocket, I can't help but feel my shoulders sag as the money disappears—finally, absolutely—from sight.

"I expect you believe you've won some share of freedom for yourself, living out of the way as you are." He gives his pocket a pat and looks to me, as if waiting for a remark from my corner. When I offer none, he presses on. "Of course, you are still so young. I remember how it was, to feel so flush with vigour and new ideas, to believe that your worth rested solely on how well you could conduct yourself beyond the yoke of another's protection. But you have to understand, you're not like everyone else, like me, like Marta. You have a gift, a quality that makes you a jewel among women, and should you make a greater attempt to nurture it, to have your hand guided with better care, then there's no limit to what you could..." To finish his statement, Ryall pulls the fingers of his right hand into a fist and throws them out like the five arms of a starfish. And with that simple movement, his vision of my future life, of my celebrity, is so vividly described.

"And when I am overwhelmed?" I ask, ignoring his hackneyed descriptions of my singular talents meant to sway me towards his side. "How jewel-like will I remain, in your estimation, if I again lose control? If I again attempt to take my own life? Or ever, should all sense desert me, the life of another?" I see him wince. He has never been one to appreciate bluntness, but I doubt I could properly convey my own thoughts and feelings if I were to dress them up in layer upon layer of flattery and nonsense.

"You have always been so critical of yourself. But how could you be anything but blameless?" Ryall says, his protest bounding off the walls before dying beneath the strange acoustics of his home. "Too much stress, you know. I have always said that it cannot be good for the nerves, and you..."

He falters into silence as his weight shifts forward and he begins to pace around the outer edge of the room. His steps lead him around the circumference of the library, past great shelves of books so neglected I wonder he doesn't paper the walls with pictures of the leather-bound volumes and save himself—or his staff, I should say— the trouble of caring for the ancient texts. "The amount of stress and fatigue you must endure, I cannot begin to contemplate."

The fingers of my right hand twitch. They need something to hold onto, a bit of fabric or lace to keep them occupied. I touch them to my left sleeve, and they seem to find some comfort there.

"I remember how you looked after your sittings, such strain on your fair features. And when you began to fall ill...Well, they were dark days. Very dark days, indeed."

"As opposed to the brightness that inhabited my life when you first took an interest in me?" I dare to raise the line of my sight, so that he pauses in his circuit, eyes alight, while the darkness of his hair seems to almost absorb the illumination put out by the lamps set into the wall above our heads.

I hear Ryall draw in a great breath, followed by the hiss of air forced out between his teeth. He says nothing, and so I take leave to continue.

"I am well aware of the catalyst behind my initial rise to fame. A small, pretty girl. Young and slender, from a good family. Well educated. And the lone survivor of an unprecedented massacre."

He looks away from me. I suppress a grim smile at my ability to rattle him.

"A suspicious massacre, at that," I go on, warming to my topic as I witness his discomfiture at the turn the conversation has taken. "No sign of intruders. No weapons. No blood. But four dead bodies, their throats sliced open, the flesh seared." My own sight falters for a moment as an image of the young woman, her figure stretched across the length of the table, slips into my mind. And so the memories begin to mingle, the fresh and the old, twisting in and around each other, until I can no longer separate what happened a dozen years ago from the events of a few days before.

"I'm so, so sorry." His voice is a mere whisper, and yet I put up my hand, as if to block the words with my palm.

"I am sure you are. You've told me often enough. And yet, you used me just the same. As my mother did, as my aunt did." My smile returns, but the effort it takes to lift my cheeks into the smallest of grins is near excruciating. "She was always there, at every sitting. But I don't think she ever found it in her heart to forgive me."

Ryall tilts his head until he peers up at me from beneath a black brow. "Forgive you? For what?"

"For never making contact with her husband, my uncle. She would push me to try harder, to extend my reach, as she so eloquently put it, but..." I sigh, soon followed by a shrug. "Now she is gone. Perhaps she is finally reunited with Uncle Roger. Perhaps she's even gone so far as to absolve me of my former failure."

I look up soon enough to see the muscles along his jaw tighten and release. His glance flicks towards me, and for a brief second, his defences weaken, and should I wish to, I could simply slip into his thoughts, search through them with all the ease of someone thumbing through the pages of a novel. And before my mind has made the slightest of moves one way or the other, I slam into something hard, a wall so well constructed that I feel the breath rush from my lungs at the impact.

"Thea," he says. I hear his voice, but I cannot see him. My head is a whirl, reeling in shock from his ability to keep me out, to prevent me from seeing something he does not wish for me to know.

By the time my senses return to me, I find that Ryall is now beside me, almost in front of me, near enough that I want nothing more than to turn my head away. The smell of him is almost too much to bear. It comes from his hair, from his skin, from his clothes, the pomades and the perfumes, all of it cloying and sickly, and all of it carried on the scent that is so distinctly his.

My mouth works over a puddle of saliva that refuses to go down. With the bile pushing upwards, my teeth lock against each other, nearly grinding as I battle away the urge to be sick all over the floor at my feet. It's then that Ryall raises his hand, his left hand, one finger extended ahead of the others, to touch my cheek.

A shudder in my knees, and I think they may fail me. Not from any overwhelming flow of passion through my limbs, but because at the moment his skin brushes mine, a low whine enters my head, in fact seems to trickle in from some hiding place behind my ear, a thin stream of sound that will not grow louder, nor will it relent and allow me to regain control of myself.

I hold my breath while Ryall's thumb traces a line along my jaw, the same jaw that is still frozen with the effort of keeping all signs and symptoms of illness from escaping. He'll travel to my ear next, his fingers pausing long enough to tease what strands of hair have worked themselves free of the pins. And then I will feel his palm on my throat, the heel of his hand at my collarbone, the tips of his fingers dancing across my skin, so tender, so light, as if I should take a compliment from the reverence with which he touches me.

"Don't," I say, or I breathe, so distrustful of my convulsive throat that I dare not lend any strength to my voice. I could push him away, if I wanted. I do raise my hand, my fingers unfurled and ready to grasp his own hand and throw it away from me. But instead I step back, once, twice, and find myself pressed against the library door, the same door that Chissick must be standing on the other side of at this very moment. I imagine that if I put forth the effort, I would be able to sense his presence, to touch the fringe of his thoughts. But Ryall closes in, and I discover that it is his heightened energy, the blood racing through his limbs, lending a brightness to his face, his eyes, that overwhelms all else.

"You are not afraid of me? Not still?"

My wish is to hold off the pain that threatens to bombard my skull. I feel it now, hardly a pinprick, so small that it could be nothing more than my fear of it causing me to overreact at the slightest twinge beneath my skin. I close my eyes, my eyelids shuddering with the task of forcing out the distractions. I listen to Ryall's breath, concentrating on that single thing until I'm able to sort through the whisperings that congregate in the corners of the room. They want to scream at me, but I'm able to hold them off, perhaps because I'm stronger today than I'm willing to admit, or—and what is more likely the truth—

because provoking my sanity is not high on their list of interests this evening.

My tongue slides across my lips, seeking to moisten them, but my mouth is too dry, my breath too quick for the attempt to be met with any success. "I am not afraid of you," I say, my voice stronger now than a moment ago. "You were never worth my fear."

A blank look on his face before the barb strikes its target. His eyes widen, just for a second, before he staggers back. "You're cruel." His hand, the same hand that touched my cheek, finds its way to his chest, his fingers splayed above his heart. "I loved you."

And he waits. He waits for his declaration to elicit some great reaction, but all I can give him is a sigh, followed by the slightest shake of my head. "Lovely words. Nothing more."

Pre-empting any response he can make, I reach back, my hand grasping for the doorknob, the sweat on my palm greasing the cool metal of the hardware before my fingers are able to work it properly.

Some part of me expects Chissick to tumble into the room as I make my departure, but he has stationed himself in the hallway, about three feet from the library door. The position of his arms and legs tells me that my sudden return interrupted him mid-stride, and except for the lack of a cigarette, I realise he is near to the exact position he was in when I found him upon my doorstep several days before.

"Oh," is all that he says. But even that is an exaggeration. For I don't make out his voice, only the shape of his mouth as it mimics the vowel that I cannot hear.

Behind me—even without looking I know that he clings to the space I recently vacated—Ryall reaches out as if to halt my progress. His fingertips brush my sleeve, when he must see Chissick, and the hand falls away. A frisson of something travels up the length of his spine, stiffens his shoulders, realigns his neck, raises his chin. The plea that was about to be whispered for my ears alone dies before it is sounded. Ryall clears his throat and adjusts his collar. His return to the role of host is a reluctant one, and as he regards Chissick for the second time this evening, I assume it is nothing more than sheer force of will that revives the smile on his perspiring face.

It is clear that Ryall wants to be gone. One look at Chissick, and he assumes that his position in my life has been usurped. But still the desire is there, to cling to me, to win me back to his side with a soft crooning in my ear, his words of love, an ever-growing list of promises made to me, as if my renowned ability, the very power that attracted him, could not possibly know what his mind, what his very soul truly wanted.

"Ah, I've neglected my guests for too long," Ryall says, all reluctance to leave me again, to leave me with another man at my side. He moves forward with a glaring intention to take my hand, to grasp my arm, to claim possession of me, but he stops himself. His hand works through the air uselessly. A brief nod, a tug at his collapsed collar, and he turns away.

Chapter Thirteen

Though Ryall has taken his leave of us, I make no move to follow him back towards the main rooms. I hear the chatter of the guests, no single words or phrases discernible, only a laugh here or there, the clink of a glass, the opening and closing of the front door.

Chissick remains beside me. I have to give him some credit for not launching into an interrogation about my private dialogue with Ryall, though his curiosity has risen to such a palpable level that it radiates from every part of him, strong enough to make me blink.

"I am sorry," I say, for no other reason than it appears to set Chissick at ease.

He looks back, makes certain that Ryall is out of sight. "Is that what brought you here tonight? You needed to speak to him?"

"No, that was an unanticipated delay." I match the direction of Chissick's glance, and when I'm sure that we're alone, I reach out and touch his arm. "Are you ready?"

He nods once. Not a single word from his lips about what he needs to be ready for.

I walk forward, down the length of the narrow hall. The servants' stairs are before me, and there's a brief hesitation while I decide whether to follow the path in front of me or to go through one of the doors that stand closed on either side. Noting the lack of a bannister, I place my hand on the wall and tug at my skirts, raising them enough so that I can move at speed without fear of tripping over my hem.

As I move briskly to the next floor, I give myself a moment to consider what Chissick's thoughts must be at this time. Perhaps he assumes that I know my way through the house because of a message obtained from one of the many spectres drawn towards me, but the truth is something much more banal. Though it's been years, I've traversed these stairs before. My hand slid over this same wall, and when I step onto the landing, even the sound of my heel striking the oak floor rings forgotten memories to life.

But his hand was so cold, despite the sweat that lined his palm, and you wanted to pull away, but something in his touch, in the way he looked over his shoulder, in the way he looked at you, was enough to dispel your fears, for a time.

"You are such a lovely thing," he said. And again, there was his touch. Circling your wrist, over the smooth skin of your forearm, until his fingertips grazed your elbow, and then...

"Miss Hawes?"

I look around, unaware that I'd stopped moving. Chissick is in front of me now, and the stairs are so close that one step back, and there would be nothing to catch me before the fall.

"This way," I say, nodding to the left, towards the only door on that side of the landing.

Chissick allows me to lead the way. Every few seconds, I glance back to see his eyes narrow upon me, as if to reassure himself that I'm still there in the gloom, that the second set of footsteps tapping along the boards before him are indeed produced by a creature of flesh and bone, and nothing less substantial. A small smile touches my mouth, and I begin to think that maybe he's spent too much time in my company.

So much time that he knows when to draw up beside me, how much space to allow me as we move together, until the light of the hall is once again behind me and I face the outline of my own shadow upon the papered wall of Ryall's bedroom.

A quick survey of my surroundings and I realise that no one unaccustomed to Ryall's habits would be able to recognise the room as belonging to a peer. The furniture is shabby and mismatched. The drapes are heavy things, laden with dust, or perhaps it is the detritus of their own slow decay. The untrimmed wick of an oil lamp sputters with the smoke of a weak blue flame. And even in the semi-darkness, there is no mistaking the hideous paper that decorates all four walls.

"Ryall never married," I say, as if that statement alone should explain the state of his private quarters.

"No children?"

I shake my head. "Well, nothing legitimate, at least. That, and he's always been something of a child himself. For him to have a son or daughter of his own... I don't think he'd relish the competition."

While Chissick seems to be involved with examining the door frame, I busy myself with the removal of my gloves, one finger at a time, finally tugging them free and folding them over each other before tucking them into the waistband of my skirt. The small chore is nothing more than a distraction, a way to divert my attention from the images currently tumbling over themselves behind my eyes, all the better to examine them without giving any one of them more attention than it deserves.

"He keeps the papers pertaining to his business matters in his study," I tell him as I move towards the nightstand. I flip through several books and newspapers before bending down to search through the drawers. "His secrets, however, he's always preferred to keep here, in his bedroom."

I look back to see Chissick standing in the centre of the room, his arms at his sides, his expression blank. "And what particular secret are we currently looking to uncover?"

I abandon the nightstand for its twin on the other side of the bed. "To be honest, I am not sure." I'm distracted by a small book, sporting a cover of soft brown leather and pages that crinkle from heavy use as I flip through them. I recognise Ryall's hand, and when I pause to scan a few lines of his own poorly composed poetry, I scoff and toss it back to where I found it. "Sissy sent us here. She sensed his connection with—" I glance up at Chissick and away again. "—the woman you took me to see. And when I was downstairs with him... Well, it was the strangest thing. It was as if a wall, a barricade had been constructed around some of his thoughts and memories. Of course, I've encountered something like it before. You," I say, and shift my full attention on to him as I make my way around from the other side of the bed. "There are things you don't want me to know. Things you would rather keep private."

He says nothing to this, but I hear his breathing, more rapid now than it had been a few seconds before. And his eyes; those blue orbs are darting about rather quickly, as if testing the boundaries of my face without wishing to look completely away.

"And that's nothing out of the ordinary," I assure him. "Most people are capable of such strength of will. But with Ryall, it was different. I am not even sure he was aware of it, and that's what worries me most of all."

Chissick clears his throat and begins to speak, his voice stronger than before. "What do you mean?"

"I mean, someone doesn't want me rattling around in Ryall's head. Someone, whether with his permission or not, has effectively locked me out of a portion of his mind."

He blinks, as if startled. "Such a thing is possible?"

I nod. "Apparently so."

I leave him, a companion to his disbelief, as I begin to move about the rest of the room, not touching anything, but simply allowing my own thoughts to focus, to settle. The images return, flashing with a speed that renders me almost breathless. As the pain builds to a level that is just shy of intolerable, I pull back, the sounds, the colours fading to a mere flicker.

I let a final glimmer slip through, and I gesture to Chissick, leading him towards the fireplace.

"Over here," I say. "You're blocking the light."

He obeys without question, and I sense his proximity as my fingers glide along the underside of the mantel, clearing away a fine layer of soot that floats down to the floor with all the weight of a feather. A small sound of triumph erupts from me when I come across an edge that is not quite flush with the rest of the woodwork, but it takes some effort to open the panel, so much that I rearrange my posture, bracing one foot on the grate while I heave until the stubborn, warped wood breaks free. The sudden release sends me staggering back, but there, sticking out of the corner of the mantelpiece, a small drawer, tilting towards the floor beneath the weight of its contents.

Chissick should be the first to move. He has only to lean forward and allow the light from the hall to illuminate the depths of the drawer and whatever secrets it contains. But, no. Instead, he douses whatever curiosity he may have and reaches out with his free hand to steady me, though I managed to regain my balance some seconds before. And yet his hand remains on my arm, a chivalrous gesture, if I'm inclined to be generous. But no word of thanks falls from my lips, and as if stung, he takes his hand away, bows his head, offers up an apology.

"Please," I say. Nothing but that single word, begging him, really. But for what, to do what, I can't say. So he steps back, and I return my attention to the drawer, or more accurately, to the objects hidden inside.

They are letters, mostly. Hundreds of them arranged into neat stacks, and beyond the letters, pushed back into the farthest recesses of the compartment, a pile of trinkets: a single satin glove, an earring, a thin ribbon tied around a lock of dark hair. A regular horde of trophies, collected from every lover, every paramour in Ryall's long history of relationships. The age of the letters is inconsequential. It's the emotions that still emanate from them, and I think should I hold onto them for too long, like a contagion, those feelings, those florid phrases and declarations of undying passion will infect my own person. So there is little eagerness on my part to search through the stacks of sonnet-ridden missives, but something pulls me on, something tucked away in here that I must find, an essence, faint and rapidly fading, that carried me all this way in the first place.

There's no ceremony, no yielding to etiquette as I give my skirts a shift and settle down in front of the cold fireplace, the pile of letters gathered in my lap like a prize, something I'm reluctant to part with. Above me now, Chissick hesitates before lowering himself to his haunches, then to his knees, his eyes darting towards the door as if he expects a battalion from Scotland Yard to discover our crime at any moment.

"Are you planning to read through all of those?" His nod takes in the papers now spilling out from the boundaries of my lap, and I glance at him before picking up the topmost letter, running my fingers over the edges of the envelope, and tossing it aside.

"No, I am not." Another letter discarded, another one snatched up from the collection. "At least, not at this moment."

"But you knew those letters were there."

I pause. At this rate, I'll still be combing through the overstuffed envelopes come next Christmas. "Well, I knew something was there."

Seeking for something with which to occupy his smothered curiosity, for a reason to remain where he is, Chissick picks up one of the discarded letters and, after unfolding the two closely-writ pages, begins to read. But he doesn't continue for more than a minute. A curse, or something very much like it is exhaled on a breath, and he refolds the letter, pitches it away with no little show of embarrassment. Yet give him a moment, perhaps two, and there! His arm extends again, his inquisitiveness piqued by that first missive, and soon, he is scanning the lines of another, enraptured by the most private declarations of love from a young woman to her beau.

Further through the stack, I come across an assortment of cards, calling cards, and a few portraits, as well. All of them are of young women, all of them reclining, doe-eyed, seemingly unaware that their skirts are arranged in such a way that a few inches of ankle is on display, or the soft curve of an upper arm. But these pictures are only an overture to what I find a moment later, a small stack of portraits, evenly-sized, as if all of them are part of a collection, and all of them shuffled together and tied round the middle with a frayed bit of string.

"Dear God," Chissick mutters once he recognises what it is I hold in my hands. For these are no portraits of fine ladies revealing a bit of ankle and shoulder, but girls clad in nothing more than the pins in their hair, the rings on their fingers, and the smooth, alabaster skin they've worn since the day they were brought into this world.

It isn't until I remove the piece of string from around the pictures that Chissick moves to take them from my grasp.

"I'm sorry," he says, his fingers closing around mine. "You shouldn't be looking at such..."

"Such what?" I ask, a question that is rapidly chased by another. "And why not?"

He glances down at the pictures, then tears his gaze away, dragging it back to my face. "Well, because it's improper, for one thing."

How cruel it would be of me to ask for a second thing, if only to watch him stumble and stammer while his gaze struggles not to dip down to those portraits a second time. "It may have escaped your notice at some point during our acquaintance, but I am a woman. And as shocking as it may be for you to believe, I have seen myself naked on more than one occasion, so you'll pardon me if I am not offended by anything these *ladies* have to offer."

If there is a blush in his cheeks, the lack of proper light hides it from view. Releasing my hand, he nods. A sign that I may continue, if I please.

Indeed, there's nothing here that I have not seen before. The curve of a buttock, the swell of a hip, an arm draped demurely, covering one breast and yet leaving the other completely bare. And none of the women make eye contact with the camera. They behave as if they're not even aware that their portrait is being taken: gazes downcast, cheeks turned so that their faces are almost in profile, their eyes—the only things that would prevent them from resembling little more than statues in a museum—curtained by eyelids, by eyelashes, by eyebrows plucked to perfection.

I shuffle through them as I would a deck of cards, until they're indistinguishable from one another. The backdrop for every picture nearly identical, and there is always a settee, cushions, layers of drapes that I imagine to be rich in colour, perhaps a deep burgundy or even a dark green. And the girls show little difference between one another, except for a few slight alterations in the shade of their hair, the trimness of their figures, they could all be products of the same bloodline. And they are all young. No longer children, but neither have they reached the fullness of womanhood. And, I must say, I'm surprised by the predominance of brunettes, making my brief appearance in Ryall's history almost something of an anomaly.

I'm halfway through the stack when something makes me pause, my fingers tightening on one of the photographs as I drag it back before my eyes. The girl's features are softer than the ones in my memory, so much that I almost fail to place her. And then the image appears, gaining clarity, of a fine dress, of soft-spoken words to her acquaintances on the street, of a single bare hand knocking on a plain wooden door.

I know what else I will see as I continue to sift through the pictures. I flick through three more, four, five, and settle on the fifth as a sigh slides out of my mouth. Here is the woman's companion, the one who answered the door, who welcomed her friend with such a great show of benevolence.

"What is it?" Chissick asks, his voice quite near to me, but still several inches above me. "What do you see?" He glances down at the photograph for a moment, but his gaze is soon darting away, seeking another object on which to bestow his attention.

"I know these women," I say, and shake my head at my own half-truth. "Or, I've seen them, in passing. But something about them... I felt myself being drawn to them." As if I recognised Ryall's taint upon them, I neglect to add.

By now, Chissick has resigned himself to the role of companion, rather than protector, for he has taken up a post beside me on the floor, his gaze skimming over each portrait with a detached interest that struggles to equal my own. I lay my hand on the next to the last picture in the collection, but before I uncover it, I grit my teeth against the sudden thrum of pain that presses out from behind my temples, one ear pressed onto my shoulder, as if that is enough to block out the sibilant whisper that raises the hairs on the back of my neck.

This is what I came for, is it? All of the voices, all of the visions in my head led me here, led me to this secret drawer, to this stack of photographs, to this next to the last picture, to this moment when I uncover the portrait, and my hand freezes, a breath sliding out of me as Chissick stifles a groan.

It would be comforting, perhaps, if there were more differences between the figure in the portrait, and the figure laid out on the bare wooden table. But if there were, she might not have been able to catch my attention quite as well as she does now. It's startling how much I remember of her, from the tapered elegance of her ankles to the mysterious emotion hidden away in her smile. And now my eyes are searching her throat, unmarred here, a beautiful column that supports a head turned to one side, half of her face cast in shadow. But it is undoubtedly her, the dead girl on the table. And now I'm left to ponder how irksome fate can be, that it brings me here to prove, without a doubt, that she was yet another recipient of Ryall's attentions.

The other pictures tumble from my hands, scattering like crisp leaves across my lap, a few of them sliding onto the floor where they may remain for some time. I have no way of knowing. All I can see is the photograph in front of me, its dog-eared corner. I turn it over, and the looping scrawl of a name, of all the names to find there, singes itself onto my memory.

Isabel Capaldi

There's a kind of music in the name, in the way it rolls off the tongue. So much that I find myself pronouncing it under my breath at first, and then louder, my voice gaining strength as the initial shock of the discovery begins to fade.

But I must admit that the surprise isn't as severe as it should be. If I hadn't already known, if I hadn't already possessed some small clue as to what I would find in this house, in this room, the idea of coming here would never have entered into my head. Ah, another manipulation of Fate? Or are all of my movements under the control of something more sinister?

I stare at the name for another minute, not reading it, but admiring the quality of the handwriting, the elaborate dips and curves, almost a reflection of the figure posed on the other side of the card. But it is not Ryall's hand this time, though the various curlicues and adornments are familiar to me. I have seen this person's handwriting before, and I feel a heated rush of frustration at not being able to match it up with its corresponding memory.

"Well."

It's neither a clever nor fitting thing for me to say, but it's enough to break the silence that has fallen over us, as stifling as the heat that draws the sweat from my pores. A quick search through the rest of the letters, but there is nothing else that stands out to me at the moment. The picture is all. The picture and the name, tied together, tied in with Ryall now, and always tying itself tighter around myself.

It is a sound from Chissick that pulls me from my thoughts, a strangled sort of cry that carries such a panoply of emotions that I do not think I could identify a single one if given endless hours to examine it. I look towards him in order to trace the line of his gaze, but I'm disappointed to find him gazing at nothing in particular, his eyes cast down, his chin so close to his chest I cannot make out his neck at all.

"That man," he says, still without looking at me. "Your Ryall. What does he know about...? Did he...?"

And even though none of his queries reach completion, I can already interpret the direction of his thoughts. "Ryall is not a good man," I tell him, and before I continue, I see a flicker in his eyes, of revelation, or at least of the promise of some such thing. But I shake my head, ready to stifle any accusation he may be about to make. "But that doesn't make him a murderer."

"And you're sure of that?"

For the first time in our acquaintance, I feel the doubt radiating from him. Not so much due to any lack of faith he has in me, but because he wants this ordeal to be done away with. He wants to know what happened, and he wants that to be the end of it.

"I have no proof." I spread my hands, palms up, before him. "Only what I sense, what I am able to relay to you. Nothing more."

He mulls over this for a full minute. Behind him, set far in the background of our scene, I hear the steady thrum of life. All of Ryall's guests, still gathered one floor below us, creating a noise that calls to me with the promise of drowning out the low hiss of sound currently pressing into my eardrum.

As if sensing my sudden disconnection from him, that I have no more insights of Ryall's character to offer him, Chissick begins gathering up the discarded papers, pausing for a moment over the pictures, before he simply stuffs them into the middle of the growing stack. I fail to pay him any attention, knowing that he must need these moments to absorb everything he's seen tonight. And this might be my mistake. For so engrossed am I in imagining myself elsewhere, that I don't notice a particularly accented rustle of paper, followed by a few seconds of silence, before he whispers something unintelligible and rises to his feet.

"Miss Hawes."

The power of his voice, substantial enough that it never fails to grab my attention, no matter how occupied my mind may be with other matters. I tilt my head back to look up at him, his face strangely illumined in the candlelight that trembles at his feet.

"Did you write this?"

I'm rendered silent by the accusation, though I'm not even sure I can call it such. His tone is conversational, so calm that I could almost fool myself into believing that he'd inquired about my health, or made a random comment concerning the weather. But I notice the single sheet of paper in his right hand, the other letters and documents all clutched beneath his arm. I hesitate, not because I'm reluctant to answer, but because I don't know what answer he expects me to give.

The paper is plain, the handwriting illegible from this distance, in this poor light. It could've been authored by anyone. And then his wrist turns and I'm able to make out a few lines of the script. Very neat, it is. And so small that the average reader would be forced to use a magnifying glass in order to decipher the words so tightly squeezed into the margins. My mother had always been appalled by the quality of my handwriting, Marta as well, and it's only deteriorated since those first years of my paltry education.

"Yes," I say, my voice such a small thing now. I wait for any sign of emotion to pass across Chissick's face, to distort his features. I would take anything, I think. An arched eyebrow, a glint of sadness, of fury, of shock. But his face remains a blank canvas, and he glances at the letter a second time, fully awash in the realisation that he's prying into other people's business.

"You knew him better than you implied." He says this more to himself than for my benefit.

"I guess I should be flattered, that he thought well enough of me to hold onto it, after all this time."

He refolds the letter and hands it back to me, but I shake my head. No need to see it again. I have only a vague memory of what was written on that page, more than half of it no doubt dictated by Marta, and I've no wish to drag it back to its former clarity.

Grasping the front of my skirt in one hand, I rise to my feet before Chissick can put out a hand to help me. "Ryall had a strong penchant for young women," I say, the bluntness of the statement registering a change in Chissick's face. "Young women who were preferably untouched. Though, he was willing to lower his standards from time to time, when it suited him."

I take the letter from his hand, my fingers running over the worn edges of the paper before I walk over to the lamp, thrust a corner into the juddering flame, the light fading and then shuddering brightly as it attacks this new fuel. As the flames climb high enough to reach my fingers, I fling the burning page into the empty fireplace, watch the corners of the letter curl inward, turning black before settling into a small pile of smouldering ash.

"I'll be glad if I never have to see him again."

And there it is, my entire history with Lord Geoffrey Ryall laid bare. Beside me, Chissick shifts uncomfortably, and I know how much he's able to glean from that simple statement. I know it without having to raise my eyes to his face.

"Miss Hawes," he says, and there is a break in his voice, enough to finish me. "The girl, Isabel... Well, I think you should know..."

I close my eyes. Already, the words are tumbling about inside my head, the words he has yet to say.

"You loved her."

He hesitates. "Yes."

"Your sister."

"Yes."

I imagine I can hear the tremblings of his own heart, the unsteady pulse that shakes his arm all the way to his fingers. He is too quiet, and I look up to see his lips parted, as if there is so much more for him to say.

"You understand," he says, his voice pitched higher than normal. Still, he has yet to take a breath. "I have to find out what happened to her."

A small nod, my face turns back towards the fireplace. "I know."

"She was all I had left."

I know this, too, but I don't bother saying it aloud.

"And you'll help me?"

What choice do I have? Already, I'm drawn in too deep.

"Her name was Capaldi?" I ask, so neatly avoiding his question that he doesn't blink an eye before he answers.

"Yes, it was my mother's name. She preferred it, I think."

There is still a tendril of smoke writhing upwards from the fireplace. Leaning forward, I scatter the ashes with my toe.

"I am sorry," I say, and watch him turn around, pace to the other side of the room.

Too much, it must be, for him to absorb in one evening. His sister... Lord Geoffrey Ryall... and even myself... all of us inextricably linked, a connection that seems to have been several years in the making. And now he must be wondering how he fits into the puzzle, his mind going over each and every fresh question with the same frantic energy as my own.

When he faces me again, there are new lines of strain around his eyes, deep troughs flanking his mouth.

"It's strange," he says, such fitting words at a time like this. "For so many years, I feel as if I've been chasing after you. And I could never understand why." The last words spoken with a laugh, of all things. "And I still don't, really. But it all comes back to you, doesn't it?"

I can't bring myself to form a reply. And there isn't a need to, because he forges on without any signal from me.

"It can't all be coincidence. It simply can't. There's something happening, isn't there? Something drawing us together?"

"I don't know." I glance at the oil lamp, the flame soon to be asphyxiated in its own smoke. "Perhaps we should go now."

I give the room a final cursory glance, retrieve the stacks of letters and photographs from the floor, snatch my gloves from the waistband of my skirt. Chissick walks beside me, only stepping back to give me space as we move into the hall. I hear the creak of a floorboard, behind me—or behind us, I should say, as when I turn around to look back, I lock eyes with one of the maids.

Her dark eyes widen as she takes in the sight of us up here, strolling out of her master's bedroom with a parcel of documents in our possession. I suspect she is about to raise some sort of alarm, and already my mind struggles to form an excuse, but in that moment before the girl opens her mouth, I find that there is no need for me or Chissick to say anything at all.

Because that is when we hear the scream. A man's scream, cut short by a strangled sound, and then nothing but the most wretched silence.

Chapter Fourteen

I imagine that some years from now, I will remember it differently. The pungent odours of perfume and pomade will not strike me as having been so harsh, nor will the spicy scent of perspiration lay so thick on my upper lip. The press of bodies will be the same, the tight circle of guests gathered around the two figures on the floor, the one kneeling over the other. But will I remember my first thought as I move near enough to peer over the shoulder of a woman whose breath reeked of spirits? That particular detail, I believe, will be better left forgotten.

Chissick is quite near to me, but I'm struck with a sudden wish to send him off on some trivial errand, anything to take him away from the tableau before us. But as the kneeling figure stirs to life, his shoulders rounding beneath his jacket as he pushes back onto his heels, I know that nothing short of my own peril would remove him from my side.

It is a man on the other side of the circle who is the first to speak, an oath muttered beneath his breath as Lord Ryall's body is revealed first to that section of the room. That single whisper of profanity is enough to instigate a buzz of voices from all around me. Another cry goes up, this one from the man formerly on his knees, his deep rattle of a voice running down a list of orders made to no one in particular. He gesticulates wildly, as if this physical movement will lend authority to his words, but no more than a few people pay heed to him, everyone else too busy marveling at their own shock to do more than stand still and murmur.

"I want to go," I say to Chissick, but if he hears me, he makes no sign of it. In fact, I feel his weight shift as he leans forward, the better to see over and around the people in front of us, the better to see the dark gash that nearly severs Lord Geoffrey Ryall's head from the rest of his body.

"Miss Hawes." His eyes are bright when he looks back at me, and I see the mingling of emotions that I have no desire to identify. "Do you see?"

I want to think that he would understand by now. I don't have to look. I don't have to rise onto the balls of my feet or crouch down to find a window in the crook of someone's arm. I know very well how Ryall is laid out, down to the bend of his wrists and the strange, unnatural curve in his lower back. I know that his eyes are open, that his face registers no expression of horror or fear. And this, I know, is what startles the assembled guests more than the crime itself—that Lord Ryall looks to have welcomed his last breath with a smile.

"Chissick, please." I grasp for his arm, but only succeed in snagging the edge of his cuff. I feel him begin to pull away from me, and... No, I'm mistaken. He is not moving away from me, but instead trying to lead me into the centre of the circle, towards Ryall's body.

"I want to leave," I say again as my heels dig into the floor.

"What?" When he looks at me this time, I see some of the old concern return to his gaze. "Are you...?"

"I am not well. I want to leave."

"But..."

"I will leave without you, if I must."

It is the threat of separation that is enough to make him abandon his former endeavour. Lord Ryall is rendered unimportant as Chissick takes my arm and does his best to shield me from any curious eyes as we pull away from the circle and find our way to the door. For a brief, fearful moment, I wonder if our departure will be impeded by the approach of a constable or any other emissary from Scotland Yard. But it seems that immediacy is our friend, for no one has yet thought to close the doors or to make any effort to catalogue the number of guests in case there is future need for a list of suspects.

Chissick and I step out into the night, from one form of warmth into another. Out of the corner of my eye, I see him wipe at his face and throat with a handkerchief, a scrap of white fabric that he shakes out before returning it to his pocket. He has no hand on me now, and I'm left to keep pace with him as we turn from one street to another, neither of us paying attention to our direction, but simply moving forward and away from the smudge of shadow that I struggle to leave behind.

"How—" he begins to ask, but I cut him off with a flick of my hand.

"Not now," I say, wincing at a new pain behind my eye.

"But he is dead?"

I'm surprised at the note of question in his voice. Could a person survive with half of their throat sliced open? "He is dead," I assure him. Completely and unequivocally.

"Miss Hawes, do you know what happened?"

I make no reply.

"Miss Hawes?"

I find that I'm unable to look at him, yet I notice how his steps draw him closer to me, until his arm is brushing against my own and I think that I could lean into him for support.

"Please," I say, my voice so low it is nothing but air passing between my lips. "Please, don't say anymore. Just walk with me, for a little while."

"Of course," he says, before he takes my arm, his fingers solid upon my sleeve. "We will walk."

***

Even the appearance of the sun above the crenellated rooftops does little towards waking the slumbering figure now propped against my shoulder. I glance heavenwards, long enough to take in the colour of the sky, that silvery haze above everything that promises no relenting of the season's uncharacteristic warmth, and I wonder if I

140

should take the trouble to wake him. But in the end, I decide against it. One of us, at least, should be allowed some rest. I'm sure that my turn will come, but for now, he can sleep for the both of us.

The churchyard stands before us, or lists towards every corner of the horizon, I should say. The various stones show no preference for a particular direction, a few of them shooting bolt upright out of the ground while the others tilt every which way. A few more of them are broken, their dearly departed pieces hidden beneath overgrown tufts of grass, of soil, of whatever bits of refuse managed to blow in and find a place to settle on the uneven ground.

The grass is dead, the colour of its decay disguised by the layers of grime and soot that have descended from the same sky I had been so intent on studying a moment ago. The wall beneath us is a tumbledown thing, bricks fallen into heaps, the better ones long since pilfered away, the rest left in piles that have eroded down into something nearly indistinguishable from the patchwork buildings that rise up in the background.

It is on one of these mounds of deteriorated masonry that Chissick and I have situated ourselves. Our backs rest upon a stronger portion of the wall, while over the last hour, his left side has slid nearer and nearer to my right, until his arm presses against mine, his head tilted down almost onto my shoulder. A soft buzz of sound comes from the back of his throat, and when I move to wipe my brow—my face becoming more saturated with perspiration the higher the sun climbs through the sky—a breath, almost a gasp, and the buzzing falters before quitting entirely.

"Miss..." His greeting is truncated by a yawn, and when he notices how close to my person his own figure has shifted, he sits up abruptly, his poor balance almost sending him sprawled onto the pavement in his haste to regain some small amount of propriety between us. "I'm sorry."

"It's half past nine," I inform him, and avert my gaze long enough to allow him a bit of privacy while he performs an abbreviated morning routine: brushing his hair back from his forehead, straightening his collar, wiping dust and dirt from his sleeves, from his legs, before he finds his hat—that depressed piece of haberdashery—fallen down to the pavement, neatly camouflaged against the backdrop of broken bricks and dirt.

"I'm sorry," he says again, as he turns the brim of his hat between his fingers. "I only intended to close my eyes for a moment." He clears his throat, claps his hat onto his head and turns to survey me in the bright morning light. "And have you slept, Miss Hawes?"

"Yes," I lie, swift and easy. And here I'm rewarded for my deceit by the expression of relief that erases a few of the lines from between his eyes.

"Good," he says, nodding. "That's good. I had hoped..." He leaves his thought unfinished, his gaze drifting away from me, towards the first row of headstones, not ten feet from the tip of his boot. He studies them for no small amount of time, and I allow myself to roll my shoulders beneath the confines of my dress, stretch out my arms until I feel a satisfying crack in my right elbow. When he looks at me again, I can already sense the new direction his thoughts have taken. "You know," he begins, and dips his chin until he's watching me from beneath a furrowed brow. "You know what happened?"

The slight lift at the end of his speech marks the phrase as a question, but as I withstand the urge to fidget beneath his scrutiny, I realise he is not in search of an answer, but making a statement of what he must already know to be true.

But still, I stall for time. My hands reach up to prod at my sadly deflated sleeves, crushed by both the heavy moisture in the air and their most recent appropriation as a pillow. My gloves have also suffered, the black silk stained and wrinkled, and as I turn my right hand, I notice a hole on the inside of the thumb.

"I would have to venture a guess at a few of the particulars," I say, my attention still caught by the tear in my glove and the pale skin of my hand that shows through the flat black of the fabric. "But, yes, I will admit to having a fairly clear idea of what happened last night."

"But with all those people about, surely someone would have seen..."

His words falter at the expression on my face, on the sharp, quick shake of my head. "We're not looking for a moustachioed villain, bearing a wicked sneer and a jagged blade. No one would have seen anything, apart from Ryall being alive in one moment, and then dead in the next."

"But—"

"Enough," I say. The word is spoken gently, but it succeeds in its purpose. Chissick presses his lips together, his tongue prodding once into the inside of his cheek before he is still. "My head hurts and I have no wish to argue with you this early in the morning."

The fact that he does not rush to apologise does him credit. And so, in the ensuing silence, I manage to shift my skirt about my legs and make it onto my feet before he has an opportunity to lend a hand or a crooked elbow in my direction. A turn of my head and I can feel my hair tumbling loose from its pins, lank and nearly colourless in the brilliance the humidity lends to the daylight. I push the worst of it back behind my ears, snag a few of the dangling pins that strike my neck and cheeks, but I cannot do more. Not until I've had a rest, or a meal, or the sun again departs from the sky.

"Oh," Chissick says, a tentative sound from him, as if testing if I will allow him to continue without interruption. His hands fumble over the exterior of his coat before he reaches inside and removes a thick packet of letters and photographs, all of them tied together with a frayed bit of ribbon he must have rescued from the floor of Ryall's bedroom. "I would not want you to forget these."

I take the packet from him, the cards and papers warm to the touch. Before I have even allowed my gaze to linger on any word long enough to read it, I can already sense other people's thoughts and feelings, flowing from the pages like water. I give my already throbbing head a shake and begin to flip through them, less from any sort of curiosity but more to give my hands something with which to occupy themselves.

"We did learn something," Chissick speaks, his voice warring with the congestion of voices inside my mind. "This Ryall, he must have known Isabel."

"No," I say, without looking up. One by one, I flip through the photographs again. But this time, I'm looking at the back of them, or more specifically, at the carefully written names that grace each and every one. "Just because Ryall had a photograph of your sister in his possession does not mean he was ever acquainted with her. Well, at least beyond what she revealed in front of a lens."

I reach the end of the stack, draw in a deep breath, and start over. The names... The names mean nothing to me. But it is the writing itself, each beautifully formed letter that seems to provoke a new sort of ringing within my head. I recognise this handwriting. And with each photograph that passes between my fingers, I feel an incredible fury build up within myself, a companion to the increased pain behind my eyes as I struggle to scrutinise each stroke of the pen that created those names. Because I know the handwriting. I have seen it before, countless times, and yet it is as if something will not allow me to touch upon the memory of it.

A sharp swear leaves my mouth after my third pass through the photographs, and I realise that I must force myself to stop or else risk further injury to my head. Even my vision is inhibited by the pulsing ache behind my brow, and so I return everything to its former place, the edges of the stack tapped against my palms, the ribbon wrapped around once, twice, and finally knotted between my trembling fingers.

"I need to pay a visit to Marta," I say, before I tuck the packet beneath my arm. "I need to speak to her, to warn her." I look at Chissick, and I wonder—oh, how I wonder what he must see on my face at this moment.

"There will be more, won't there?" he asks, and before I can even inquire as to his meaning, he presses on. "More people, more deaths."

I try to compose a lie, ready to send it off the tip of my tongue to assuage that flicker of fear in his eyes. But as I open my mouth to speak, I find I cannot give the words a voice.

"Miss Hawes?"

"Yes." It takes every ounce of strength I still possess to keep myself from looking away. "I believe so."

"How many more?"

"I don't know." And as soon as I say it, I see the slight recoil pass through him, as if by uttering those three short words, I have devastated him.

"Very well," he says, and touches his fingers to the brim of his hat, giving it the slightest adjustment on his head before he holds out his hand. "Do you mean to pay your call to Miss Summerson now, or would you rather…"

Again I shift the hem of my skirt, caked in filth as it is, and seek a steady place on which to take my first step forward. "I see no reason for delay," I inform him, and when his gaze takes a quick measure of my appearance, I raise my chin, tilt my head to one side. "She's seen me in a far worse state. And more times than I would prefer to count."

He says nothing, only makes another offer of his arm, one I accept. "Thank you," I tell him, but my words seem to pass over and around him without leaving even the faintest indentation. And at that moment, I wonder how much more death there will be before this is at an end?

Chapter Fifteen

Twelve hours have now passed since we left Ryall's house. His body, no doubt, has since been removed from its place on the foyer floor. A doctor would have been called in to examine the prone figure and declare him deceased, and I assume that a coroner would follow. The police have been called in by now, and some of the guests—those who chose to linger—have already been questioned as witnesses. There will be no suspects announced, not yet. No motive for the death has been discovered. And of course, once they look closer at the body, at the quality of the wound that ended his life...

But this is nothing more than conjecture on my part. The scene I've invented is so tangled up with the truth of the matter, I'm unable to separate fact from the imaginings that swirl about in my head. Giving that same weary head a shake, I blink out of my reverie and tell Chissick which street we need to turn onto.

For the last few minutes, Chissick has maintained a steady grip on my arm, his fingers tucked into the crook of my elbow.

"Are you certain you're feeling well enough?"

It is not the first time he has asked after my health since we started towards Marta's, and I'm doubtful it will be the last. And yet he words it differently with each repetition—How is your head? You're not feeling faint, are you? The heat, is it too much?—fooling me, he must think, into believing that each query is independent of the last. And so I play along with his game, responding with a nod here, a few words there, enough to pretend the art of conversation is alive and well between us.

"This way, Miss Hawes. You almost missed the turn."

For a moment, I wonder how long it has been since I've eaten. I consider asking Chissick for confirmation, but the last thing he needs is yet another item to add to his catalogue of worries. But I'm sure it has been a full day and a night since anything has passed my lips. No wonder I fail to recognise the street beneath my feet, or even the houses that sprout upwards from the pavement, until the faded green door of one house in particular is staring me in the face.

"Shall I wait for you out here?" Chissick asks, but already I'm raising my gloved fingers to the brass knocker, the hairs prickling on my arms as his hand falls away from my elbow.

It's a mark of how little Marta has travelled over the last few years that a simple knock on her door should thrust me back, with no small amount of force, into the midst of my childhood. Two raps with the knocker, and there's Katie to answer the call. But here, already, is where past and present diverge. In the past, Katie would never have answered the door. She was too young then, keeping herself to the kitchen on most days, always clad in a dress three sizes too large, and an apron that could've fit around two girls her size. And here is another sign of the changing years, that I must ask permission to enter the house I used to call my home.

Katie greets me today with a beaming smile, the corners of her mouth stretched wide enough to nearly leap past the boundaries of her face. She's still a small creature, even after all this time, but she bears her physical deficiencies with a great deal of cheer.

"How do you do, Miss Dorothea?" Katie bobs a belated curtsy as her gaze flits to the man beside me. "And, um..."

"Is Marta in?"

With a great demonstration of reluctance, Katie returns her attention to me.

"Of course, Miss."

She ushers us inside, then stops mid-stride and turns around. Her hands reach out as if she's offering an invisible gift. "Oh, should I tell Miss Marta you're here? She'll want me to put you—" Here, her glance takes in Chissick, as well. "The two of you in the drawing room, I'm sure."

A part of me almost feels offended by this show of formality. To be escorted to the drawing room, like a common guest! "No need to trouble yourself on my account, Katie. But you could take care of this young man, bring him a cup of tea and something from the kitchen."

"Oh, of course!" Katie springs forward, her hands splayed open as she rises onto the balls of her feet and grasps Chissick's shoulder for support as she reaches to take his hat from his head. So committed is she to the task, that I fear she may knock him off his feet. But the hat is successfully removed while all of Chissick's limbs remain intact.

"Katie, is Marta ready to receive visitors?"

"Oh, no, Miss." She laughs, Chissick's hat pressed beneath her arm. "You know better than I what sort of hours she keeps."

I do, indeed. "I'll show myself up to her room, if you don't mind. And please see that my friend is well looked after while I am gone."

It's a chore towards which Katie shows little reluctance. Chissick's hat clutched even more tightly against her thin chest, she chivvies him into the drawing room, all the while interrogating him as to how best he likes his tea.

Her chattering dies away as I move towards the stairs, my hand grasping the rail for support. I didn't think to ask if Marta had decided to change bedrooms during my absence, but I follow the faded carpet runner to its end, outside the room I remember as belonging to her. Nothing more to do but land a soft knock on the door, followed by a much louder series of raps that finally elicits a response.

"Yes, yes? Who is it?"

It's a robust voice that answers, tinged with some annoyance. And finished off with something that might have been a yawn.

"Marta?" I say, my forehead pressed on the door. "It's Dorothea. I'd like to speak with you for a moment, if it wouldn't be too much of a bother."

A series of noises for a response now, the clattering of a glass, a thump—perhaps of a shoe landing on the floor—and a sigh, loud

148

enough to be audible even through the heavy panel of oak that separates us.

"Come in!"

I'm startled, at first, by the changes made to the room since I last set foot inside of it. Of course, I couldn't have expected Marta not to keep pace with the latest interior fashions, but the profusion of palms, cheap bamboo, and papier-mâché leaves me to assume that only someone possessing the talents of an acrobat would be capable of navigating the maze of ornaments and three-legged tables that litter every corner.

Something else that catches my attention: there is some organization to the mess. Several trunks are flung open, their insides lined with clothing, and other items have been gathered into discreet piles. Shoes laid out with their partners, books and newspapers stacked along the wall, and most telling of all, the wardrobe that stands empty on the other side of the room, its innards removed, folded, catalogued, and ready to be packed into one of the trunks or suitcases that surround the end of the bed like an archipelago.

And there, in the middle of the bed, sits Marta herself, marooned in an ocean of stockings and shawls and tangled scarves edged with beaded fringe. She looks remarkably altered from the last time I saw her. Wearing a plain dressing gown, her hair flattened from sleep and trailing over her shoulders, there is little of the entrepreneur about her now. And when she opens her mouth, the fullness of her Manchester roots dances off the tip of her tongue.

"Christ, you look like a corpse." Another yawn and I'm gifted with a view of every single tooth in her arsenal. "And I can't say that's a dress one should go about in while making their round of morning calls." She looks me up and down a second time, eyes blinking as her attention settles on my face. "Where were you last night?"

"I paid a visit to Lord Ryall."

"Oh, right. Right." She waves a hand, ready to dismiss me as her interest slides back to the task before her. But I watch as the corners of her mouth turn down, in fact her entire face seems to drift towards her chest as she gives my soiled dress, my untidy hair and exhausted features a more careful scrutiny. "Am I to assume you've only just departed from his home?"

"You may assume what you like," I tell her, my voice steady, despite the tiredness that has now infected my hands and feet with a peculiar numbness. "However, the truth of the matter is far less scandalous, at least as far as your imaginings will venture."

Her mouth tightens at this, but instead of making any further inquiry, she settles back onto her mound of cushions and pillows as she fingers the collar of her dressing gown. "You going to give me a proper greeting, or are you going to frighten away the rest of the morning with that bloody frown of yours?"

I rearrange my features for her benefit, enough so she won't notice the way I lean upon the door, the way the hem of my skirt marks the shaking of my legs. "I would have sent a note, but I thought it better to catch you unawares."

"Mmmph." She picks up a handkerchief, vibrant yellow silk, and folds it into a neat square. "Too much about you is enough to catch me unawares." She dabs her fingers at the puddle of sweat gathered at the base of her throat and dries them on the edge of her nightdress.

"Shall I open a window?" I offer, though I doubt I've the strength to walk to the other side of the room and beat at the casement.

"And let in the stench from all outdoors? Good God, no!" She snatches up another handkerchief, tugging it free from the pile with enough force to tear the thin fabric to shreds. "And what is it that's gone and brought you here at such an ungodly hour? If it wasn't a stay at Ryall's that has you looking like they've dragged you out of the Thames, then you'll have to pardon me for feeling a bit suspicious of your motives."

Through all of this, I've not moved more than a few paces from the door, the towers of clutter threatening to fall in on me from all sides. "I simply wanted to speak to you." Another cursory glance around the room, at the half-filled cases, the feeble attempts at packing. "Are you going someplace, Marta?"

"Oh-ho! You haven't heard?" Her cheeks swell upwards as her smile broadens. "It seems that a certain Lord and Lady Buxton have heard about the goings-on at a certain sitting conducted by none other than my little Franny." She winks in my direction, indicates my part in the proceedings with a regal wave of her hand. "They want to play host to a whole week's worth of sittings and demonstrations, and all of it coming out of their pockets." Her shoulders push back, and her chin rises, buoyed by her fledgling pride. "Well, it's more Lady Buxton's idea. Silly thing, went and lost her son a few years back and thinks that he's been up to haunting a cupboard, or some other such nonsense. But she's had a run of mediums through there, and not one's been able to leave an impression, so now it's Franny's turn to make her mark. To be truly honest, I think it might be too soon in her career to be performing in front of the... well, the higher-born, I'll say. But when an opportunity presents itself, who am I to turn my back on it?"

She laughs at this, almost a charming laugh, but when I cannot bring myself to join in, the handkerchief droops from her fingers while her gaze finds its way to my face. "Oh, Dorothea. What's in your head this morning?"

I reach down and pick up a glove, turned inside out, and fiddle with the fingers to quell my own nervousness. "Too much."

Marta chuckles softly, but I can hear the strain behind it. "Still haven't been sleeping lately?"

"Not well, no." I'm in no mood to lie this morning.

"I thought not. Lord, you look to have aged about ten years in the last week." She shakes her head, clicks her tongue against the roof of her mouth. "And what about eating? Red meat and wine, you know. Does wonders for a system that needs brightening up."

"I am fine, Marta. No need to concern yourself over me. I am not a little girl anymore."

I wait a few minutes, and she clears her throat. At that moment, a grey shroud passes over my sight as a high, clear cry sounds inside my head.

"Thea," she pronounces in a rough whisper. "What's wrong?"

Reluctantly, I close my eyes and pick out the strongest voice in my head, prodding it until it's louder than all the rest. A frightening, solitary note, more plaintive than I've heard in some time, whispering into my left ear.

"It's nothing." My teeth clench as my gaze seeks out the floor, ready for the fall I think must be about to come. Already, I'm dealing with the punishment for my mistake. Allow one voice to be heard, and the rest of them begin an unholy clamour for attention, cackling between sibilant whispers, hissing vulgarities that pull at the knotted muscles between my shoulder blades. "I'll be fine. Really." I shake my head, as if disagreeing with my own words. "Not enough sleep, but I'll be fine. I'll be..."

In a moment, she's on her feet, clearing a path through the piles of junk to grab my wrist, squeezing until I'm afraid she'll feel the scars I took such care to hide beneath my sleeve. In a harsh voice that feels moist against my ear, she says:

"You've still got it!"

"No." I pull away from her, a small movement, while my eyes dart from side to side, careful not to trip over anything that might find its way underfoot.

"Some people want the spectacle," Marta continues. "That's what they pay for, but you bring 'em something else. You know, I felt chills just now, wondering what was going on inside your head. I mean it, the hair jumped right to attention on the back of my neck, and all without you hardly lifting a finger. That's the power you have."

"I don't want—" But before I can even decide what I want, she cuts me off.

"Lady Francesca is nothing, do you hear me? Nothing. You say the word, and I'll make you my first concern. Get you back up in a decent house, decent clothes that actually fit you, latest styles and all."

No, no, no. That's not what I want. Not at all. I never wanted the fame, the fortune. Pretty dresses made from pretty fabrics and adorned with pretty scraps of ribbon and lace, my hair pinned and curled, scented creams for my hands, perfumes for my skin. But there's no use in telling this to Marta, not again. And yet it's always the same things she has to offer, because I'm sure she never really hears what I have to say.

"You tell me what you want," she says. "Anything, and it's yours."

Oh, to be teased and tempted in such a way! Anything, she says, and yet my mind can fix on only one request, one that has been gaining clarity and definition ever since it entered my head a few hours before.

"I want you to tell me how you came to make Ryall's acquaintance."

She rears back, shocked I think, and—in a rare instance, how I shall have to treasure it—quite speechless. A perfect opportunity for me to continue uninhibited.

"Well, I'm sure I've already told you—" She's interrupted by the stack of photographs, landing with a muffled thump on the end of her bed.

I give her a moment to lean forward, to peruse the first few pictures at the top of the pile. She doesn't go so far as to touch a single one of them, and when she glances at me again, her face looks older, more tired, I think.

"Did he give these to you?"

I shake my head.

"You took them?"

"From his bedroom."

A brief widening of her eyes, but she must decide there are more important matters to discuss than how I came to acquire some of his more personal belongings. "I've known him for quite some time."

"Before you met me?"

There is a slight tightening at the corners of her mouth. I think she may be about to lie, but instead she nods, an almost imperceptible movement, and I sense there must be some internal dialogue within her own head apart from the conversation she is carrying on with me. "Yes. Well, I was not always interested in this larking about with spirits, as you may or may not already know."

I did not know. I suspected that Marta's background might not have always been as reputable as the front she currently puts forward to the public, but considering the tragedy marring my own past, I was not going to make her feel uncomfortable for her own youthful missteps.

"I had a house, and I kept a very select group of girls. Lovely birds, intelligent. Not one of them would have been out of place in the poshest of drawing rooms. They knew how to speak, how to act. And Ryall... Well, he was one of my best customers. He always preferred my youngest ones, but it was nothing unseemly, mind you."

"Of course," I say. The only thing I can say if I want to avoid offending her, which would no doubt put a swift end to her narrative.

"I remember there was one girl, Emily, a very pretty thing. Ryall took a strong liking to her. It wasn't until after a few months of him paying her more than the usual amount of attention that I guessed something *unusual* was going on between them." She tugs at the collar of her dressing gown, but I notice the straightening of her shoulders beneath the thin fabric. "My girls were good, some of the best, but they certainly weren't any of them skilled enough to have a toff like Ryall sniffing around for longer than a season."

She clears her throat, dabs at a fresh layer of perspiration shimmering on her temples, and allows my mind the freedom to move forward towards the next point in the conversation.

"She was a Spiritualist."

Marta nods. "Of course, I'm not one to pass judgement on what others choose to do with themselves when they happen upon a few spare hours, but he was paying my girl for a particular service, and if that service wasn't being performed..." Her head tips from left to right, a fair recreation of the argument she must have held with herself all those years ago. "Well, it all squared itself away, in the end. And I'm not ashamed to admit that it felt good to step into something of a more respectable line of business."

"Respectable, yes."

She must hear something in my tone, because her eyebrows push upwards as she regards me from her place on the bed. "Scoff all you like, but it kept you warm and fed through many a season. You may be keen to disparage your former livelihood to all and sundry, but traipsing around as you are, looking like Death is nipping at your heels isn't doing much to support your arguments."

"The writing on the back," I say, eager to drive our conversation forward while my strength still holds. "Do you recognise it?"

There is a frustrating reluctance in her movements as she reaches for the top photograph, flicks it over with a single finger and glares down her nose at the name scrawled there. "Looks to be a woman's hand." Her mouth curls at the corner as her nose wrinkles. A slight turn of her head as her eyes close, and I know she wants nothing more to do with it.

"But have you seen it before?" I press.

"Perhaps," she says, always ambiguous. It's part of her trade, to be so frustratingly enigmatic, to keep people teetering on the edge and so always willing and wanting to come back for the next act. "Perhaps not. I'm no good for remembering that sort of thing. Details and such. There are better heads for poring over such nonsense."

I leave my post near the door, my balance wavering once as I move towards the side of the bed and sweep up the scattered photographs, careful to count through them and return each one to the stack tucked beneath my arm. Her disinterest in them may be feigned. Should I leave one behind, she could snatch it up as if it were a piece of unearthed treasure.

"A shame," I tell her, my voice calm, my eyes focused on

arranging the pictures and letters to my liking. "Any little clue would have been welcome, but if you are truly unable to remember anything..."

I glance up long enough to see her mouth chewing over something, as if she were capable of masticating her unruly thoughts into something more straightforward. "You want something." It is not spoken as an accusation. I must give her that.

"Many things, but I doubt more than two or three would meet with your agreement." I'm breathing more heavily now, and I press my legs forward onto the edge of the bed, the better to support them and give me a reprieve from their incessant trembling. "First, I would ask you to leave England." Now that I've given the words life, I cannot pause for longer than it takes for me to draw in a breath. "If you promise to leave before the end of the week, perhaps? That would be four days, right? If you leave, I promise to take on whatever task you ask of me once I've deemed it safe enough for your return."

The offer sounds paltry even to my own ears, but there's no denying the spark of interest in Marta's eye. She considers it, for a moment, but her expression hardens, her unpainted mouth drawing into a tight line. "Here now, what exactly are you going on about? And what's this about you deeming it safe? Safe for what?" Her arms cross over her chest. "Don't you be telling me you've gone off your head again. I had enough of that the first time."

"There are other places besides London," I tell her, going on as if she hadn't spoken a word. "What about Paris? Or Cadiz? Or anywhere, really. And you can take your Lady Francesca with you. Go on a tour, if you like. But stay away from here. For a while, at least."

She returns to pondering. For something to do, she begins snatching scraps of clothing from the end of bed, gathers them into her arms and carries them over to an open trunk, dumping them in without ceremony. I watch her as she makes a show of tidying and straightening some of the mess, tossing a pair of slippers into a suitcase, sorting through a pile of gold and silver bracelets.

"Lord Buxton has offered me a great deal of money," she explains as she slams down the lid of a large trunk, her fingers fumbling with the latches that adorn its front. "And I'm supposed to toss all that out the window? Because you want me to up and run away with my tail between my legs? This could be Franny's big break, you know. I'll not risk this chance at real prosperity, at rubbing elbows with royalty and all that, simply because you've gone and picked up a bad feeling."

"A moment ago, you said I gave you chills."

"Yes, well." She stands up, out of breath now, and I notice the dark stains of perspiration beginning to form beneath her arms. "A rank bit of mutton will give me chills on the right day." A brief chuckle follows these words, her attempt at assuring me that she is in no way comparing me to a hunk of spoiled meat. "Now, you tell me exactly why you think I should be leaving London, why I should be all ready to throw away such golden opportunities, and then..." She raises one hand, palm forward. "Then we'll see about working out a little bargain of sorts."

The images are there in a moment. Indeed, I very much doubt they ever left. "I don't believe that London is safe, anymore."

"Oh, and this is such a change from how it used to be?"

I pull in a breath as a bead of perspiration slides down the back of my neck. "Ryall is dead."

This, I see, clamps her mouth shut. But my victory is short-lived, as her jaw works over the argument she is no doubt about to throw, like a gauntlet, at my feet. "No shock there, really. I'm more surprised that the man lived for as long as he did."

"Marta." I wipe the moisture from my forehead, the back of my hand sliding across my face. "I don't know what I am supposed to say to make you believe, to convince you." I shut my eyes, hold my breath until I feel a pressure on my chest. "I think you may die, too," I blurt out, my voice low. "By the same hand that killed Ryall. And my family."

She studies me for a few moments, and takes to smoothing down the front of her dressing gown, picking at invisible pieces of lint. It's not like her to be so fastidious, and so her current behaviour acts as a bit of preparation for whatever uncharacteristic thing she may be about to say.

"All right." Her lips press together, forming a pout in the perfect shape of a rosebud. "But I want your word I'll be seeing you back on stage within a month's time, and that you'll continue doing absolutely everything in your power to make my Franny look good. If from here on out, every séance turns out to be nothing but twelve dumb ducks sitting around a table, waiting for a ghost to come dragging its chains across the floor—"

"I promise, Marta. When you return, everything in my power."

Her eyes sharpen. I fear she can smell the evidence of the lie, seeping from my pores.

"And you don't believe I should be looking to make this a permanent change of address?"

"No," I admit. "But I am quite certain that at this moment, it's not safe for you here. For any of us, really."

If she has any doubts, she keeps them to herself. And then her face softens, not with relief, but with the promise of new business ventures, of all the cities that must lie before her, crowds of people, and all of them stumbling under the weight of the spare coinage that fills their pockets.

"And you're sure this is for the best?" she asks, and now I know, I know that she's already judging how long it will take for her to finish packing up her things, now for a voyage beyond the limits of London, of all England, rather than a mere trip to the other side of the river. "What if nothing happens while we're gone? What if our absconding, as it were, turns out to be nothing more than a waste of my time and money?" All business, she is.

"Then I'll be sure to drop onto my knees and praise God for sparing us all any additional grief."

A small smile from that, but it's short-lived. "And what about taking Franny out of the city so soon? You know that you've always been my favourite and all, but if this ends up making her look like some kind of fool, like a fraud, running away after a single unexplained incident..."

"Don't worry," I say, the lie so bold, so blatant that I wonder how she can put her faith in a single syllable. "I promise that your Lady Francesca will have her career, one that will shine with an incandescence far brighter than what you ever imagined for my own."

I fear I've pushed too far, as Marta's head draws back, eyes narrowed as if to better survey the untruth that drifts through the air before her. But if I'm afraid that she'll change her mind and deny my request, I'm allowed to release my breath as she relaxes her own shoulders and dismisses me with a shake of stockings in my direction.

"Go and get yourself some rest," she says. "If you're set to make a return to the stage, I'll not have you dying before the first curtain rises."

Again, I breathe. The air in the bedroom seems to have reached such a thickness that I suspect I'm drawing in more moisture than air with every inhalation. I turn away from her, my gaze fixed on the door, the letters and photographs wedged firmly against my side. As my fingers reach for the doorknob, I stop and turn back, my grip tightening as I see a brief wave of black spots in front of my vision.

"One more thing," I say. My voice is weak, but if Marta is in a mood to be generous, I have no wish to squander it. "Why did you take an interest in me? I was only a child, an orphan by the time we met. Was it a mere whim of yours? The scandal associated with me, or...?"

I leave the question open, inviting her to respond with as much information as she is willing to provide. The wait is almost unbearable. It is not until I begin to think she will not speak, that she will not give me anything that I see her gaze drift towards a point beyond me, her focus on a period of time years before.

"It was Sissy."

A wave of pain threatens to rise up and engulf my thoughts, but I stamp it down quickly, my breathing becoming more laboured with the strain.

"She directed me to you," Marta continues. "Said that you had quite the talent, especially considering what a young thing you were at the time."

I push back through my memories, tangled things that they are. "But I didn't know her then. In fact, you were the one who first took me to see her."

"No." She shakes her head, and her gaze rests on me. The look in her eyes is mingled with an expression I've not seen since I still wore a pinafore over my dress. "She was well acquainted with your family, from what I understand."

"My family?" In my mind, I can still see the shadows and feel their menace as they condense and rush towards the people seated around the table.

"Your mother and her sister. They were great patrons of Sissy's work, if I'm not mistaken. Of course, once they found out you had a gift, well... She didn't need to be taking herself all the way down to Sissy's neck of the woods any longer."

My hand grips the doorknob with renewed strength. "I never knew." It comes out as a whisper, and quite honestly, I'm amazed I can even manage to remain standing.

I cannot think of anything else to say. And so I leave, without uttering a word in farewell, without wishing her a note of safe journeys or fine weather or anything else that etiquette would demand from me. The door creaks as I pull it open—I cannot tell how much of my weight now rests in the hand that clings so steadfastly to the brass knob—and I step out into the hall, my lungs gasping for air, desperate to escape the stultifying atmosphere of Marta's bedroom.

It takes a flash of movement to stir me from my thoughts. Out of the corner of my eye, I see a swish of vividly coloured skirts, hear the soft strike of heels on the rug as Franny slips through another doorway and ducks out of sight. But I cannot spare her any attention now, nor do I care if she overheard any of my conversation with Marta. I force myself to push forward, down the hall, down the stairs, down, down, down, until I hear nothing but Katie's frantic exclamation and the heavy thump of boots as Chissick follows me out the door.

Chapter Sixteen

I try not to pay attention to how I must look, my gloves hanging from my hand, buffeted by my leg with every other step. My head is bared to the afternoon sun, my hair adhered to my scalp with such an abundance of sweat that I wonder if I couldn't wring a cupful of water from the sodden strands. Inside my shoes, my feet itch, and several hours of walking have caused my ankles to swell.

I could say that Chissick's appearance fares no better under comparison. A tonsure of hair sticking out from beneath the edges of his hat, darkened points that cling to the sweat of his skin. And—oh!— that cap, looking more like a deflated sheep's bladder with every wearing. The black wool jacket, showing signs of wear at the elbows, patches of grease where he's taken to fingering the buttons. The splatters of mud on his trousers. A streak of horse manure on the heel of his left boot, the scent of it always chasing him from one street into the next.

And there is still more, if one takes the time to look for it. The small streaks of ink that mark my fingers, evidence of my thumbing through the letters and photographs again and again until the pages have begun to wilt from the oils and perspiration of my skin. Lean in close enough to Chissick and you'll see a few crumbs lodged in his beard, a souvenir from his time in Marta's drawing room, and the myriad edibles foisted on him by the eager Katie. And there, on the hem of my skirt, a splotch of wax, a reminder that I'm still in the same dress from yesterday. For isn't this the same fine gown I wore to Ryall's house, when I sat on a dusty floor with nothing but the stub of a poor candle for light?

As we leave the more reputable streets behind us, I notice a thickening to the atmosphere. The streets are narrower, the buildings stacked one on top of another, and the water...

Even as the river threatens to evaporate before our eyes, still there is so much moisture here. Trickling down walls, stagnating in gutters clogged with garbage and the bits and pieces of rotted vegetables leftover from a poor day at the market. All around me, the water roils and flows and steams. Every breath, I think, adds a few more drops of water to the air.

On the corner, we pass a small stand, still boasting the remains of a few rotted vegetables. It's been cannibalized, supported now by only a few slats of wood, a few bent nails that will no doubt be retrieved before the next evening falls. And upon this skeleton sits another, of a much more human make. Instead of wood and rusted nails, this one is draped in skin and a few layers of brown, coarse clothing.

The old man is lame, judging by the crutch laid across his lap, held by two white-knuckled hands I think would not give up their possession should Saint Peter himself step down from Heaven and tap him on the shoulder.

For a moment, I fear that the invalid might have already passed on to his appointment with the saints, but a twitch takes hold of his cheek. A spasm travels through his jaw, and the lips draw back from black teeth as he sniffs through a thickness in his head that culminates with the rumble of a cough from his sunken chest before he is still.

I do not realise I have halted—in the middle of the street, no less —until a word from Chissick, his renewed grip on my arm, draws me forward once more. I pull my gaze away from the old man and allow it to rest on the fingers of my right hand, wrapped around the string that holds the packet of letters.

Our progress through these streets is slow, a sign of Chissick's reluctance to return me to my home, to leave me to my tiny, sweltering room on the second floor. Stepping away from me and turning around, he reaches into his pocket and produces his leather wallet.

"Here."

From out of the wallet appears a small card, not one embossed with gold lettering or bearing a family crest, but a plain card, upon which has been written a few lines in what I assume to be Chissick's own hand.

"What is this?"

"Please, take it."

And I do. I glance at the writing, at the numbers and letters that seem to have been written with no clear purpose, until they begin to take a new shape, and I understand that I'm looking at a street address. Chissick's address, I'm certain.

"Thank you," I say, and tuck the card into my sleeve.

When I look up, it is to find he has turned his own eyes downward.

"Miss Hawes, if you ever need..." But what I may need is lost in the twitch of his mouth and a deep furrowing of his ruddy brows.

"Of course."

"I do not want to leave you," he says. "Not in your condition."

"Allow me some time to change my clothes, to rest, and I will come to you. We'll have dinner," I suggest, and he nods in agreement. "Some food, I think, should be most restorative."

"I look forward to it," he says. "A few hours?"

"You have my permission to call on me if I've not appeared on your doorstep before dark."

He does not say goodbye, not with any discernible words. There is a slight nod of his head, and his hand almost arrives at the brim of his hat, but both actions fall short of completion, and so he turns away, his arms settling into an awkward pose at his sides before he clears another corner and is taken from my sight.

And as soon as he is gone, my own legs resume their march. I can see the edge of Mrs. Selwyn's door from where I stand, but I've no desire to submerge myself in the sable depths of her house. But so consumed am I in contemplating a new path that will lead me in a circle around that wood and brick edifice, that I don't pause to watch where I set my feet, and I slip on a small clump of cabbage leaves left to rot in the middle of the street, one knee striking the pavement hard, the other struggling to straighten while my hands describe small circles in the air, a small ballet of sorts that helps me to regain my balance.

But a new sound enters my head once I'm planted on my feet again. A high peal of laughter, so close I almost mistake it for one of the voices I carry around with me. I raise my eyes, and there stands a boy, muddy pants rolled up to reveal scabby knees set into a pair of bowed legs. My gaze quickly marks off the other requisites: dirty hands and face, unwashed mat of hair in an indiscriminate shade, a squat stub of a nose that fits into his face as well as an unripe tomato, and a mouth...

Oh, I'll never forget the mouth. Nothing but a crooked slash above an equally crooked chin. There are no lips to speak of, only the place where his face splits apart, and crammed into that aperture, yellow teeth that crowd his pale gums like overlapping tombstones. And from between those two rows of teeth, such a laugh finds its way into the air between us. He pushes out the sound, starting as a rattle behind his rib cage, and then travelling upward, out of his lungs, his throat, before it's thrown out at me with all the force of a punch.

So much force that I rear back, wanting to duck as if the boy's pale fist had found its way towards my head. But this only serves to heighten the boy's amusement, and now he is doubled over, hugging himself with spindly arms as he coughs and chokes and sputters, his eyes squeezed shut, his lipless mouth twisted into a vicious echo of a grin.

"Please, don't."

My thin voice carries every mark of the harassed victim, giving the boy leave to continue laughing, until I reach down and wrap my fingers around a dusty edge of broken brick. I've no talent for throwing things, so I aim wide to keep from accidentally striking the boy. And when the rock whistles past his head close enough to stir a few of the dirty hairs above his ear, he looks at me, his mirth momentarily halted. I take this minor reprieve to rise up to my full height—as paltry as it may be—push out my chin, and gather all the rest of my anger and fear into speaking one word that I know will do its job before it has even left my mouth.

"Run."

And watch the boy, displaying the very definition of the word! Oh, he can't move fast enough now, skinny legs pumping, arms bent, elbows ready to knock at the first thing to get in his way. I could laugh out loud if there wasn't still some fear inside of me, enough to make me shiver, even as the sun beats down on my rounded shoulders.

Because, really, I didn't want to miss.

***

One hour of sleep, that is all. My dress is changed, my hair taken down, brushed, and returned to its pinned and braided knot at the nape of my neck. I have splashed my face with water and stepped out to purchase a ham sandwich from one of the few vendors left in this part of the city. And now I'm settled on a bare patch of floor beside my bed, my skirts hiked up as I fold my legs beneath me.

The photographs are scattered in a heap, along with the letters, without any reverence for the hours that must have been spent scrawling their words into existence. I have read through all of them, once and then again, my eyes now burning and my mind humming with the collection of feelings and overwrought declarations on display. Most of them have told me nothing. They are notes of love, for the most part. The language poorly spelled, the penmanship often not much better than what I would expect to find scribbled on a child's slate. Ryall's long catalogue of companions, all sorted here like a hoard of trophies.

As tedious as I find most of the missives to be, there are a few gems I've uncovered, raw jewels they are, lacking a proper cut and polish. A few words from a barely literate Catriona reveal what I had begun to entertain as the briefest of suspicions, that the photographs are a display of wares, all of which are for sale, the particular services offered fully dependent on further negotiation.

I look again at the image of Miss Isabel Capaldi, Chissick's sister. She is younger than he is, both in the photograph and the memory I have of her unlined face, so serene above the terrible wound that had ended her life. Their names do not match, though now that I consider her profession, I do not wonder at her wish to bear a different surname than the one gifted to her at birth.

My fingers slide across the other images of other girls. I have no need to touch them, but I think back to Chissick's previous query, his wanting to know if I needed to touch an object to make a connection. And so my fingers continue their journey, and my breathing slows, and the pain in my head—now an ever-present thing—throbs in time with the beating of my pulse.

How many of these other girls are already gone? Their throats sliced open, their life, their spirit flowing out of them as their blood does not. Or is Isabel the only one?

I think of Ryall, and the wall inside his head, stronger than stone in its ability to keep me away from his thoughts. He knew something. He knew something I'm not supposed to know. And I wonder... Was Isabel privy to that information as well? Could that be why they are both dead, both murdered by the same—should I say "hand", considering the culprit?

I sit back on my heels, my eyes closed as my hands fumble in my lap. There are too many questions. I made the mistake of entertaining a few, and now they rush into my head, one after another, and at such a pace that I cannot give the first one its proper attention before another has usurped its place. Perhaps, I tell myself, another visit to Sissy is due. I could push the burden of some of these questions onto her rounded shoulders, watch her swollen fingers flutter over the tiles as she pulls a few answers from the ether. But Marta's revelation of

Sissy's acquaintance with my mother and my aunt still rankles me, and I suspect that if Sissy did not see the need to inform me of her association with my family at any point over the last decade, I can't trust she would be any more forthright with me now.

Another breath, another minute of listening to the pounding of my pulse in my ears, and the chaos of my thoughts begins to lessen. When I open my eyes, the room seems unusually bright. It is midday, and the shadows cast by the sunlight that pours in through the window are at their lowest ebb. A shift forward, and I gather up the papers and the photographs, caring little for any sort of order as I form them into a haphazard stack. I have to rise up onto my knees to reach the last of the pictures, and it is when my fingers brush over one of them that I notice its subject.

The well-dressed young woman from the street, with the dark hair and the fine posture and the warm smile for her friend. And that friend...

My attempts at picking up are demolished as I sift through my stack, flicking the discarded papers onto the floor as I search for that other picture, the one of the young woman who had opened the door to her visitor.

When I find it, a breath slides out of me. Blonde ringlets over soft shoulders, a light-coloured gaze that dares to acknowledge the camera without artifice or guile. I turn the photograph over, my eyes searching for the name that I already know must be written on the back.

Edith Wing.

At least one of her photographed companions is dead, and the man who counted them with his belongings is gone as well. But Miss Wing? As of a few days ago, at least, she was very much among the living.

I stand up, resolve fueling my movements. I will go to her. I will see if she is still alive, and if so, I will search through her thoughts and dredge every piece of information I can from her fair and lovely head.

Chapter Seventeen

I lose my way only once. The streets are a different animal in the full light of day: alleys and byways that were menacing and narrow in the darkness now seem almost pleasing to the eye with a bit of sunshine warming their broken cobblestones. But once I arrive in the correct street, locating the house is a simple enough matter. The door is the same plain, unpainted wood I remember, devoid of any sign or placard to distinguish it from its more mercantile-minded neighbours. I knock twice, and then once more, louder, in case the first were drowned out by the sounds of the street behind me.

The door is opened without preamble, and there is the young woman from the photograph, so alike and yet so dissimilar from the image of her I carry in my mind that a moment must pass before I can reconcile it with the face now peering out at me from amid the backdrop of shadows behind her.

"Miss Wing?" I pronounce, then clear my throat and say it again, this time without the inquisitive lift at the end of her name.

Her light eyes dart first from my face, to my hands, and return upwards. But it is not only my visage that is treated to this rapid inspection. I notice the flick of her gaze as it takes in my posture, my clothes, along with the lay of the street behind me before her head tilts and those pale blue eyes dare to blink before they narrow between blonde lashes.

"Who are you?"

Her distrust is such a palpable thing that I almost reel from the force of it. But I remain in place, my hands clasping and unclasping several times before I put an end to the nervous movements and slide my gloved palms down the front of my skirt.

169

"My name is Dorothea Hawes. I was hoping to speak with you about... Well, I believe we may have had a mutual acquaintance?"

The pale eyes widen, her lips parting as if in preparation of some speech, but there is nothing. And so I clear my throat a second time, and I forge ahead.

"Please correct me if I am wrong in assuming that you are familiar with Lord Geoffrey Ryall?"

The reaction is instantaneous. The hand of hers that I can see, the one gripping the edge of the door, tightens until her knuckles change swiftly from a scrubbed red to a shade of mottled white. The door begins to close, her eyes still wide, her gaze still fixed on my face until the gap between us is only a few inches wide. But before she can shut me out, I jam my foot into the doorway, and I grit my teeth as the slab of wood jars against my instep.

"He is dead," I say, before she can say another word, indeed before she even notices that one of my limbs is the impediment that prevents her from slamming the door in my face. "I need to speak with you." My words gain speed now that I have her attention, whether she wishes me to have it or not. But before she can shove me back out into the street, I must say everything and anything I can. "He is dead, and I need to find out what killed him, because if I do not, you may very well be next."

The pressure upon my booted foot relents. The door, however, remains partially closed, Miss Wing blocking the narrow gap with her slight frame.

"Who are you?" The repetition of her previous question baffles me at first, and she raises her chin, the small gesture lending greater meaning to those few words. "Who sent you?" she clarifies, and I realise she is already straining to gauge the amount of danger levelled against her, before I'm even given the opportunity to outline the specific threat.

"No one sent me," I tell her, my conscience pricking at the hint of falsehood underlying those words. For have I not been slowly working my way towards this young woman's threshold, circling it as a hunter stalks its prey, while fricative whispers urge me onward in my progress? " I am a Spiritualist," I tell her, seeing no reason to prevaricate on this matter, at least. "Some might refer to me as a medium."

Her mouth gapes for a moment before her jaw snaps shut. "So how's that? You talk to ghosts and monsters and such-like?"

"That is what the newspapers used to proclaim, when they were feeling complimentary."

Again, her gaze leaps towards an area somewhere behind my left shoulder. Her lips draw together, and I notice her teeth—tolerably straight and with only a faint yellowing to them—as they nibble at the corner of her mouth. The rest of her face is fit for a miniature, all delicate lines and youthful proportions, eyes large and clear as they continue their survey of my own figure.

What she sees there must not be enough to impress. I note the look of indifference that wipes the lines from her brow, eyelids lowering as her attention settles on my face. Surely, I think, she must wonder what attraction I held for such a discerning connoisseur of the fairer sex as was our Lord Ryall.

"I've not got all day," she declares. And yet the door opens to me, not wide, but enough to admit my slender frame. Once inside, I'm forced to blink until my eyes settle to the meagre amount of light permitted through the shuttered windows. A minute passes before I can trust my sight to lead me far beyond the door, and yet I hear a bustle of movement from somewhere off to my right, a loud clunk and a scrape before a swirl of sparks announces the stirring of a fire on its way towards resurrection.

The fresh glow of embers suffuses the room with a soft orange light, along with an unwelcome warmth that exerts a pressure not dissimilar to the weight of a hand upon my chest. Instinctively, I move to back away, but the room is smaller than I anticipated and so I find myself knocking my elbows against the door before another step brings my hip into hard contact with the blunt corner of a table.

"You can sit, if you like."

This, spoken with such an evident desire that I will in no way avail myself of the use of either of the two rush bottom chairs set perpendicular to the fire. My host, on the other hand, feels no such qualms against reclining in my presence. A twitch of her skirts and she is seated on the chair nearer to the fire, the heavy iron of the poker still in her hand as she reaches out to prod the sluggish flames with its hooked end.

"You'll not be getting an offer of tea and light refreshments, if that's what you're waiting for."

I'm still near to the door, my sleeve brushing the latch as my hands fidget for a moment, restless beneath Miss Wing's attention. And yet, she has not once looked in my direction since taking her seat, and I find it is this lack of acknowledgement that succeeds in unnerving me while I struggle to arrange my thoughts and dampen the lingering discomfort that seems to swathe my entire skull in a dull, throbbing pain.

"I've come..." I say, but my voice falters and I must take another breath and start over. "I've come to ask a few questions of you, only a few, if you will allow it."

I watch her fingers as they tighten and relax around the thickest part of the poker. "Ask away. I've nothing to hide."

The lie is a bold one. She wants me gone. Gone, and never to lay eyes on her again. But she shifts in her chair, tugs at the edge of her sleeve, and with that slight movement, I notice the cracks in her armour, this show of bravado nothing more than a shield hastily assembled, and as swiftly demolished should I wish to put forth the effort required to unsettle her.

"You were acquainted with Ryall," I say, and it is not until the words are spoken that I realise how quick I am to abandon the use of his title.

Another swift jab to the fire, a blackened log splitting in two before the flames brighten amid a burst of sparks. "That wasn't a question, but even if it were, the fact that you're here in my house, prying into the more sordid bits of my life tells me you would already know the answer to it."

And now, she looks at me. Her eyes seem to have taken on the glow from the fire, and I ignore the heat now pulsing out from the fireplace as I step forward—one, two, three paces and I've covered more than half the breadth of the room—so we may regard each other with greater clarity.

"I found a photograph of you, among Ryall's possessions."

She ponders this for a moment, her bottom lip sliding in and out of her mouth as she turns the poker between her fingers. "And I assume the nature of this photograph," she says, and clears her throat. "I assume it's not something you'd show off to your mum?"

I raise my eyebrows. She nods once, the abused bottom lip pushing out until her mouth takes on a pout I can imagine would have been used to great effect with Ryall, along with others of his ilk. "I see."

At that moment, I wonder what indeed she does see. Her eyes glaze over, and I sense the way her mind drifts over an assortment of thoughts and memories, stored away until now. And then her gaze clears, her examination of my person resuming, but this time with a more accusatory edge, as if I should feel some remorse for coming here and forcing those memories upon her.

"And you say you found it? He didn't give it to you?"

My fingers flutter, the nervous movement travelling upwards through my arms until I shake it off with a sharp roll of my shoulders. "I was there, when he died. Many people were," I amend, before she can construe something criminal from my presence at his home at such a time. "But I came across a collection of photographs, one of which is of you, and another of a young woman who is now also deceased. Murdered." I push the word into the air between us. "And in the same manner as Ryall."

She returns her attention to the fire, the poker prodding at a stubborn bit of wood until it cracks and splinters. I notice she is not burning logs, but rather dry, broken boards, some of them still sporting bits of nails and other metalwork, as evidenced by the blackened pieces that litter the ashes at the edge of the hearth. "So your visit today," she begins, punctuating each word with another jab before she finally gives up the poker to its place by the fireplace. "I should take it as a service, perhaps? You'll be expecting some gratitude for tottering all the way down here to warn me of my impending demise?"

It is fear that prompts this speech. I feel it rolling off of her, filling the room around us until I think it should be heavy enough to smother the fire she stirred back into life.

"I expect no such thing." I swallow, take a step forward, and do my best to blink away the warmth that assaults my eyes. "As I said, I wish to speak with you. To ask some questions, if you would allow it."

Edith tilts her head back, and I notice a flash of pink as her tongue slides across her lips before taking up residence in her cheek. "Ask what you like," she says, her words sounding thick as her tongue continues its survey of her molars. "I can't imagine I've any particularly startling revelations to impart."

"You'd be surprised," I breathe, but when she looks in my direction, her brow furrowed, I shake my head. "Nothing, only..." I clear my throat. "Did you know a woman named Isabel? Isabel Capaldi?"

I say nothing more, allowing that name to slip into her head, to unfurl itself like a net and drag through her memories, in the hopes it will snag something pertinent.

"Oh," she says, her tongue still prodding at the corner of her mouth. "Oh! Izzy, you mean. Lovely thing. Wanted to be an actress, if I remember right. Her mum was one, and fairly successful, too."

"Did she ever mention her family to you? A brother, perhaps?"

A shake of the head, a return of the pout.

"But you both had your portraits done?"

"Our portraits." She scoffs. "As if we had Gainsborough in to do our likenesses, eh? All feathered hats and flocks of sheep?"

A bubble of laughter begins its ascent from somewhere in the region of her chest, but a glance in my direction and the levity is subdued.

"Not Gainsborough, then." She lifts her hands, palms up, fingers curved slightly, as if making an offer of the emptiness held inside them. "I don't remember the chap's name, the one with the camera. My sincerest apologies there, as I'm sure that's something you're after. But there was nothing remarkable about him. Dull face, dull hair." She shrugs, and her face brightens. "Wouldn't it be a thing, if all the miscreants, all the ones with villainy on their minds, what if they were like actors in a play, all cast to look the part?" Here, she straightens up in her chair, spine stiff, shoulders back, while her gaze focuses on some point in an imaginary distance. "'Oh, see that one with the harelip and the lazy eye? Get the coppers after him in a trice!'"

"Who else was there?" I ask, cutting across her final words, my voice struggling to rise above a whisper after her boisterous performance. "Was Ryall ever in attendance?"

Already, the lips purse, the head shakes from side to side. "No, no. And why would he be? As always, we were the ones left to take care of the unpleasant side of things, no matter that the room and all those lovely cushions and draperies we posed on reeked of sweat and mildew, or that we got a cuff upside the head should we have voiced a single word of complaint." She shakes her head again, the movement more violent this time. "It was just us. A few of the girls, the man with the camera… Oh, and her Majesty would occasionally deign to make an appearance. That is, if she thought our Missus was being too slack in her duties."

"Her Majesty?"

Edith waves a hand. A flick of her fingers to illustrate that while

I'm not privy to the joke, she will neither take the trouble nor the time to enlighten me.

"Mrs. E. That's what she preferred." And before I can pose the next question, she raises her shoulders in a small shrug. "I know nothing else about her, so don't bother inquiring." She attempts a smile, but I notice a return of her previous fear, appearing as a glint in her eyes, one she's unable to smother before it draws her lips into a tight line. "Well, it was only them, and us. And then the pictures went out, and the men would ask for the girls they liked—all through the Missus, of course; we never had a say in it—and that was that. All arrangements neat and completed."

And now she will not meet my eyes. The floor holds a greater claim on her attention, followed by the tips of her boots, sticking out from beneath the stained hem of her dress. Her fingernails—blunt, chewed down to the quick—are the final recipients of her gaze, and with that focus I notice a slight rounding of her shoulders, her back curving forward as her entire form seems to pull away from me.

"What of Ryall?" I ask, hoping to catch her before she has withdrawn entirely. "Did he ever ask for you?"

I watch her fingers as they pick at a sliver of dead skin on the side of her thumb. "He did. Once. He seemed to lose interest rather quickly, but perhaps that's just his character." She looks at me, as if expecting me to shed some illumination on Ryall's quirks, but I ignore the conversational worm dangling at the end of her hook.

"And Isabel?" I press forward, my mind immersed in the tangle that occupies my head. Desperately, I attempt to pluck at a solitary thread, in the hope that it will unravel the entire snarl. "Did she know Ryall? Was she ever one of his choices?"

"It's possible." Her head tilts to the side as she considers. "But doubtful. I was under the impression he preferred those with a fairer sort of colouring." This, spoken with a keen glance at my own pale head.

There is silence after this. Of course, it isn't quiet at all. There's still the crack and snap of the fire, the slow creak of the house around us, the rustling of some creature creeping about inside the walls. And further out, the bustle of horses, of wheels, of boots and slippers on the pavement, of shouts and whispers and the faltering hum of a city as the Thames—its very lifeblood—drains away from it.

"Is there anything else?" Edith's voice drags me back, back from the receding waters of the river, from the pain that flickered in my head as quick as a single heartbeat, and back into the sultriness of the small, dark room in which I still find myself. "Or are you all out of questions?"

"Would you..." I begin, and I close my eyes, squinting hard until the pain fades to something more manageable. "Would you have wanted Ryall dead, for any reason?"

"No," she says, without a thought, and I realise it can be nothing else but the truth. "He wasn't a bad sort, really. There are worse than him, much worse. And most of them still with the ability to walk the Earth."

My hand reaches back behind me, searching for something on which to lean. The burst of energy that brought me here is nearly dissipated, and I'm so tired. "Thank you," I tell her, the words feeble and empty. They're spoken for no other reason than to foster my departure from the house. "I've taken up enough of your time today, and I should be on my way."

A nod of my head, a gesture towards the door. Edith rises from her chair, one hand sweeping down the front of her skirts, her posture erect as she takes on the role of charming hostess about to make her farewells.

"Good day to you, Miss Hawes."

"Thank you," I say, forgetting that I had already said it a few seconds before. "If you remember anything else, anything at all..."

I offer her no direction, no way of contacting me should she wish to offer any additional information. I'm already turning towards the door, my hand grasping for the knob as my eyes squint in preparation for the brilliant daylight I know lies beyond the panel of wood.

"Miss Hawes," she says, and my grip on the knob tightens, though my steps pause. "The woman we called 'Her Majesty,'" she continues. "Mrs. E? I know it may not be much help to you in your inquiries, but... Well, it was merely a joke, her nickname. We called her that because of how she dressed, you see."

I turn around. Now, more than anything, I simply wish to leave. The ache in my head has altered in some way, and over and over again, my thoughts keep straining to escape to the edge of the Thames, to the mud and the silt layered there. "How she dressed?"

"Like the Queen, all in black. In mourning," she adds, when my expression does not change. "And they said she'd dressed like that for years and years, and all over a dead husband or such."

The pain... It nearly blinds me. I fumble with the door, my fingers searching without guidance, the knob cold beneath my hand—even through my gloves—as I wrench it open and stagger out onto the pavement.

I must see Chissick. It is my only coherent thought, driving me forward like a hand at my back. I must see him, I must see him. Before the pain in my head becomes unbearable, before the last of the tangled images in my head unfurls itself... I must see him, and I must tell him, because *I know.*

Chapter Eighteen

Brick by brick, I feel a wall sliding into place. I cannot fight it. It happens too quickly, the blocks slamming down, shutting out the light but for a few small chinks. It is those imperfections to which I cling, narrow but brilliant shafts of illumination, each of them carrying a flash of memory: the familiar slant of handwriting on the back of a photograph, the rustle of black silk edged with crepe, the intonation of a prayer, a sudden chill that draws up the gooseflesh on my skin.

But I cannot shape any of these fragments into something greater, and with each attempt, another brick appears, and another piece of knowledge is lost until all that is left is the pain in my head and the exhaustion that holds my body in its trembling grasp.

And then the bells toll out the hour, announcing to the world that it is three o'clock, and here I stand on Mister Julian Chissick's doorstep.

His is not a grand house in any way, nor was it ever. Two narrow storeys, so similar to its neighbours on either side that I have to keep my gaze fixed on the number above the door to prevent myself from drifting over to the wrong stoop.

I pause on the stair, one hand braced against the doorway as I search for a knocker or a bell of some sort with which to announce my arrival, but there is nothing but a gaping wound where a knocker had once resided. And so I'm left to beat on the door with my fist, four knocks and a pause, four knocks and a pause. It becomes almost something of a litany, until I press my ear to the wood and hear the sound of heavy boots on a staircase, the steps growing louder before the knob turns and the door swings open before me.

I expect Chissick to say my name, to offer some kind of a

greeting, but instead he stands there, the laces of his shoes straggling around his ankles, his braces twisted over his shoulders in his haste to put them on. His jaw still sports the previous day's growth of beard, and he looks at me as if he's looking through me, believing me to be nothing more than an apparition turned up on his doorstep.

"I am sorry," I say, in lieu of a proper greeting. "I thought I had given you enough time to rest, to recover."

He runs his hand through his hair, still uncombed since this morning. "No, it's fine."

If I expected him to say more, I'm sadly disappointed. Without another word, he steps back, ushers me inside with a small dip of his whiskered chin.

My eyes blink as they acclimate to the semi-darkness that cloaks his front hall. My steps find some strength now I'm indoors, and the absence of direct sunlight seems to act as a balm to the ache in my head. "I would have been here earlier, only I called on someone before I came here, a Miss Edith Wing." I pronounce the name, and wait for a reaction from him. But I can see that his thoughts are still mired in a fog of exhaustion, and so he has yet to attend to my words. "She was one of Ryall's girls, one of the women from the photographs." Still— Still!—he does not look up. "Chissick, she knew your sister."

The change in him is abrupt. A rigidity that affects his limbs, his spine, travelling up through his neck until his head turns, his gaze focusing on nothing I can discern as he straightens up to his full height. "And?"

I blink again, each flickering of my eyes matching the frantic pace of the pictures changing inside my head. "And she knew..." But what she knew, the details of the conversation are already slipping away from me. Another brick drops into place. Another light is shut out. "I cannot remember. Something is trying to prevent me from recalling. But I knew..." I look up at him, my voice, my expression, my very posture shaped into an apology. "When I left her—Miss Wing—I saw it all, right before my eyes. But someone has tampered..." I blink. "It's right there, and I can't seem to focus on it."

"Well, please," he says. "Come in." Those words spoken despite the fact he's already closed the door behind me. He glances left and right, his gaze settling on an open doorway, and the room beyond it, cold and dark, furniture hidden beneath sheets, a fireplace stuffed with broken crates and a few dusty volumes.

He walks towards me, and I notice the buttons on his shirt, misaligned, and the collar sticking up on one side. And his eyes, still swollen with sleep. A sleep I must have snatched away from him. "I woke up a few moments ago. Um, if you could wait here, not more than a minute."

He runs up the stairs, taking them two at a time, and I soon hear the clomp of footsteps above my head, the bang of a drawer, or a door, and he appears again, shoving his arms into the sleeves of his coat as he returns to my side.

"Your shoes," I point out, glancing at his tangled laces.

"Oh, right." He drops to one knee, and when that boot is taken care of, switches to the other. "I'm sorry," he says as he pulls himself up, hands straightening his collar, running over his hair, settling on the cockeyed buttons of his shirt. "I didn't realise how tired I was." A quick check of his pockets, and he dashes towards the door, but he pauses with his hand on the knob, his fingers flexing and releasing as he turns around once more, his red-rimmed gaze fixing on me. "Wait, where are we going?"

"To eat," I tell him, while he fiddles with his collar. "I find I am in great need of sustenance."

"Of course." Another flick of his collar, which refuses to react to his ministrations. "But this Miss Wing, how did you find her? You were able to call on her, at her home?"

I wave my hand, a sharp dismissal of his question. "It was coincidence that drew me towards her, nothing more. The important thing is that she is still alive, at least for the moment."

A line appears between his eyes, and I notice a trembling in his jaw, an attempt at masking a yawn from my sight. "You should not have gone without me," he says, his eyes no longer on my face. "You had no idea what could have been waiting for you there."

"A woman was waiting for me there. Young, alone, and afraid. That is all."

He nods, mollified. "And she helped you? You were able to see who is behind all of this?"

"Only a glimpse," I tell him, and I feel the heat of guilt flush upwards into my cheeks. "But it will come again. I am close now, and whoever it is, they're frightened."

I watch his jaw set, his throat tighten as he swallows. "To eat," he says suddenly, echoing my previous statement. "Neither of us will be worth a damned thing if we're both dead of starvation."

My eyes widen at his language. He must still disapprove of my having gone to see Miss Wing without him. He steps past me and opens the door, the dusty corridor flooded by a broad shaft of afternoon light. I raise my hand to my face, and beside me Chissick ducks his own head, as if the brightness is a solid object that must be pushed against.

"Chissick," I say, and he glances towards me, his eyes narrowed. "Your hat?"

"Oh, of course." He steps back into the gloom, long enough to snatch his hat from a peg near to the door. He claps it on his head, gives his collar another tug, and offers me the crook of his arm.

I cling to Chissick's sleeve as we descend the narrow steps outside his door. I'm ready to speak again, my beleaguered mind straining to return to the details of my conversation with Miss Wing, but my thoughts are interrupted by a voice from behind my left shoulder. I glance at Chissick, but before he can put voice to another word, Trevor passes out of the glare of the sun and into view, his hat squashed beneath a crooked arm that bears no jacket or coat. A faded grey shirt appears to be the only covering the upper half of his person will tolerate at this time of day, and when he sees me, a brief touch of thumb and forefinger to his brow is all the acknowledgement I receive.

"Jules." He gives Chissick a nod and the full force of his attention. "I didn't know if I'd find you at home this time of day."

"You caught me just in time." I feel Chissick's arm tense beneath my grip as he speaks. There can be nothing but ill to come from a visit from Trevor. Upon my first meeting him, there was the length of a dead body between us, and so his appearance now, on the heels of my visit with Edith Wing and as the pain in my head threatens to leave me crumpled into a heap in the dust, can bode nothing well.

"I thought you'd like to know," Trevor speaks, his every word prefaced by a breath that seems to draw in all of the available air. "There's another body." He winces, his gaze flicking towards me as if he would wish me anywhere but within hearing range of this pronouncement. "I wouldn't have thought to bother you with it, but it's the same wound at the throat as the other one. The same... everything."

Chissick scuffs his heel across the dirt and grit of the pavement. A breath slides out of him, and his arm sags under my fingers. "We were about to find a place to eat, but—"

"If you want to take a look before the peelers arrive and leave their mess and footprints everywhere, you might want to think about postponing your meal."

"How far?"

"It's Southwark," Trevor says, and clears his throat with a gruff, wet sound that rings in my ears for several moments afterward. "It's down by a pier, a dilapidated thing."

Chissick nods, and turns towards me. His hands find their way to my shoulders, and I can feel his thumbs pressing on my collarbone. How light and frail a thing I must appear to him. "Are you well enough, after last night?"

"Yes, I am." It is such a lie, but it comes so easily that I feel I have no other response to make.

"Right, well." His fingers fall away from me, and there's a sudden coolness in place of his touch. "That's not far from here, not far at all." He rubs his chin, his knuckles scratching at the fresh layer of beard that hides the lower half of his face from view. "A bit of a walk? You're not averse to that?"

"Of course not," I say, and I feel Trevor's eyes rest on me, before a frown and a low groan mark his disapproval.

***

There's the crunch of gravel beneath my feet, and the sour smells of rot and something I recognise as being stagnant. And still, there is no breeze, nothing as wholesome or refreshing as that. And this brings me to realise that it's the very air around me that is still, and holding onto every scent that has passed through this area, until my nose—poor thing—is overwhelmed. All the smells of fish and soot and piss and muck have combined into an entirely new aroma, and I glance to my left, toward the solid edifice of Southwark Bridge, and I wonder if I'll be forever forced to associate this smell with those shallow arches.

It's a small group gathered near the pier. Hardly a pier, I notice as I walk forward. A barked command, and I hear the rumble of wheels from somewhere behind me, the clatter of hooves, and I take it as a signal to breathe, to steel myself, and to clear my head as best as my mental companions will allow. Several yards away, there's a set of stone steps that descends into the sluggish water of the river. The pitted stones are caked with mud, with a yellow and green sludge that seems to shimmer even on the side where the sunlight does not reach. I wonder how much time has passed since those bottommost stones saw daylight, felt the brush of air across their surface. Maybe not since they were first constructed and set into place, however many years ago that might have been.

I notice Chissick and Trevor already standing with the other men, four figures in all, two of whom I don't recognise. I circle them for another minute, and then I close in.

184

As Chissick is the first to acknowledge my approach, it's his discreet signal that alerts the man standing to his left. And like a chain reaction, the other two turn their heads, respond to my appearance before them with the knuckling of foreheads, fingers grasping for hats they'd long removed before my arrival.

Trevor takes a step back, an awkward movement that admits me to the circle. "Not a pretty sight, is it, Miss?" he says, and pushes at his shirtsleeves, rolling up the cuffs to expose his meaty forearms.

"No, it isn't." It's something of a performance not to show I notice the shadow of suspicion in his eyes, the way he places himself between Chissick and myself, as if making a conscious effort to always keep us separate. He wipes his hand across his face, clearing away the perspiration along with his former expression, so that when he looks at me again, I only notice the sunburn on his cheeks, the skin on his nose blistered and already beginning to peel.

This heat must be near enough to lay the poor man flat. Every pore on his body seems to producing more than its usual share of moisture, so that when he raises his hand to his brow, I think I see several drops of sweat dribble from the rounded point of his elbow.

The men, four of them in all, had been speaking in low voices as I approached, but have now fallen into an uneasy silence. After all, there is a sixth member of our little group I've neglected to mention. Stretched out on the gravel, she acts as a centrepiece to our meagre gathering. The lower half of her body is all layers of shredded and muddy skirts twined around swollen legs, while the upper half is shielded from view. One of the men has sacrificed his coat to the task of concealment, so I'm left to study the feet, one with a shoe and the other without, the stockings and petticoats stained a mottled grey by the silt and sediment of the river. For there's no doubt that this body was recently recovered from the water that even now edges away from us, drawn out by the tide.

Dimly, I'm aware of what has brought all five of us here this morning. Another body. So many of them now. Should I be worried that this has become too regular of an occurrence? Chissick gestures, not to me, but to Trevor, and the top three inches of the coat are pulled back.

Matted hair is all I see, no individual strands, but thick ropes of grey that cling stubbornly to the pale, slightly greenish skin of the forehead. The hesitation that stills Trevor's movements sends a frisson of anticipation through me, through all of us, until Chissick is forced to speak.

"Just get it over with."

No more hesitation now. The coat is pulled away, up and off, and given a hearty shake before it is returned to the man who surrendered it. That I should spend all of my attention on the fate of the ill-used coat should do much towards shedding some light on my current state of mind. There, on the ground, not three feet away from me, is a dead body. But my reluctance to react to its presence is not guided by any kind of revulsion, but rather a fear, of sorts. A fear of confirmation, if I wish to be more specific. Because I already know the identity of the woman lying there. I know her face, the sound of her voice, and with startling clarity, I remember the last words she said to me.

I can take care of my own self.

If I close my eyes, I can still picture her seated on her little wooden stool, a tray of tiles balanced on her lap. But that is only a memory. Now, her face is blotched and swollen. Trails of dried silt stream from her nostrils, from the corners of her eyes and mouth. It's when I take a second look at her eyes that my chest rises and falls, and I take to pulling in each and every breath through gritted teeth.

Sissy's left eye, clouded and milky, still marbled with veins of blue, protrudes from its socket, while the other eye, the one I remember as being black and glassy, is gone. A dark slash from the gaping socket down to her jaw mars the entire side of her face. I close my eyes and look away when I realise that I'm staring at a sliver of exposed jawbone.

"Who found her?"

The question slips out, bristling with an authority I've not yet heard myself use.

In reply, the oldest man in our group, the owner of the coat, moves forward. He bows his head as he looks at me, peering up through small eyes with pale lashes. His head is crowned with a tonsure of white, and the top of his scalp is sunburned and scabbed over.

"I found her, ma'am," he says, raising his hand to his forehead, touching the brim of an imaginary cap. "The boy and I were out early this morning." He gestures to the youth beside him, a gangly thing still growing, judging by the amount of wrist and ankle left bare by his ill-fitting shirt and trousers. "Night and mornin's the only time to go out nowadays, try to catch a bit of cooling over the water. But as I said, we were just fishin' and the like, and here we were coming up on morning, and this one spotted something like was billowing out, breathing on the surface of the water. And Tom said he thought something had got itself hooked up on the corner of the old pier. Didn't you, Tom?"

The boy named Tom nods, his eyes downcast, both hands clasped and held over his groin. His colourless hair stands out at all angles from his head, flattened on one side, but sticking out like the quills of a porcupine on the other.

"Yes, ma'am. Tom saw her first, 'course we didn't know it was a 'her' at the time, but we swung the boat round, our heads all full of wonderin' and worryin' about what it could be. I didn't want to think on it being someone having gone and pitched themselves off the bridge, but you gets all sorts, 'specially in those hours before sun's up to full strength, and we weren't taking any chances, so I says to Tom, I says, 'I hope that's not a jumper!' Didn't I say that, boy?"

Another nod from Tom, who in the full light of the afternoon, wears a green cast of his own around the edges.

"See? Tom'll vouch for us, ma'am. And so it were as I said. We swung the boat round, and I rowed until I had a burning ache in my shoulders." Here, the old man moves his arms, around and around, back and forth, until I understand he's recreating the scene from several hours ago, all the way down to the stoop his shoulders must have worn as he pulled on the oars. "And I told Tom to bring out the grapplin' hook, and he took a stab at her." He stabs at the air, a move that would put D'artagnan to shame. "But that's when he did the damage to her face there, and we are sorry about that, ma'am. But you've got to understand, out there in the water, just a lantern swinging round your head for light... Right, Tom?" His head swings around and he locks onto the boy with an eager stare. "You're sorry about sending that hook through the old woman's eye, aren't you?"

This is the last straw for poor Tom, who turns his back on the assembled company, gravel spraying out from beneath his heels as he lunges towards the water's edge. He retches loudly, and the rest of us avert our eyes, thankful for the old man's attempts to clear his throat and carry on with the conversation as the boy's coughing subsides.

"He's very sorry," the old man assures us, again tipping his invisible hat in my direction. "Aren't you, Tom?" With a gnarled hand, he draws the boy back into the circle, clapping him on the shoulder. The action carries enough force to nearly send young Tom running back towards the river. But instead, he wipes his mouth with his shirtsleeve, and pushes several strands of sweaty hair out of his eyes.

"Yes, ma'am." The boy's voice is pitched high, higher than normal, I suspect, as he still appears to be holding his stomach in check. "I never meant to... I didn't..."

Perhaps it's the way the young man trembles, the weakness in him that draws the words of comfort from me. I tell him it will be all right, that I'm sure he meant no harm, that he was a good lad and that he did a good job. And I'm almost tempted to trawl my pockets for one of Marta's coins and make a present of it to the boy, but I wonder if it would somehow be deemed vulgar, and so I falter into an awkward silence, and the boy trains his gaze on the tips of his muddy boots.

"Well," the old man says when no one ventures to speak for more than a minute. He says the word again, while his pale gaze darts here and there, as if searching for any part of the story left untold. "Well, we hauled her up all right. You wouldn't think it would be such a hard job for two, but hanging off the corner of the pier like she was, and them skirts holding water like..."

Unfortunately, he can't think of anything known for its absorption, so he stammers some more, his eyes still shifting in search of his previous thread. "Why, there was a moment or two when I'd thought we'd lost her. It's the fat ones, you see, the way they put a strain on the nets, tearin' 'em to shreds if you're not watchful. But we got her in all right. We got her in." He slaps his thigh, his grizzled chin nodding up and down for several seconds. "And then I sent Tom here running. A right little messenger boy when he wants to be, earns himself quite a bit of coin with those legs of his. And I told him, I said, 'Now, we don't want any of those police mixed up in this business, leastways not 'til we've got our bearings settled about us.' And here Tom runs into this good gentleman here." A nod towards Trevor, which quickly moves to include Chissick and myself. "And now here comes these fine —Yes, fine young people."

As the old man flounders into silence, I find that it takes a concentrated effort on my part not to look at Chissick. Yet I feel his eyes on me as I move closer to the body, and the tone of his thoughts hovers around him like a fog. All I have to do is trail my fingers through it, and I can sense his uneasiness, and stronger than that, his wish for privacy. But here we all are, under the open sky, and suddenly I'm labouring under not merely the four pairs of eyes trained on the back of my head, but under the inquisitive gaze of the entire city.

They watch as I kneel down, down and down, until I'm close enough to sweep the clotted hair from Sissy's forehead, my fingers breaking apart clods of mud that had worked themselves into a tangle. Still clearing away strands of hair that cling to her skin like seaweed, I travel down to her jaw, skirting over the wound in her cheek, the empty eye socket that stares up at the world with more menace than her own, original eye ever managed to convey.

Down and down again, and now I'm fighting with her collar, twisted around her neck, the fabric stiff with dried mud and what I can only wish is blood. But there is the telltale bloodless wound, the wide slash that splits her throat in two. The skin is strangely puckered, and when I prod the loose flap of skin with my gloved finger, a gurgle rises from the dead woman's throat, as eerie as a strangled cry, before a surge of thick, dark sludge bubbles out of the wound.

Young Tom is already running by the time I look up, one hand covering his mouth as he hurls himself towards the edge of the river.

"Dammit," Chissick breathes behind me, almost beside me now as he drops down to his haunches, his shoulder pressed against my own.

The other two men, sensing their sudden roles as outsiders to this scene, move themselves away. The old man follows young Tom towards the water, though in a healthier state than his companion, while Trevor busies himself with muttering over a cigarette and a handful of soggy matches from an inside pocket, matches that his own abundance of perspiration has rendered useless.

I wait until I'm certain that Trevor has passed beyond the range of spying before I reach again towards Sissy's collar, this time pulling it open, tearing at the fabric until I've bared the top half of her bosom and the small canvas pouch wedged between the folds of her cleavage. Around the back of her neck, holding the pouch in place, is a thin bit of cord, and I make a failed attempt at pulling it apart before Chissick slips the handle of a small pocket knife between my fingers.

As soon as the cord is severed, I weigh the bag of tiles in my hand. Should I wish it, I could summon an image of every person to have had their fortunes told by the grimy letters held inside. Even now, without any effort, I feel Sissy's fingers trailing over the rounded edges, the blankness of her thoughts as she allows the information she needs to flood her mind.

A bit of curiosity is all it takes. I close my eyes, and there are the faces of her final customers, perhaps the last people to see her alive. But there is nothing from them, only the typical feelings of fear, of hope, too simple to be of any interest. So I push further, and there is my own face, seen through Sissy's eyes, and I suppress a shudder as my own sensations from that morning reach across the distance. And now more faces are passing by, everything a muddle as the control slips away from me, and the faces lose definition, the emotions that Sissy draws from the tiles become baser, more confused. It's a struggle to pull myself back, but before I can separate myself from her entirely, there is a glimpse of something, but hardly even that. A shadow, a feeling so faint, as of walking into a room only lately abandoned by another person.

"Miss Hawes?"

My hand tightens around the canvas bag. An odd feeling comes over me. I reach one hand to the ground beside me, almost cool in the shadow of my own body, and the other hovers, as Sissy's would have done at one time. Over her arm, her abdomen, her chest, up to the wound, always the wound, where the rivulets of water and sludge still trickle down from the open flesh, spilling onto the gravel, the same gravel that bites into my knees, creating bruises I'm sure will be with me for some time.

"She knew," I say, not looking at Chissick, but at Sissy's gaping throat. "She knew who did this. She saw her face." And as I gather my courage, enough to keep the grief at bay, I drop the bag of tiles into my lap and pull off my gloves. There is sweat on my palms, between my fingers, and I wipe my hands across my skirt before I touch her.

And I do touch her. Skin to skin. But the coolness I expect from her flesh isn't there. The body is warm, warmer than my own, and as my fingers forge a trail across her collarbone, inches from the wound, the shadow of my hand merges with the darkness lingering beneath her damaged jaw. At this moment, the sun could burn bright enough to set the world on fire, and it would do nothing to banish the chill that takes hold of me.

"What is it?" Chissick asks. Strange, that his voice should seem so far away.

I pull my hand back, and there, hovering in the air, a smudge of shadow. But another look, and I see that it's nothing less than an absence of light trailing from my fingers, writhing for a moment, before it twines around my palm, running like ink along the seams of my hand.

"Dear God," I whisper.

It's a curious feeling that takes over me. Chissick is beside me, and yet I cannot trust myself to acknowledge him, afraid that by looking at him, by sending a few words in his direction, he'll shimmer and fade out, just as my hand does before me. Trembling, I tug at my skirts, struggle not to tread on my hem as I stand up.

"Miss Hawes?"

Before I can be sure of my own balance, Chissick is already on his feet, his hand on my arm, his fingers seeking out my wrist.

"You're not well, Miss. I shouldn't have allowed you to come here. Let me take you home."

But his words fail to penetrate the fog that descends on me, bringing with it a pain that had never truly departed, but was only lying dormant, waiting in the recesses of my mind for the next opportunity to strike. And it strikes with a fury, a constant pressure that doesn't relent but squeezes tighter and tighter, my head in something like a vice. Now Chissick's hand tightens, a grip strong enough to break my thin wrist into splinters. And I realise that he is holding me up, preventing my imminent fall towards the ground.

And I do fall, despite Chissick's attempts to keep me upright. I hit the gravel with such force that the breath is pressed out of my lungs, and before I can draw in another to replace it, the shadow flows along my arm, rises up in front of my eyes, steals around my throat, and I'm gone.

Chapter Nineteen

Light...

It flickers behind my eyelids, in reds and yellows and putrid greens that bring a flood of bile to the back of my throat. There is a distinct memory of gagging, and of being rolled onto my side so the sick could dribble out of my mouth, instead of running back down my throat and causing me to choke. I cough once, and the pain that invades my head is enough to bring on a renewal of the flashing colours, the feeling that my skull will split into pieces before I'm lost to the darkness once more.

***

The second time, there is little light. Neither are there any swirls of colours to send my stomach into rebellion. A muscle jerks in my arm, and following this, as if called to life by that small spasm, there is the sensation of someone pounding on the back of my head with a blunt instrument. An attempt at opening my eyes fails so miserably that I feel the burn of tears along the seams of my eyelids, but another try gifts me with a sliver of sight that reveals nothing more than shapes without definition, blurs and shadows that ignite a spark of frustration inside of me. Contrary to my will, my eyes close, the tears burning a path of warmth along my skin, the last thing I feel before the darkness envelops me.

***

I stretch out my hand towards the light, my fingers flexing, nearly bending backwards before I curl them into a trembling fist and feel my nails press into the slick of sweat gathered in my palm. The movement becomes an exercise, stretch and curl, again and again, until I feel like someone deprived of the use of their muscles for a long period of time.

The feeling does not dissipate, and as I lie there—for I'm aware enough to notice that I'm lying on a bed that is most certainly not my own—I become acquainted with other feelings, or more accurately, one feeling that seems determined to drown out every other sensation that vies for an audience. It's an odd thing, almost unsettling, to wake up wrapped in a cocoon of exhaustion. One would think that sleep would be enough to dispel such a malady, but here I am, listening to the irregular thrumming of my heart, holding my breath as I wait for the jarring beneath my ribcage to take on a more even rhythm.

My hand finds its way to my throat, three fingers seeking that dip below my jaw where I can count out the rapid fluttering of my pulse. I turn my head to one side to allow my fingers better access, and that is when I see Chissick sprawled across an armchair, within arm's reach of the bed. Most of him is silhouetted against the window, the lamp on the bedside table casting enough light to illuminate the side of his leg, the one draped over an arm of the chair. Behind him, daylight shines through the shutters, casting rows of distorted white lines across the rug.

I watch him for a minute, my pulse still pounding away beneath my fingers, and wait until my sight clears enough to focus on the steady rise and fall of his chest. Sound asleep, I think. His head tucked into the crook of his shoulder, a shoulder raised to prevent his slide and tumble out of the chair. His coat, that black monstrosity of wool and perspiration, lies in a heap on the floor, leaving him in his shirt and braces, his collar unbuttoned and his sleeves hanging loose around his freckled forearms, the scrubbed fabric showing its wear in the bare threads that have worked their way out of the weave.

I've no wish to disturb him. Slowly—because I doubt my body

could function at a faster rate—I slip my arms to my sides, shift my weight onto my elbows and drag myself into something that almost resembles a sitting position. The mattress groans beneath me, a short burst of sound that ricochets through the room like a gunshot. I wince, and Chissick's eyelids rise up like curtains.

He sees me, I think, before he's quite certain of the scene before him. And then he rubs his eyes and passes his bare forearm across the lower half of his face, the finale of a yawn still visible as his hand returns to his lap.

"How do you feel?" he asks, and swings his leg off the arm of the chair, his booted foot landing heavily on the floor. My teeth clamp together at the sound, and with a tremble, my arms fail. The mattress lets out another protest, more of a whine this time around, and I shut my eyes as the room transforms into a blur.

"You're not well."

I hear him as if from far away, and I have to wait for his voice to reach my ears. When I open my eyes again, I'm staring at the ceiling, at a yellowed smudge of water damage that frames a crack in the plaster.

"I know."

It's barely a whisper, but he nods to show that I'm heard. The next words fight for dominance on the tip of my tongue. I could ask for a description of what transpired after I fainted beside Sissy's body, no detail abandoned, though I very much doubt the facts would vary from any picture I could form in my head. And yet the question slides out unhindered, and Chissick bows his head as he shapes a reply.

I fell, he tells me. Crumpled to the ground as if my strings had been cut. He refused all help, left Trevor to deal with Sissy's remains and hired a cab that brought the two of us back to his home. Not much of a home, he apologises, and slides forward on the chair. Should he have called for a doctor? The doubt colours his voice even now. But he told himself, assured himself that I would not have wanted anyone else to be involved. And then there was nothing left but for him to stay by my side, waiting for two days.

"Two days?" The words grate along the back of my throat.

"Nearly that," he says, sparing a glance for the shuttered window behind him. "I tried to wake you, several times, but I thought it would be best if I were to let you sleep."

"No," I say, my head rolling from side to side on the pillow. "Please, don't ever do that."

Before he can apologise again, I try to move, my hands tangling with the edges of a blanket Chissick must have draped across me. I muster enough strength to push most of the fabric away, and I feel the blood drain from my head, my lips tingling before they go numb. Chissick takes on the role of caregiver, hovering at my side, and I wonder how ill I must look to elicit such a hasty reaction from him. But his movements are nothing but a practice in hesitation, and I sense he has no clear idea of what should be done.

And so he relies on an old standby, laying his hand on my forehead, first the back of his hand upon my skin, and then the palm, his touch surprisingly cool.

"You're still cold," he mutters, and there is a trace of astonishment there.

I'm prepared to argue with him, for doesn't he see the sweat on my skin? Can he not feel how the heat seems to flow off of me in waves? And yet he reaches down for the blanket I threw off, tucking it around me before I can summon the energy necessary to stop him.

At the sound of my opposition, he treats me with a look, and I almost think that like a mother hen, he'll cluck and fret and do whatever he likes. But the look doesn't last long enough to gain any strength, and his hands fall away from the blanket, flexing as if he still held the edge of the course fabric between them.

"You should at least have something to eat, to drink," he says. And maybe because this lacks the tone of a request, I nod, feeling almost sheepish as he turns on his heel and walks out of the room.

And with his departure, some of the light fades, the glow from the lamp pulling back, retreating behind the punched copper shade. Or maybe it is simply the lowering of my eyelids that hurries the darkness along, until it covers not my eyes, but floods my nose and mouth, pouring down my throat like water. It fills my lungs, rendering me incapable of screaming. But still I try to force the sound, only to pull more of the shadow inside. I feel it now, working its way under my skin, mingling with my blood. A scream does finally break free, but it's too late, because I'm being jostled from side to side, before something hot is pressed to the side of my face, searing my skin so terribly that when my eyes fly open...

I blink.

Chissick is above me, the tip of his nose not four inches from my own. There is a pressure on the left side of my face, and I feel his hand against my cheek, his fingertips tangling in my hair.

But it's the sound, a soft whine, almost plaintive, that catches my attention. I think I will never forget that sound, and only when Chissick dares to take a breath do I notice I'm the one creating it.

A sharp gasp before my lips seal together. I can feel the tears, the thickening behind my eyes before the first ones burn across the edge of my eyelids. Chissick sweeps them away before they run down and soak into the pillow.

"You're all right," he says—no, breathes it across my forehead. His eyes dart from side to side, examining every inch of my face, now held between both of his hands. He leans over me with one knee on the mattress, and when he's sure that I'm not about to expire before him, he speaks a second time.

"Was it a nightmare?"

Such a simple question, and yet I cannot give him an answer. The stuff of nightmares, it surely was, but there will be no classing it as nothing more than a bad dream.

"I heard you scream," he speaks quickly, perhaps seeking to fill the silence that fell to me. "I couldn't imagine... I'd been gone not even a minute, and I heard..." He glances towards the window, a snap of his eyes that I might've missed had I not been staring into his face. But the look is enough, and I turn my head until his hands fall away from me, until I see the shutters on the window, bulging outward as if some great mass had fallen against them.

I stare at the cracks in the wood, at the one hinge dangling cockeyed, and finally at the new pattern of light cast on the opposite wall.

"I can't stay here."

It's not much above the level of a croak, what my throat produces in lieu of a voice. And before Chissick has time or opportunity to piece out what I've said, I make another attempt at throwing off the blanket, my legs making a few pitiful kicks, hindered by too many skirts and my own illness. I'm able to see that my shoes are still on, still carrying a faint crust of dried mud around the heels when Chissick steps forward and places a hand on my shoulder.

There's little strength in it, not even enough to throw me off balance were I in better control of my faculties. But at this moment, I realise that he is holding me up rather than halting me, and another moment passes before I'm leaning into his hand, taking what energy I can from the light grip of his fingers. It's not enough, however, to keep me upright for long. The room spins, and my throat begins a frantic round of swallowing to push down the bile that threatens to flood the back of my mouth.

I fall back onto the pillow, the mattress giving up the lightest of squeaks in protest. Above me, Chissick hovers, the natural fidgeting of his fingers seeming to speak in a language his mouth has yet to master. It's not until he begins to pace, and I see the steps drawing him ever closer to the door that I make another attempt at finding my voice.

"Wait."

A single word, and it has its effect. Chissick stops moving, his fingers fluttering once before he turns around. Three strides return him to my side.

"Don't leave me alone." It hurts to say it. Not because of any pain in my throat, but because of the confession of my own weakness. "And please don't let me sleep."

So bidden, he searches the area around himself, wraps his hand around the back of the armchair and drags it several feet closer to the bed. When he sits, he's close enough to rest his elbows on the edge of the mattress. A shake of his head, and he runs his fingers across his bearded jaw. "What should I do?"

I exhale and turn my gaze to the ceiling. Already, the shadows are creeping in, the streaks of daylight losing their hold on the far wall. "Keep me awake," I tell him, and I wonder whether he takes it as a request, or an order.

"Well," he begins, hands curling about his knees, shoulders shrinking inside the wrinkled folds of his shirt. "I guess I could..." Another shake of the head, and his eyes begin a search, as if he hopes to find an answer stashed away in some darkened nook or corner.

I begin to think he'll give up before he's even started, when he finally speaks. He stops and starts several times, and in fact, the hesitations and the stammers never truly depart, but he plunges onward in a quiet, clear tone I can't remember having heard from him before.

And I listen to what he is saying, only to understand he is telling me about his sister.

He describes her as I imagine he would describe a painting, commenting on her hair, the shape of her face, the colour of her eyes. There's no mention of anything about her, the sound of her laugh, or an amusing anecdote that would encapsulate their childhood together.

I don't look at him until he stops speaking. Then he exhales, and shifts forward on the chair.

"I didn't know her," he admits, his chin dipping down to brush against the drooping points of his collar. "I never met her. Not when she was alive.

"My mother was an actress," he goes on, meeting my eyes again, as if daring me to heap shame on him for having such low connections. "At least, that's what I was told. By the time I found her, she'd spent several years dipping matches, and..." His hand returns to his jaw, and I can only imagine the state of his mother's visage at their first meeting, the phosphorous glow of her rotting flesh.

"She managed to write a brief note, nothing too personal, but seeing as how we weren't particularly close..." A movement of his right hand towards where the pocket of his coat would be, if that article of clothing wasn't still clinging to the corner of the bed, just beyond his reach. I wonder if he keeps the note from his mother in the same place as he keeps the newspaper clipping of my portrait.

"She gave me her name, my sister's name. Isabel." He breathes the last syllable on a sigh. "And you know the rest."

"I am so sorry."

My words fail to mark any immediate change in his expression. With a faint creasing of his brow, he shakes his head, opening his mouth enough to allow two words to slip through.

"Thank you." But that simple phrase isn't enough, and soon, his hands resume their fidgeting, his fingers taking hold of the edge of the blanket that hangs over the mattress, pulling at the threads until the weave begins to unravel. "It seems..." he says, stops, and draws in a fortifying breath. "It seems the both of us have been inundated with death these past few..." Days? Weeks? Years? "Well, for quite some time."

And, as if to lend greater credence to his theory, he abandons his destruction of the blanket, only to move towards my left arm, his fingers trailing across the back of my hand before he turns it over, glides his thumb over the scar on my wrist.

"Is it so terrible?" he asks, and my face must register some confusion, enough to make him add: "The life you have. Would you really prefer death?"

I turn my face away. A few pins still tangled in my hair dig into the soft flesh at the nape of my neck, but I make no move to pull them out. "It never stops," I tell him, and I know that nothing I could say, no sound my voice could create would ever succeed in telling him what plays through my mind at any given moment.

"And when you sleep?"

"There's nothing else. It's as if I disappear."

Chissick's eyes widen before a small nod jars the rest of his features into motion.

"The nightmares—" he begins, but I cut him off before he can finish.

"They're not nightmares. I had nightmares when I was a girl. Dreams, even. Pleasant ones, like any young child should have. But these..." I glance at the ruined shutters, at the cracks that fan out from the corners of the window frame, small black lines tracing their way through the wall's plaster. I wait until Chissick has aligned his gaze with my own, and I study his profile, the soft curve of his lower lip, the veins of red staining the corners of his eyes. And the questions form in my head, slipping into my thoughts before I can stop them.

Will he be next? Will I see his throat slashed apart, same as the others? And what of Marta? What of...?

But before I can compile a list of potential victims, a renewed pressure on my arm draws my attention down to Chissick's hand, to his fingers still treading across my scarred wrist.

"So foolish," he whispers. But whether his comment is intended for my ears or not, I snatch my arm away from him, bury it in the folds of my skirt while I give a few frantic tugs to my sleeve. He looks at me, a curious expression shaping his features, and the question is there, asking me which boundary he may have crossed.

"Please," I say, and regret using the word. "Don't say such things when I don't even possess the strength to walk away from you."

But any contrition I may have expected from him is absent. Even more than that, an eagerness seems to take hold of him. His shoulders straighten, and his cheeks—oh, poor, hollow things they've become— puff out with a kind of courage, or purpose. I almost expect a smile to grace his mouth, infuse his whiskers with life. But there's no smile there, and when he speaks, his voice registers at such a low pitch that I feel myself straining forward so as not to miss a single word.

"Miss Hawes," he says, and I realise that days have passed since I last heard him speak my name. "I can't imagine what you must think of me, what kind of person I must appear to be in your eyes." His head droops, his bottom lip sliding between his teeth. "You may think I'm mad, for all I know. And I'm not sure I would blame you. My behaviour has been most irregular lately. But I assure you that my conduct over the last few days is nothing like how it was before I met you."

I can't prevent the small sound that erupts from the back of my throat. Almost a chuckle, but not quite.

"I must admit," Chissick continues, unimpeded by my minor outburst. "There have been times when I was convinced there was something leading me inexorably towards you. I would hear your name in conversation, see your face in random places, and I began to think that it was a way of keeping you always on the edge of my thoughts. Just when I would think I'd forgotten you, a friend would mention your being in the paper, or that they had gone to one of your demonstrations, and there you would be again, as if you had walked right in front of me."

His eyes leave my face for a moment, to study the empty swatch of space beside me.

"But it did succeed in bringing me to you, because when I found Isabel, when I found out what had happened to her, yours was the first name I thought of."

He looks at me again, his mouth moving without sound, hesitating.

"When I was still with the church, I found myself drawn to people who had fallen on hard times. Women, like my mother, who had once been on the stage and turned to more prurient activities when there were no more parts to be had. Men, like my father, who had taken to drink, to abandoning their families..." He scratches his beard, his fingernails digging into the already raw skin underneath. "There are times when I think I sought out the church in order to somehow absolve some of my family's sins, to make a recompense of sorts." He shrugs, the movement pulling at the worn fabric of his shirt. "Perhaps that's also why I was so easily led away from it."

I can think of nothing to say. And so I blink, and I breathe, and I count the irregular beatings of my heart until I lose track and am forced to begin again.

"I'm sorry," I hear him mutter, his voice coming out as a mumble behind his hand. "I don't know what else I should talk about."

"It does not matter." I make an attempt at shaking my head, but my neck aches, my temples throb, and the pillow beneath me is soaked with a disconcerting amount of my own perspiration.

It falls to him to find a new subject on which to expound. His chair creaks as he moves, and I hear the swift intake of breath that should precede some new speech, but there are no words to follow.

"Chissick?"

Another breath, and I hear his voice. "I have no wish to offend, or to pry into private matters."

I stare up at him, knowing that this isn't the end of what he has to say. But he refuses to continue until I've added something to the conversation.

"What do you want to know?"

And those six words work as well as any key. But still he holds me in some suspense, slides forward on the chair, and rests his forearms on the edge of the bed. He's so close now, his breath tickling the back of my hand as he speaks.

"Do you pray, Miss Hawes?"

Oh, such a question. And yet, should I attempt to lie, I have no doubt he would be able to see through any prevarication I could make. "Not for some time, no."

He nods, as if the imperfection of my faith is well understood. "I know the efficacy of prayer has been widely debated, particularly in these days of science and enlightenment, but..." His gaze abandons my face, his eyes searching for something I suspect even I could not see should I have wished it. "I still pray, despite my departure from my former post. And before I found you, before Miss Summerson directed me towards your whereabouts, I felt that He spoke to me."

I remain still, waiting for him to continue. Because I know that he wishes to unburden himself to me, and I truly have no desire to put up any sort of impediment.

"I felt a tremendous need to find you. Not only because I was certain you would be able to help me discover Isabel's killer, but because there was a great weight pressed upon me, a..." He squeezes his eyes shut, lines fanning out from the corners as I watch him struggle to latch on to the precise words he wants to use. "To save you," he announces, and in such a tone of voice, hushed as a whisper in a church. He reaches for my hand, takes it within his own, and I wait for the first bleating of protest to slip out of my mouth.

"I don't—"

"The words came to me," he starts again, speaking over me until I've stuttered into silence. "That no matter what happens, no matter the danger to myself, I have to do whatever I can, anything and everything within my power to save you."

"Save me?" The words feel foreign and slightly unpleasant on my tongue. A tremor of fear courses through me, as I wonder if the good Lord's direction to him will entail a crusade towards the redemption of my soul.

"Yes. No matter what happens."

My hand still between both of his, he tightens his grip for a moment, so quickly that I could mistake it for a reflex before he pulls away from me and slides the chair back from the side of the bed.

"And that's all God told you? That you will save me?"

A flicker. That is all. But that single vibration in his person, and I know he will not tell me all.

"Everything in my power," he says, after another moment has slipped away.

And there, I must be content with that. "Thank you," I say, almost meaning it. I close my eyes, and I listen to the creakings of the old building as I stave off the blackness that hovers, so full of menace, at the edges of my thoughts.

Chapter Twenty

I smell the smoke before I open my eyes. It is an acrid and cloying smell, clinging to the roof of my mouth, coating the back of my tongue so that I choke and nearly gag. So pervasive is the odour that I imagine I have awoken to a room full of ash, the flames already licking their way beneath the door. But the air is surprisingly clear, only a slight thickening to the motes of dust that float through the last beams of daylight.

I wipe my hand over my face, surprised that it comes away clean, aside from a thin sheen of perspiration and the normal profusion of oil from my pores. I draw another breath into my lungs, and though I detect a tinge of smoke on the air, it is not as strong as my sleep-dazed mind had made it out to be. Dragging a corner of blanket behind me, I stagger towards the door, what strength I may have regained over the last day incapable of being measured until some wakefulness should return to my limbs.

The doorknob is cool beneath my hand, and I step into the hall, blinking at the darkness, my fingers tracing my passage along the wall until my eyes adjust to this unexpected lack of illumination. I pass over another door, and another, before I'm greeted by the faint glow emanating from the staircase. I think that I'm seeing the lights from the first floor, but the glow brightens, sharpening from a dull mist of light to the solid flicker of flame from Chissick's lamp.

I stand still at the top of the stairs, and I feel his eyes move over me, over the state of my dress, my unwashed hair hanging in clumps over my shoulders, until I turn my own gaze away from the bright lamp that is inches from his face.

"There is burning," I say, my voice low. My hand remains on the wall, as if I might leech some strength out of the very foundations of the building.

Chissick nods once, so brief a movement that I might have missed it had I not kept his figure in the corner of my eye. "It is miles from here, yet. We're in no danger."

I make no sign of having heard him. I turn away, back towards my room, towards my bed, though the tangle of dirty sheets and sweat-soaked blankets becomes more repugnant as I approach. By the time I arrive at the bedside, there is more trembling in my muscles than I had anticipated, but I touch one hand to the edge of the mattress, the other hand reaching out into the air, my fingers grasping at nothing as I direct my feeble steps towards a chair that seemed much closer when I glanced at it from the doorway. I move like an old woman, weak and palsied, my limbs eager to disobey every other command issued from my head. After a minute, my balance wavers, and I feel sick before I grasp onto the arm of the chair and tumble into the seat, my head still swimming as the urge to retch waxes and wanes.

I sit for several minutes with my head bowed forward, my elbows resting on my knees. I disregard my poor posture, or how far apart my feet are placed on the threadbare rug. Without lifting my head, the fingers of my right hand seek out the inside of my left wrist, a gentle touch that allows me to count to one hundred as I feel the blood pound inside my veins.

So involved am I in my counting that I don't hear the light scrape and slide of chair legs on the dusty floor. Chissick's low sigh, however, is more than enough to draw my eyes from their inspection of the rug, and then he is on one knee at my side, his hands reaching out to help me, and yet I sense his hesitation before I feel the brush of his fingers on my arm.

"You should be in bed," he says, his voice lowered to a hoarse whisper, and I wonder how ill I must appear that he is compelled to speak in such a hushed tone. "If you were in need of anything, I would have come to your aid."

"I had to move. I can't sleep. Not anymore," I tell him. And then, "No, leave me here," as his hand begins to lift me up and out of the chair. "I will stay here for a minute. I will not return to bed until I am ready."

He leans back from me, no apology falling from his mouth. "Would you like me to bring the light over to you?" he asks, his voice returning to its normal level. "A book, perhaps? Or a cushion? That is not the most comfortable of chairs, I know."

But I shake my head in reply to each one of his offers. I want to stay here, until I can build up another reserve of strength, until I can move once more.

Beside me, Chissick places his hands on his knees and stands up. "Would you like me to leave you, until there is something I can do for you?"

"No," I say, without looking up. "I want you to tell me what is burning."

He sighs, his breath a short blast of air that dies beneath the weight of the humidity in the room. "I don't know. A house, I believe. Or a row of them, by now. But no one has been harmed, from what I've heard."

Because there is no one to harm, I want to say, but my mouth remains closed. And I know that the same thought has already been entertained in his mind. There are not enough people left in the city, entire avenues left deserted, left to the whim of any spark or flame that may descend on their rooftops.

And even if there were still people, still able hands willing to chance injury for the sake of saving a neighbour's building, where is there the amount of water needed to smother a fire? The Thames is little more than a trail of mud now, cracked near the edges, where no fresh water has touched for several weeks.

I shake my head. "It will be here, too. We cannot stay. Everything will burn."

Another touch on my arm, but a burst of energy and I'm able to pull away from him, out of the chair, over to the table where my outer clothes—unwashed, but brushed and neatly folded—sit next to the handful of belongings that had been on my person when Chissick brought me here. I don't ask for a comb, but instead run my fingers through the tangle of hair around my head, tugging at the worst of the knots until I can twist it into a bun that I pin into place at the back of my head. My hands fumble with the fastenings on my skirt, on my blouse, but I don't ask Chissick for assistance. And I'm certain that for this task, he will not offer it.

"Where are you going?" he asks, and before allowing me time to answer, because he must know that I will give him no such satisfaction, he continues to speak. "You're not well," he says, and there is so much meaning carried on those three words that it is enough to make me pause. But only for a moment. I retrieve my shoes from beneath the bed—also brushed with some care, though their newfound cleanliness serves to highlight their sad condition—and lean into the side of the mattress as I struggle to slide my bare feet into them.

"You should leave," I tell him, without looking up from the knot I make of my laces. "It's not safe to be here."

"In London, do you mean? Or with you?"

I glance at the window. The cracks have grown since I last looked, wide enough to have sent small particles of plaster down to the floor. And the colour within them appears darker, as if the walls are filled with ink, and the fluid is only waiting for a large enough space through which to escape.

"Both, I would imagine." I return my gaze to my shoes and give my hastily donned skirt a final tug. "Where is the fire?" And when he fails to give me an immediate reply, "Tell me the place."

"Somewhere on Oxford Street, I believe."

I nod as my hands fly upwards, fiddling with a lock of hair too slick with perspiration to remain in place.

"Miss Hawes."

A last glance around the room, my eyes scanning the bed, the table, every nook and crevice for something I may have left behind.

"Miss Hawes, I can't let you go anywhere."

He stands in the doorway, blocking it should I attempt to dodge past him. Not that I would have half the strength for such an action.

"Why not?" I wish to sound stronger than I feel, but the quaver in my voice gives away everything.

"I can't say."

"No, I am sure you can't."

He lowers his eyes for a moment, and I move towards the door, towards him, my steps faltering as I push against him, his arm dropping to his side without any attempt to impede my progress. But before I arrive at the landing, before I can even look down to the floor below, I feel his hand on my wrist, his fingers tightening enough until I stop moving, as if any additional force might cause me some harm.

I look round at him, but he doesn't release me. "I need to leave."

"Why?" he asks, like a curious child.

"Because I want you to live."

He blinks.

"Julian, I'll destroy you."

And with that, I've told him everything. He must know now, how it is all my fault, all of the deaths, the drought, even the fire burning through the city as we stand here... It is because of me, because I have failed to stop this monster that is drawing its circle more tightly around me.

But my words have not the slightest effect on him. Instead of releasing me, he reaches down for my other hand, his fingers brushing across the scars on my wrists.

"How terrible is it? What you hear?"

"I wouldn't wish it on another person. No matter their sins."

"And you would really seek death, as an escape?"

I pull my right hand away from him, but my left... He pushes my sleeve upwards, exposing the pale welts that criss-cross my skin.

"I am afraid of death," I confess, and the sigh that follows rattles out from between a jaw that trembles. "The wrists... It's one of the worst ways to do it. And I didn't cut deep enough. Because as abhorrent as my life truly is, as much pain as I endure in every moment, it may be worse, after."

A strange thing. I have never before expressed such a belief in words, but the moment the various syllables have found their way into the air, they ring with so much familiarity that I could be led to believe this statement has been a replacement for my morning and evening prayers, recited from memory.

"Please, Julian. Please let me go."

He is prepared to stand against me. There is a tension in him, and I know that he is entertaining the notion of dragging me back to the bed and forcing me to rest. But before he can raise another argument, there is a knock at the front door, loud and insistent. Chissick blows out a breath and steps away from me.

"Give me a moment," he says. I see it, something in Chissick's eyes. There is a darkness, and I wonder if I have already spent too much time in his presence, that the shadows have completed their journey from the recesses of the room and latched on to their next victim. But a turn of his head, and it is swept away so thoroughly that I'm able to convince myself that the darkness was never there in the first place.

I'm alone again, my limbs now restless with the need to be gone from this room. I have been here for too long, and now it feels as if the walls are closing in around me. I attempt to pace the length of the room, but my strength is still not what it should be, and so I rest against the edge of the bed while I listen to the noises that come up from downstairs.

I hear the front door open, followed by voices. Chissick's first, and another. A woman's voice, but I'm not close enough to hear what is being said. I raise my hand to my face and wipe away the fresh layer of sweat that has accumulated across my forehead. My balance wavers, and as I put out a hand with which to steady myself, a sudden jolt of pain stabs through my skull. The pain is so intense that when I open my mouth to cry out, there is no sound, only a terrible retching sound from the back of my throat as I reel forward. Somewhere, behind the pain, I still hear the voices from below, Chissick's louder now, and the woman...

I land hard onto my knees, and my hands are on the floor, my fingernails scratching at the dusty floorboards. The wall that had been so carefully constructed inside my head, the one that had kept everything hidden from me, that had been placed there by a power not my own, begins to crumble. It is a slow destruction at first, but the bricks start to fall faster, exploding into dust as everything I was not supposed to know floods into my mind, all at once.

My forehead is pressed against the floor. There is moisture there, either sick or my own tears, I cannot tell. My eyes are squeezed shut as I listen to the tread on the stairs, lighter than Chissick's heavy footfalls. And then someone is in the room with me, bending towards me, before the pain rises to its highest pitch and I disappear.

***

Lady Francesca is seated on a chair, one leg pushed out from beyond the hem of her skirt, as if that one limb has taken to search for an escape from the warmth that is trapped beneath the heavy fabric. In her plain, grey dress, her dark hair pulled back into a severe bun, I could almost mistake her for a stranger. But the eyes are the same, still veined with red. And the voice... Any doubt as to her Yorkshire ancestry is firmly erased with the first few words to leave her mouth.

"I wondered when you'd stir back to life. Matters are pressing, and here I've been left to wait for over two hours."

Not quite a greeting, but it's enough to turn the conversation over to me. And I do take my time with it. Unsurprising, as I'm still prostrate on the floor, my laboured breath stirring a small ball of dust a few inches from my face.

"I tried to call on you at that old bat Selwyn's," she continues, unperturbed by the contrast in our positions. "But she said you hadn't been there for days."

"No." My voice is stronger than I expected it to be. Or perhaps it is because I feel the vibration of it in the floorboards beneath my cheek. "I've not been home much of late." A tremor in my voice betrays my weakness, and so I press my weight into my hands, and slowly—so slowly—push myself up until I'm able to pull my legs beneath me and shift into something resembling an upright pose. "Why are you here? Why aren't you…?" *Gone*, is the unspoken word, and yet it hangs between us as if I had shouted it out to her at the highest volume.

"Marta," she replies. And when that one word is not enough to enlighten me, she soldiers forward. "She kept me here, said I had a contract to fulfill. But I've fulfilled it, and now she can run all the way to Leeds for all I care."

"Marta left? She left London?"

"This morning," Francesca informs me, and crosses her arms over her chest with some vehemence, as if she's prepared to defend the truth of her statement.

"Finally," I say, and I allow myself to breathe.

For several moments, neither of us speaks. The room is close, and there is an odour that emanates not only from the sweat-soaked mattress behind me, but also from a few unwashed undergarments that rest in a tangled pile on the floor. Francesca turns her gaze towards the window, the muted daylight striking the lower half of her face. And as if spurred on by the illumination, her chin twitches, a movement that her lips soon pick up until the motion is joined by her voice.

"But that is not why I'm here."

I nod. Of course it isn't. I sense her duplicity, coming off her person in waves, and with each wave, another throb of pain assaults me.

"But you already know that, don't you, Miss Hawes?"

I close my eyes. I will need to move soon, but I think another minute must pass until I can trust that I've acquired enough strength. "Where is she?" And when she doesn't immediately reply, I lean forward, my weight now rolling onto my knees as I grab for the edge of the mattress and pull myself up until I'm standing. "Where is my aunt? Because that is why you are here, is it not? To fetch me to her, like some pathetic little messenger boy."

A slight raise of the eyebrows is the only reaction I receive for my brief outburst. "I don't know what it is they all see in you. Marta never stopped crowing about your accomplishments, and Mrs. E..." A snort or a huff, I'm not entirely sure how to label the sound that comes out of her nostrils. "It was like the sun rose and set on you."

Mrs. E. Better known to me as my aunt, Mrs. Ann Everett.

The wall is gone, and I can see everything now. Aunt Ann, dressed all in black, always seated at the table with us when my mother hosted one of her demonstrations, of which I was always such a reluctant participant. And there was the handwriting, the looping scrawl that graced the backs of the photographs, the shape of every letter so familiar. But of course I had recognised it. Hadn't I seen it a hundred times in my youth, decorating the various notes and invitations that passed between my mother and her dearest sister?

"At the sitting, at Mrs. Damant's..." I pause, long enough to take several breaths before I find I can speak again. "I felt something." I look at her, sitting so coolly in the chair that had been Chissick's seat while he waited at my bedside. I try to think of Chissick, to send up a thought as to his current whereabouts, but between the ache in my head and the confusion of pieces clicking together in my mind, I cannot spare a moment's pondering for him. "My aunt was behind that, as well?"

"She wanted to test you, to see how much control you could exert over the spirit."

"And she was willing to risk your life—*you* were willing to risk your life—for a mere test?"

Her hands clench and unclench in her lap, but the rest of her remains still. "I was being punished. I had defied her, foolishly. And she needed to assure me how wrong I had been to doubt my trust in her." She closes her eyes, and for a moment, I hear her string of apologies spoken into my shoulder, her voice clogged with tears as she begs forgiveness from someone I can't see.

The bed is beside me, the edge of the mattress pressing deep into my thigh. But I will not allow myself to sit, especially not while Lady Francesca is still in the room with me. "She should not even be alive. She was there, the night..." I remember it. The darkness that invaded the room, taking my mother first while she still clung to me, before it sent out its tendrils to the other people seated around the table. "I saw her die."

But Lady Francesca is already shaking her head. "She is very strong."

"Stronger than death?"

A sharply inhaled breath, and I see her shoulders push back against the confines of her plain dress. "Perhaps."

I let go of the bed. My balance threatens to desert me, but I remain standing. "But why am I not dead?"

The question is not intended for my visitor. In fact, I very much doubt she would be able to provide me with any sort of satisfactory answer. But it is the same question that has plagued me since I was a child, since I watched my parents die at the hand of the shadowed creature I have always felt responsible for admitting to this world.

"Mrs. E wishes to see you." She stands, her chin lifting to better look down at me.

"Why didn't she come here? Why send you?"

A small shrug. All of her movements seem so delicate, so subtle now that the guise of Lady Francesca is put away. "She wants you to come to her of your own volition. I think she wants you to have a choice."

I allow my chin to dip towards my chest, my expression tightening as another wave of pain thuds through my head. "How generous of her."

She turns, and I understand that our interview must have already come to an end. But before she reaches the door, she pauses, and I notice her hesitation, her desire to be gone from this place and yet to linger for another moment warring within herself.

"Tell me, Miss Hawes. Do you dream?"

"I beg your pardon?"

"Dreams, you know. In your sleep." She spends another moment studying the grime that mars the hem of her dress before her gaze switches to my face. The strain that was previously lacking in her appearance is there now, the vestiges of sleeplessness, drawing deep lines into her face. And there, in her eyes, I see the veins of red that creep ever closer to the dark brown of her irises, so soon to be overtaken. "I don't have them anymore."

And for a moment, I'm lost. Foundering, even. But her attention returns to the small square of floor in front of her, and then she's speaking once more, her voice adopting the tone of someone conversing only with themselves.

"Ever since that night, I close my eyes to sleep, and all I see is darkness until morning. I used to dream every night, vivid things, but..."

Again, she looks at me. For what, I'm not sure.

"Do you dream, Miss Hawes?" The same question as before, and this time, I know that I must give her an answer.

"No, I am afraid I do not have that pleasure."

This must be enough to satisfy her, for she returns to her examination of her skirt and the floor around her. "It's so warm in here," she says after a minute slips away, as she presses the back of her hand to her forehead.

"I am sorry I can't offer you anything." I spread my hands apart, a gesture meant to convey that there is nothing, not even a drop of water in the room that I can give to her.

"Mrs. E tells me I will have a new life," Francesca says, skipping from subject to subject with such quickness that I struggle to follow her. "I am to be quite prosperous, you know. Never wanting for anything, rubbing elbows with royalty and all of that." She folds her arms across her chest, her hands gripping her elbows with some strength. "Your Marta is a fool. To her, it's nothing but tricks and sleight of hand. But Mrs. E has shown me how much more there is, if one can learn to master it."

I shut my eyes, even before she's finished speaking. "You're mistaken." It is all I can think to say. My weariness is too great to even consider forming a stronger argument.

"And I'm sure that Marta doesn't care she's lost me," she continues, growing more petulant with every pass her hands make across her upper arms. "She'll always have the memories of you to fall back on, her little favourite."

I give her no sign that I'm attending to her words. Let her talk. It's what she wants, to hear her own voice, the voice of Francine Butterman, a girl so long buried beneath the trappings of Lady Francesca that she's afraid she might have already disappeared.

"You don't know how difficult it is," she says. "How trying, always being held up in comparison to someone else, and always falling short." A flicker in her eye, and I know she is speaking of more than Marta.

"I am sorry," I tell her, but she waves it off, reaches up to adjust a pin in her hair.

"I'll have my success." This, spoken as she plants her hands on her hips. "I spent too many years, taking my chances at being accused of fraud, but I wasn't about to be dragged up in front of the magistrate because some old biddy wanted to knock about with a table, thinking she was having a chat with her dead husband."

She presses her hand to her throat, and I notice the tension in those fingers, ragged nails poised to scratch at her own skin. I expect her to look at me, but now she averts her eyes, and I see the shade of memory pass over her face, and I know that she and I are both recalling that same evening, when the shadows almost took her from this world.

"I didn't think it was real, before I met Mrs. E." She flinches at her own words, and still she won't acknowledge my presence. "I remember reading about it in the papers, how so many of you were uncovered as fakes, nothing more than common thieves, fooling the gullible into believing anything you wished them to, really. But then she came along, and she taught me how much more there is to the world, how terribly small we are in comparison."

She takes a step backwards, away from me, and I think she would take another, but the wall puts a rapid end to her progress. One hand behind her now, against the sooty plaster, and the other reaches out to me, or rather, it keeps me at a distance, two fingers crooked, a visible sheen of sweat on her palm.

"What..." she begins, only to stop and run her tongue across her bottom lip. Her teeth appear, biting down on that same bit of flesh her tongue moistened. "If you don't dream, what is it that you see?"

Oh, such a question to ask. Such a question to *be* asked. I could tell her that I see all sorts of things. Sometimes a terrible amount of light, and colours. And I see faces, people I've never met, things I cannot always bring myself to believe are real. And yet I know the truth. I know when I see one man strangling another, and I feel the pressure of his hands, and more than that, the darkness inside of him.

"Same as you," I say, without blinking. "Nothing at all."

"But it doesn't frighten you?"

I blink. "Yes, it does."

It's an easy confession to make, but one that seems to do little towards reassuring her.

Her head tilts towards me, her mouth working in silence over the question before sending it into the air. "So you've never known anything different than this?"

"No, I haven't." The remark, minor as it is, nearly undoes me. I find I can no longer look her in the eye, and so I settle for studying a ghastly streak of ash that still stains the far wall.

"But what happened?" she persists. And I wait, allow the silence to return, a stultifying cloud that rests on my shoulders, pressing me further down, until I think the floor may collapse beneath the burden of it all.

It takes some time, I think, for Francesca to understand that she will have no more response from me. And so she takes it upon herself to speak, to carry along the thread of conversation I so abruptly abandoned.

"When I was in the cabinet," she says, and nods along with her words, as if verifying the truth of them. "I heard such screaming in my head, and I thought I would never hear the end of it. But the strangest thing, it was as if there was some part of it, something that..." There is a small sound of frustration as she searches for the right word. "Something that tempted me, made me want nothing more than to give myself over to it." She looks over at me suddenly. "Do you know what that feels like? I asked Mrs. E, but she wouldn't say. But do *you* know?"

"Yes."

She closes her mouth. Her hands find their way back to her hips, and with a slight shift to her posture, some of her bitterness returns, brick by brick, a wall built up between us. And I pull myself away, allowing her the luxury of this mental distance.

"Well," she says, and there's that same lift to her chin, a bit of Lady Francesca returning for an encore performance. "I'm sure I shouldn't take up any more of your time. Mrs. E is waiting for you, and she wouldn't like it if she found out I'd been the cause of some delay." She nods, once. "I'm perfectly able to show myself out."

"Wait." It is spoken in a whisper, but it is enough to halt her progress through the door. "Where is she? Where am I to meet her?"

"The last place you saw her." Lady Francesca almost smiles. "She

QUENBY OLSON

is there, even now."

After this, there are no standard farewells, no words spoken on a false note of promise, to call on one another the next time we're in one another's neighbourhood. Neither of us would believe a syllable of it. But when I'm alone in the room again, there is a niggling premonition, a touch as light as the bead of perspiration that slips across my skin, that this is not the last time my path will cross with hers.

So sure am I of this fact, that I believe there is not a single thing that could contrive to shock me. Should Tower Bridge choose this exact moment to fling itself into the Thames, not a modicum of surprise would register upon my features. My prescience is so strong that when my thoughts push outward, beyond the confines of the bedroom, I already know the exact line of Chissick's crumpled form, and the darkening shade of the blood that stains the floor beneath him.

Chapter Twenty-One

Tripping downstairs with my skirts wrapping around my legs, all of my movements fall out of synchronization with one another. The room I stumble into is empty, and here the staleness of the air has me gasping for breath. The warmth from the insulating layer of dust, from windows shuttered, from the sickly flame of a lamp sending its streamer of smoke into the air, all work towards dulling my senses until I fear I may faint away before I've taken another step forward.

But I do manage a few shaking steps, one hand still clutching at my skirts, the other passing in front of my face to better clear away the haze that has gathered in front of my eyes. So muddled is my sight in the gloom that I'm forced to rely on my other senses: my hearing, poor as it is, and also my hands, trembling as they curl around the corner of a roll-top desk while my legs seek to regain their strength.

I move around the desk, but everything is quick to become another barricade. Even the slithering of my heel in a smear of blood is simply another hindrance, preventing me from moving to the other side of a threadbare armchair before it is too late.

Too late... Too late...

I push the thought out of my head, though the whispers that echo in its wake gain strength, until a single, solitary note rises above everything else, an accompaniment to the sight laid out before me.

Chissick is quite near to the wall, his spine curved awkwardly as if he had attempted to fit himself in the small space behind the chair. One arm is flung out behind him, and I notice a hole in his shirtsleeve, from where the fabric must have snagged on the edge of a broken brick in the fireplace as he fell. His face, for the moment, is obscured by a leg of the chair, but there is nothing to cover the streaks of blood that fan out from the side of his head, their acrid darkness unfurling from behind his skull like the petals of a flower.

I grasp the back of the armchair for balance, not only to compensate for my own dizziness, but for the subtle listing of the floor on this side of the room, as if the wall is sinking, the whole thing ready to one day tip itself into the neighbouring street. There's little space for two bodies in this corner, and so I grope my way to the other side of the chair, nearer to the fireplace and the cold ashes that coat the blackened hearth.

Perhaps it is my refusal to acknowledge Chissick's upper half, the wound on his head that must be there, that allows me to take better stock of the scene before me. A few feet away, to my right, I see the wrought iron shovel that must have been snatched from its place beside the fireplace, its edge still decorated with coagulated blood and a few reddish hairs from Chissick's own head.

It takes little effort to summon a picture of the scene that must have played out while I had been upstairs, nearly unconscious on the floor. Lady Francesca arriving at the door, and Chissick—oh, how I could curse myself for ever allowing our acquaintance to extend beyond our first meeting!—attempting to keep her away from me, until she slipped past him and grabbed the weapon from the fireplace when he made to remove her from the house.

And then she walked upstairs and took up a position beside my prostrate form, seating herself there for two hours while Chissick bled out only one floor below.

A blink of my eyes, and I force myself to return to the present. I'm still standing, my free hand hovering uselessly at my side. I do not know what makes me so reluctant to touch him. Slowly, more because I fear I cannot remain on my feet much longer than for any desire to close the distance between us, I lower myself to my knees. His legs are the nearest things to me, one of them straight and one bent at an awkward angle. I crawl forward until I can take hold of his wrist, but my own heartbeat is too erratic for me to make out the pace of his own pulse, if he even has one. I reach up and across his abdomen, over his ribcage until my fingers brush along the edge of his collarbone and settle in a hollow place beneath his jaw.

His skin is cool to the touch. Seconds pass, and I rest my forehead on his shoulder, the pain that saturates my skull throbbing with such intensity that flashes of coloured light crowd my vision. I will count to one hundred. I tell myself this, while my fingers press against him, waiting for some sign of life to make itself known. I drag out each number, my voice a mere rasp upon the worn fabric of his shirt.

And, there! A slight fluttering, almost imperceptible, but enough to put a hold on my next breath. So I wait—wait!—and there it is again, and stronger, enough that I allow myself to exhale, and with that expelled air, my shoulders slump, and a burning heaviness rises in the back of my throat, almost choking me.

But I cannot give way to emotion, not now that I know he is safe. My hands scrabble upward, over his jaw, until I'm cradling one side of his head as I examine the wound that graces his scalp. His hair is clotted with blood, but as my fingers prod the damaged flesh, I realise that the mark left by the shovel is not as deep as I had feared. The skin, however, is a ragged mess, and fresh blood oozes under my ministrations, gentle as they are.

I know little about the treatment and care of wounds. I glance around me, as if a great pile of bandages and antiseptics will appear out of nowhere, brought into being by the sheer force of my need for them.

"I have to leave you." I speak, my voice still a weak and trembling thing. I try to move him, shifting his arms and his legs into positions less likely to cause him additional discomfort when he wakes. By the time I'm finished, blood stains my dress, my hands, and no doubt my face. Chissick's own person bears no less evidence of his attack from Lady Francesca, and so I rise to my feet, one hand reaching out for whichever solid object is nearest as I stagger upstairs.

I pass by the room that had borne witness to my recuperation of the last few days, and begin opening and closing doors, searching for the room that must be Chissick's. I find it at the end of the hall, a large, cluttered space showing all the signs of recent habitation. There are books strewn about, resting in stacks, some of them still open, with torn bits of paper or broken pens marking the pages. The bed is unmade, though the linens seem tolerably clean, and the entire room comes off as the most used and also most cared for in the house.

My hands grasp at what I trust myself to be strong enough to carry back down the narrow flight of stairs. I snatch several of Chissick's shirts from the depths of a wardrobe. There is a slight smell of must and mildew carried by the fabric, but they are clean, and so they will have to do. I struggle with an armful of bed linens, the bulk of them dragging behind me like a tail as I slip into my room long enough to collect the pitcher of stale, tepid water from my bedside table.

I return downstairs, the spoils of my journey spilling out of my arms as I drop to my knees at Chissick's side. His shirts are all in terrible need of mending, and so I use the various holes and thin spots as places in which to tear the already weakened fabric into more manageable pieces. I douse a few of them with water before I lean over him, my hands moving restlessly in the air above him as I take in the amount of blood and mess that covers half his head.

My progress is slow, and my arms begin to ache after only a few minutes of effort. It's not until I daub at the edges of the wound itself that there is a marked change in Chissick's state. As I wipe away the congealed blood, his eyes twitch beneath his eyelids, and he draws in a deep breath before his lips move once, but with nothing spoken that I can hear.

I'm unaware of the passage of time as I work, and it is not until I'm tying a strip of cloth from one of his erstwhile shirts around his head that I glance up at the window and notice how altered the light is that pushes its way through the shutters. My eyes are strained from

224

both the constant headache that will not relent and the faint tinge of smoke that permeates the air. I cannot move Chissick from where he lies on the floor, but I make what I can of a bed for him with the pilfered linens from his room and the remnants of his shirts that aren't soaked in blood and filthy water.

"Rest," I tell him, though I've no idea if he can attend to my words. "I have to leave you now. But you will recover," I add, as I slip a wadded shirt beneath his injured head, the makeshift pillow raising his cheek from the level of the still damp floor boards. "I know you will."

There is nothing more I can say. Vague promises of my eventual return, that I will see him again before the day is at an end... I can offer no such thing. And so I use the armchair for support as I rise to my feet, my skirts sodden and streaked with Chissick's blood.

I walk towards the door, my steps sounding loud and uneven as I break the silence that weighs over the house. There are no gloves on my hands, nor a hat to cover my head. I'm only half-dressed, in clothes that could not even be salvaged by a proper laundering. It is funny, I think, that the state of my dress should be what occupies my thoughts at such a moment. But what should be the focus of my current musings? An injured Chissick lies on the floor behind me, and ahead of me exists something I do not believe I yet have the power to contemplate.

I grasp the edge of the door frame, pausing long enough to pull in enough air to fill my lungs. The road before me is blurred, and so I blink once, twice, but a moisture invades my eyes, and I feel a burning along the edges of my eyelids. I glance heavenward and I see tendrils of smoke, and above them, still darker clouds, and all of them moving out of synchronization with one another, so that they swirl and crash against themselves, a roiling ocean of dark smoke and sickly smog, the latter lending its own palette of colours to the ever-changing canvas.

I cling to the outer walls, my hands brushing against brick, against wood, against roughly hewn stone as I place one foot in front of the other, until I feel the distance grow between myself and the worst of the fires. But the smell seems to buffet me from every side, the bitter odour of smoke that claws at my throat until every breath feels as if I'm pulling a bit of the fire into myself.

No need to look ahead, I tell myself, my gaze pinned to the ground, to the tips of my scuffed boots as they wink in and out of sight from beneath the hem of my filthy skirt. Step after step, I walk until my legs no longer feel as if they would respond to any orders my poor, demolished mind could conceive.

Fortunately, my feet know where to go, even taking care to sidestep every pile of refuse left in the street. For the sweepers have long since disappeared, leaving the filth to accumulate. But does it matter when there is no one left to walk the uneven cobbles?

Well, there is myself. And a few others, I'm sure. There are some left, the ones who cannot leave, mingling with the proud folk burdened by their own confidence, their belief that no such threat as ostentatious as the one hovering over the city's rooftops will cause them any manner of harm.

I'm beyond exhaustion, I think. Hunger is a trivial thing. My stomach has ceased to rumble in protest of its barren state, while my limbs respond sluggishly to each and every command my mind sends out to them. And there is the renewed pain, searing in its potency since Lady Francesca's arrival at the house set the walls to crumbling inside my head. It took only the slightest pressure, and all of my thoughts and memories broke through. Everything is illuminated now, and the clarity of it all is quite an impossible thing to bear.

I can see my Aunt Ann, never as beautiful a creature as my mother, but more quiet, less obtrusive with her particular gifts of wit and ingenuity. It was she, I remember, who introduced my mother to a fascination with spirits and sittings and the world beyond the veil. And then how difficult would it be to recognise the talent I possessed for it, the dreams and the peculiar foreknowledge I had always considered to be my great affliction singling me out in her keen eyes? A word in my mother's ear, and I was given a place at the table, where the candles flickered into dull pinpricks of blue and the cold crept over my skin like water.

I turn onto another street—this one unfamiliar—and yet my steps continue forward with such confidence, such surety that there is no other path I could take that would lead me home.

Home.

I want to baulk at the word, at the connotations associated with that solitary syllable. But it is not to Mrs. Selwyn's that I'm returning, nor Marta's, nor any other friend or relative who took it upon themselves to offer their charity to an orphan girl left to face the censure of the world after the scandalous death of her parents.

My steps gain strength as the daylight wanes, despite the hours I've spent on my feet, travelling lanes and avenues now abandoned by the city's gentler folk. The fires are some ways behind me, but I wonder how much longer until their destructive path reaches the parched lawns, the gardens left to dry into dust beneath the ever-present sun.

I try to imagine how it must look to someone glancing out their window as I pass by. A solitary figure, decorated with dried blood, dressed in clothes that display an entire catalogue of scuffs and stains and tears. My hair has come loose from its pins, the lank strands hanging tangled and unwashed over my drooping shoulders.

But I'm not as solitary as appearances would allow, for is there not a bevy of companions, all of them whispering, their chattering growing in pitch and receding as one voice presses forward, until there is nothing else for me to hear?

Home, the voice speaks to me. The word now a caress, and then a threat. *Home*, it says again. The voice is calling me home.

Chapter Twenty-Two

The house is still there. Red brick and white trim, sandwiched neatly between a dozen other homes indistinguishable from one another but for the brass numbers above the front door. The brass needs polishing, I notice, the dull surface of the metal reflecting little of the light from the streetlamp that rises out of the sidewalk, less than ten feet away.

I grasp the railing and feel it give beneath my weight. Perhaps the bolts are loose, or perhaps I have misjudged my own strength. Or lack thereof. I move from one step to the next like a woman much older than myself, my shoulders bowed, both feet together before I trust my balance enough to release the right foot and plant it solidly on the next stair.

The door is different than I remember. From the street, the colour appeared to be the same dark green that my mother had favoured, but standing here, so close I believe I could lean forward and press my forehead onto the painted wood, I notice it is now an ugly shade of brown. I blink a few times, until I can see the bubbles in the paint, the cracks where it is peeling and I can glimpse a few streaks of the original green beneath it.

There is no key for the lock, at least none in my possession. My fingers brush over the latch, and I entertain a fleeting thought that ever since that fateful day nearly a dozen years ago, I've never been given any knowledge of to whom the house belongs. But it is nothing more than a simple twist of my hand for the door to open before me. And there I stand on the threshold, afraid to set a foot onto the span of floor where my shadow now stretches out before me.

I must admit it is at the forefront of my mind that this doorstep, this simple collection of ascending stones flanked by an iron railing, is also the place where a young coster stumbled upon the body of Christopher Hawes, his deceased form already beginning to smell in the heat of early summer. My father, stripped of his dignity, of his very life, by a bloodless wound in the soft flesh of his throat.

I don't have to close my eyes before the scene is laid out before me. The coster's nervous cries, how his breath pushed at the curtain of fog that swirled around him. And more men arrived, only a few, as it was still early in the day. One of them checked for a pulse, a redundant action, judging by the depth of the cut that almost severed the victim's neck in half. The chaos held off until the arrival of the constable, and then it became an event, shouts sounding from every corner, the death of a gentleman. Murder! Murder! And all while the shadows writhed, shadows that shouldn't have been there in the mist and the fog, shadows that shouldn't have disappeared as the first rays of the sun speared across the rooftops.

But they're all gone now. No trace of an unnatural shadow, not even a smudge clinging to the crevice around the door frame. Of course, a dozen years have passed since my father breathed his last here. The emptiness should calm my nerves, but still, there is a familiar uneasiness that presses on the base of my throat.

The open doorway presents a darkness so close I'm convinced the brightest lights of Heaven wouldn't succeed in banishing it. My shoulder now set against the frame, I hesitate, having no wish to take that first irrevocable step forward. But the fear is almost palpable out here, though I'm still undecided as to whether I'm about to walk into it, or if I will bring it along with me.

Clearing my throat, I pull in the deepest breath I can manage, biting down on it until I suspect my lungs might rupture from the pressure. When I exhale, more than mere air slides out of me. I feel a resistance slipping away, and free of these latest encumbrances, I close my eyes and walk into the imagined dark.

There is no offending odour to prick my senses, only the smells of dust and, though I'm unsure it can be counted as an aroma, a staleness that hangs in the air, so heavy that my next breath feels as if it's being drawn through a cloth pressed over my mouth.

But the heat overwhelms me. Within seconds, it's enough to muddle my thoughts, the warmth possessing a numbing quality that leaches all of the energy from my limbs, until every step is an effort. How long has the house been shut up? Since the day I left? Without a draft to shift the air, the heat given free rein to build upon itself, day after day, until what I now inhale feels like the cumulative warmth of a decade's sultry days.

I wonder why my own behaviour should take on more of a secretive quality, now that I'm hidden away inside. A few seconds of scrabbling through my pockets, the scrape of a match, and there's a burst of light between my hands. I watch the flame flicker and threaten to die out before my trembling fingers set it to the blackened wick of a candle taken from a dusty sconce fastened to the wall, the light fading to blue before a few motes of dust spark it into a yellow teardrop of illumination.

It is the flash of light that alerts me to the presence of another person in the room. It was only for a moment I saw the face, a whiteness of pallor sickly enough to match my own. I catch sight of the mirror on the wall, my own reflection faded to that of a ghost's by the film of dust that clings to the surface of the glass.

A moment passes before I trust myself to breathe, and my pale eyes meet their own twins above the guttering flame, and the question is there, waiting for my reply.

Where is she?

I can't bring myself to admit that I don't have an answer. I feel nothing, as if there is no other presence inside the house apart from myself. Perhaps my aunt is not here. Perhaps Lady Francesca was wrong, whether intentionally or unintentionally, and I'm all alone. And so I may even be able to entertain the option of escape. Simply turn around and walk away. Out the door, across the macadam, away,

away, back to any available room that will admit me, to the cold comfort of a bed that is not my own.

But have I really convinced myself that I will be any safer somewhere else, lying atop a filthy blanket, dabbing at the sweat that gathers between my breasts, counting the seconds that bridge every breath while I wait for the next layer of perspiration to form? Will the voices desert me there? Or will they remain here when I make a run for it, trailing behind me for a few paces until I finally lose them somewhere around Oxford Street?

It's too much to hope for. And so I return my attention to the hall mirror, the door still hanging open behind me, my heels scraping only inches away from where my father's head once rested on the stoop.

There is nothing else now but to move forward. And I do, ignoring the staircase and the rooms above. Their bare walls and floors hold little interest for me, riddled as they are with the vestiges of unimportant memories, nights curled up in my bed, standing in the doorway to my mother's bedroom, watching her dress for dinner, the ivory column of her neck glowing in the candlelight as she reached up to fasten the clasp of a necklace.

The parlour is to my right, the door opening easily beneath my touch. This alone should make me pause, that the house seems so inclined to welcome me, every door swinging on hinges that glide as if they had been freshly oiled moments before my arrival. Even the floors seem reluctant to offer a creak or a groan, anything that would make me aware of my own presence.

And perhaps this is the building's gift to me, that it should allow me to pass through its rooms uninhibited, and so smooth is my entry into the parlour I could almost be fooled into believing that should I continue towards the wall, I would simply drift through the man-made barrier, my flesh dissipating into the ether.

But I don't go so far as the wall. I halt partway into the room, near where there would have been a table, wood and round and bare, with the fingerprints of a dozen pairs of hands pressed upon it.

There are more memories, but if it was my wish to while away an afternoon in careful rumination, my intentions are cut short by the soft tread of a woman's step in the hall behind me.

My Aunt Ann's tread, but I'm loath to admit if the sound is recognizable because I have a wonderful gift of memory, or if I'm underestimating the extent of my own prescience.

"My dear, dear Thea."

That she uses my first name, my Christian name—and even the shortened form—should not be marked as significant. I heard it from her mouth no fewer than a hundred times before I was yet ten years of age. But the tone of her voice startles me. Its familiarity is unnerving, as if we had spoken with one another only a few hours before, her final words still a prominent echo inside my head. And yet I've no time to dwell on the strangeness of everything around me, for another sound must take precedence.

An inhalation of breath. That is all.

When I speak, I'm surprised at the amount of confidence in my voice, in the way my shoulders straighten beneath her gaze.

"I watched you die," I say, the words sliding out without a hint of interrogation. It could be nothing more than a comment on the weather, so calm is my tone. I turn towards her and I see nothing but darkness. Dark hair, dark clothing, but for a glimmer of green and gold in her eyes, their changeable colour picking out the light from the candle on the wall.

"Your eyes lied to you." There is a slight lift at the corner of her mouth, and I'm struck once more by the resemblance between her and my mother. Though, my mother was taller, I believe. But it's been so many years, and I have grown so much in the interim, I can no longer be sure.

"But my mother, my father? The reverend?"

She moves forward, not towards me, but nearer to the shuttered windows, her steps taking her on a circuitous path about the room. I hear the soft swish of her skirts, the strike of her shoes on the bare floor, and yet there is a dull quality to the sound, as if I'm hearing it from a great distance, or through some invisible barrier that lies between us.

"Your mother never fully appreciated your talents." A shake of the head, a click of the tongue, and there! With that simple commentary on my mother's failings, I'm thrust back to my childhood, to the petty complaints and biting words that were often traded back and forth, back and forth, until they had been polished and refined like the most brilliant of gems. "You were a trained creature, brought out before the assembled company and told to perform a few tricks before being shut back inside your gilded cage."

She glances at me, and though she is still several feet away, I notice the shadows that linger beneath her eyes. Not a colour in their own right, but more an absence of any other shade, as if her face were a portrait the artist had neglected to finish.

"If I could have been allowed to teach you, to guide you..."

And now she pauses, yet the sounds that accompany her progress seem to be delayed. So the rustle of her dress, the dull echo of her final footfall reach my ears a moment after I witness the same cessation of movement with my eyes.

"You have suffered so much, and sometimes I ask myself if more could have been done on my part to prevent it."

Her next move takes me by surprise. She steps towards me, her hands reaching forward as if she will take hold of me, as if she will embrace me. But I lift one hand, my palm outward, and it stops her so suddenly that I watch the stunted energy ripple through her like someone struck.

"I watched you die."

It is no longer than the length of a breath, but in that short amount of time, her entire manner is altered. That quirk of a smile I had witnessed earlier, the almost maternal benevolence shown towards me crumbles away before she returns to her path around the edges of the room, around me.

"I was caught unawares, that night." Her right arm sweeps in a graceful gesture, and again I'm able to see the table, the glitter of my mother's jewels, and the sheen of her gown. "I had not thought he would be able to come through so soon. But I had been inattentive, and my sister insisted on keeping such a tight rein on you."

As she moves, I watch the play of light across her features, at the lines and creases that decorate her face. She has aged, more than what a few years of steady living should provoke in a woman's appearance. But there is something strange about her visage, something I could almost describe as artificial. For while her skin is marked with age and wear, the smooth face of her youth—the face more in line with the look my memories attribute to her—still resides beneath the surface.

"Your mother..." She begins again, now that the subject has been broached.

"My mother is dead, among others. Tell me what you've done."

She shakes her head as she turns her back to me. "You don't understand, the amount of power that exists just beyond our reach. All one needs is a way through." She looks back over her shoulder, showing me the sharp lines of her profile. "You are that way through. The spirits, Thea. They cling to you, congregate around you. Wherever you are, the barrier between worlds is at its thinnest, and once you've learned to control it, to pick and choose which entities you wish to allow passage through..." She spreads her hands open, and all manner of possibilities are laid out before me.

"That night," I begin, repeating those two words as the realisation dawns upon me that I may never be able to reference that evening in any other way without it breaking me. "Something came through, something you say is possessed of extraordinary strength."

I cannot allow her to see how disturbed I am, but I must encourage her to speak, to coax her into telling me everything. For with each and every word to come out of her mouth, I feel a small piece of my own guilt slip irrevocably away from me.

"It was more, so much more than I could've asked for." There is fear, I think, underlying her words. But also a kind of reverence, and I find that more frightening than any horror she might have chosen to exhibit. "But I wasn't ready for it, and so he was left unchecked, for a time."

The expressions of those who had been gathered in my mother's parlour, in this very room, are things of which I think I will never be rid. I remember open mouths, soundless cries of terror as their lives were stolen from them. "Unchecked" seems like such a paltry word, better used to describe a youth's foolish indiscretions or a wayward patch of ivy, rather than an event that culminated with the deaths of four... No, not four. I look at my aunt, standing a few feet away from me, face and arms and legs very much animated with life.

"It took some time to regain my own strength," she explains. "You cannot imagine. And all while attempting to harness him, to bring him under some semblance of control."

Behind her, the candle flickers. My eyes remain on her face, and it is with that subtle change of illumination in the background that I notice the lines that fan out from her eyes, from her mouth, and even flanking her delicate nose. They shift, it seems, writhing across her skin in time with each breath she takes.

"And then there was you." She looks at me, facing me directly as if she were my reflection in a full-length mirror. "I thought I'd lost you. And you, you're integral to everything. So much more important than my sister ever let you know." A pause, long enough for the jab against my mother to settle in the air above us. "All I wanted was to keep you safe, to keep you alive."

On that final word, a thought sparks to life inside my head. Before I can stop myself, my hands clasp in front of me, my thumbs taking turns gliding over the raised welts that cut across the skin on my wrists. But the thought slips away from me in a moment, and my aunt steps forward, rapidly closing the distance between us as she reaches for my hands.

"I am so, so sorry I could not be there for you, and when you were most in need of someone by your side." She squeezes my fingers until I feel the bones ache beneath the pressure. "Then, when I had finally recovered enough of my strength, I discovered you under the care of that Marta Summerson."

As soon as the words are out, she must realise she's gone too far. And so she recedes, my hands are released, and my space given back as she begins her circle of the room all over again. Her gaze, though, she keeps averted from me, and I wonder if she must sense how the shadows move over her, twisting and reshaping themselves in every dip and hollow of her skin.

"To hear of you being on the stage, no better than some common —" Her lips press together, and her chin lowers until there is hardly any light visible between the line of her jaw and her chest. "But I did what I could, sending Lord Ryall to you, making sure to always know of your whereabouts."

I open my mouth to speak, and for a moment, I almost cannot find my voice. Watching this woman—for though she resembles my aunt in every feature, there is something disquieting about her presence that prevents me from fully acknowledging her connection to me—as she prowls about the room feels akin to watching a seasoned actor tread the boards, and so how can I bring myself to interrupt such a skilled performance? And yet the words must be spoken, and she is standing there, waiting for me to provide my portion of the dialogue.

"You never thought to show yourself to me? In all that time?"

"Oh, Thea, dear. You have to understand! For such a long time, I was of no good to anyone. And as time passed, I could not trust how you would receive me."

My teeth clench. I cannot let her see the distaste I feel for her, and I cannot let her see the pain that even now squeezes my skull. For the darkness that has sheltered within her for the last twelve years has now set my mind to screaming. But I must keep her talking, anything to keep her talking, because I know that it cannot be much longer now. Even though I can barely control the direction of my thoughts, there is one that remains clear, and it is that I must keep her talking, I must distract her, for as long as my body will allow me.

"The girls." I force the words out, my jaw still rigid. "The girls in the photographs. What had you to do with them?"

Her posture stiffens before I've even finished speaking, and I see a measure of that pettiness I had already witnessed her exhibit towards my mother return to her.

"A fortune is a fortune. My husband chose to acquire his through some less than reputable means. Does that diminish its value in your eyes? My *sister*," she pronounces, injecting no small amount of venom into those two words, "believed it to be a blight on my status. But do you believe there is a single well-appointed gentleman in all of London —in all of England—whose fortune does not bear the taint of scandal?"

That she feels compelled to defend herself when I've raised no accusation against her is more than enough for me to identify the guilt she must carry in her own breast. I give her a moment, quickly followed by another. She does not anticipate a reply from me, and so I do not take the trouble to offer one for her perusal.

"Some photographs of a few girls, hmm?" She sniffs, shoulders pressing back, elbows pushing out from her sides as if she is preparing to anchor herself in place with those slight joints. "If only you were acquainted with the worst of it."

There is darkness, slowly seeping from her pores. Or perhaps it is only my eyes seeing false things as the pain tightens its grip on my skull. I blink in hope of clearing my vision, but the shadow remains on her skin, gathering in the creases, small rivulets joining with others as they trickle down... down... down... until I think her sleeves and her cuffs may be soaked in it.

The sensation is a strange one, watching the entity move over her, so close to her person that I have trouble differentiating between the two. But I cannot stop watching her, even as I hear the uneven tread in the hall outside the parlour. Aunt Ann is in a better position to see him as he enters the room, and so instead of witnessing his entrance, I'm instead able to watch the mingled shades of surprise and confusion as they play across her features.

My curiosity sated, I turn towards him as well, and I see the glint of the pistol he holds in his hand. In his right hand, I notice. Because every detail, no matter how mundane, seems to impress itself on my mind in this moment.

"Chissick," I breathe, and I fear I could collapse into a mound of soiled clothing and quaking limbs if it were not for the brightness in his gaze, holding me in place. "Please. Stay right there. Don't come any closer to either of us, if you would be so kind."

Chapter Twenty-Three

Chissick holds the gun against his thigh, his arm seemingly relaxed, his stance casual, but I have no idea how quickly he could move if given reason to do so.

There is blood, I notice, staining the skin on the back of his hand. Farther up, and I see the marks of it on his shirt, dried to the colour of rust on his ruined collar. And even higher, there are the makeshift bandages still wrapped around his head. But the blood there is old, from when I left him hours before, and so I try to calm myself with the knowledge that the wound has not taken to bleeding freely once again.

"How did you find us?"

It is my aunt who speaks first. There is no surprise in her tone, but instead a heavy dose of chagrin—bordering on weariness—at Chissick's sudden arrival. There is a part of me that wishes for nothing more than to step back and ponder all of the happenings that have led him here; this poor man who came into my room at Mrs. Selwyn's only days ago, bearing a battered bowler and a yellowed newspaper clipping in the recesses of his jacket.

"Someone told me." His eyes never flicker towards mine, and for that, I give him a great deal of credit. But I watch as he swallows, the quick rise and fall of his Adam's apple against his filthy collar. And I see the perspiration, too, shining on his brow, his upper lip, mingling with the paleness of his complexion to create an image of someone hardly strong enough to remain standing on his feet.

What a pair the two of us must make! The weight of a feather could succeed in laying the both of us flat, and yet here we are, facing off against something that has killed at least a half dozen people.

"I've kept an eye on you for some time. Mister Chissick, is it?"

239

He makes no reply. I watch his hand tighten and relax around the handle of the revolver, and then he is still.

"Your reputation precedes you," she continues, and I still cannot determine how irritated she is by his presence. Did she anticipate his arrival? It hadn't occurred to me until now to even wonder if her dabbling with such otherworldly beings has gifted her with the ability to see beyond what the eyes can perceive. Or perhaps... perhaps she had been too full of hope that her Lady Francesca had put an end to him with a single swing of a cast iron shovel.

She tilts her head to one side, a small gesture that gives the impression she is surveying him. It is a movement that contains the power to unsettle, not for any particular act or gruesome spell committed by it, but simply because it is a motion made for gentle conversation, for drawing rooms and for the wink of gaslight on jewels and for painted fans. Not for use by a woman who stands before us with the shadow of death crawling across her palms.

"I lost several of my girls to you, you know. I never could have predicted that a dull, dry bit of sermonising would be enough to steal them away. And where are they now, hmm? What glamourous life have you sorted out for them? Toiling away in factories, I'm sure. Making cheap lace for middle-class housewives. Or maybe even bouncing their own babies on their hips, before their stinking, loutish husbands come home to beat them, bed them, and pass out on top of them."

His face remains closed, a lack of expression carefully held in place to prevent anyone from guessing his thoughts. At least, this is all I can assume in the brief tick of silence before my aunt takes a step forward, her chin lifting before she renews her assault.

"Is that what you wanted for your sister? For Isabel? What a promise that would have made! 'Give up the parties, give up the adoration. Make a home in Shadwell and peel potatoes for the rest of your days.'"

I hear the hiss of air as Chissick draws in a breath through his teeth. "Miss Hawes," he says, but he does not look at me. His gaze is still on my aunt, on the darkness that seems to pulse like a living thing as it condenses around the tips of her fingers. "Are you well?"

The question forces my mind to pause. And so I have to take a moment to think before I can return an answer to him.

"No."

"But for the moment, at least? You won't...?" A quick dart of his eyes, from my aunt to me and back again, and that is all the acknowledgement I receive.

"For the moment," I say, my voice quivering slightly. "I believe I am still breathing. And you? Your head, does it pain you?"

A twitch at the corner of his mouth, though I cannot tell if it is the evidence of a wince or of a stifled grin. "Like the very devil."

My aunt, I notice, watches this exchange with no small amount of interest. She steps forward, towards Chissick, and as she moves, it seems as if all the darkness, all of the shadows in the room shift with her. "You worry about her, don't you?"

He clenches his jaw, causing the tendons in his neck to tighten, but still he gives her no reply.

"But what about you, Julian?" I see him flinch at her casual usage of his Christian name, as if such familiarities from someone such as her should not be permitted. "Who is there to worry about you? Your family is gone. And your church, your chosen brethren, why even they disapprove of you, of the company you choose to keep around you. Drunks and whores. Gamblers. Murderers. You think you can save them, don't you? You think you can save everyone, yet you couldn't even save Isabel, your own flesh and blood."

My gaze drops to the revolver. Even in the poor light of the room, I can see the white of his knuckles as he grips the handle with renewed strength.

"I don't believe you're afraid of me, afraid of what I could do to you." She is close enough to him now that should she raise her hand, she could strike him across the face. But she does not need to touch him. A flick of her fingers and the shadow slithers through the air, twining around itself as it slides with the softness of a caress around Chissick's throat.

"Ryall wasn't afraid of me," she says, and now she is close enough to him that her breath should stir the wreath of darkness that cinches around his neck as he pulls against it. "And your sister, she had the nerve to laugh at me, to spit in my face when I threatened her and everything she cared about. And she cared about you." The last few words are carried on a whisper as the blackness claws its way up along his throat, over his chin, until I fear it will press itself over his mouth and smother him unless I can think of something, of anything...

"And Sissy?" The words are nearly a shout as they tear themselves out of my throat, loud enough to ensure that I can pull my aunt's attention from her latest quarry. "What was her crime against you?"

Her reaction is instantaneous. The shadow relents, and I watch as Chissick collapses to his knees the moment the pressure around his neck is released. But now she is walking towards me, and with each step that brings her closer, the pain in my head increases tenfold. By the time she is in front of me, each breath feels as if I'm trying to gasp at clean air through a veil of smoke, and the pain...

"Sissy thought she would stop me. Can you imagine that? Silly, gross creature that she was, and she thought she could somehow put a halt to all of this." She sweeps her hands out to her sides, as if what is contained in this dark, sweltering room is nothing less than an exhibit of her greatest achievements. "She found me, you know. Only a few days ago. She said you'd sought her out, for help. How you would think she could help you...?" Another step, and she is so close that I can feel the darkness as it shivers around her. "She was going to tell you about me, but I couldn't have that. It wasn't time yet. I had to wait until you were ready, until you would have only a single choice before you."

Somewhere—perhaps only a few feet away, perhaps from the opposite end of the world for all that I'm capable of trusting my senses

—I hear Chissick coughing, still gasping to regain his breath as he struggles to return to his feet. My own posture seems to have diminished upon my aunt's approach, and when she reaches her hand towards my face, I feel myself cringe away from her.

"It hurts, doesn't it?" Her face swims in blurred and contorted lines before my eyes, and that is when I realise that I must have begun to cry at some point. "But my dear, sweet Thea, it's only because you insist on fighting it. The more you strive against it, the more of your strength it will take from you."

White hot pain lances through my head where her finger touches my temple. "It was so difficult, but this is why I waited." She applies more pressure, and my vision turns black as a wave of sickness roils upward from my stomach. "I wanted to be sure you had reached the point where no one else could help you." Her finger slides down the side of my face, and it is like a knife slicing through my flesh. "Look at me, Thea." Her finger now under my chin, she tilts my face upward, but my eyes are unable to focus on anything. "I will teach you how to control it, and through you, we will gain all that we ever wanted."

When she steps away from me, the sharpest edge of the pain drains away, like poison drawn from a wound. The void it leaves is swiftly filled by a dozen—no, a hundred thoughts that boast such clarity, I'm almost driven off balance by the sudden realisation that accompanies them.

Before I'm aware of it, my fingers seek out the scars at my wrists, sliding over them as a new thought enters my head. I glance at Chissick, swaying on his feet, and then at the gun he still holds in his right hand.

"Julian," I whisper, not for any pale attempt at secrecy, but because I doubt I possess the strength to speak at a higher volume. "You must listen to me."

His eyes meet mine, and there is the furrow of a question between his brows.

"Julian," I say a second time, and it issues from my lips over something of a groan. "So many have died. They are still dying." *You must see,* I try to tell him. *You must see what has to be done.*

"And they will continue to die," my aunt chimes in, the uninvited guest to our conversation. "Unless you learn to use it, to control it for yourself."

"This heat," I continue, ignoring my aunt as she stalks in a fresh circle around us. "The drought, all of it. It is because of this spirit, because of its malevolence. And it will continue to destroy and to kill as long as it is allowed to run rampant through the city." I lean towards him, too weak to trust myself with the mere act of taking a step forward. "It must be sent back, Julian. It has to be stopped."

"No, no, no." My aunt's voice is a whisper, barely registering as a sound as she returns to my side, and with her presence, the pain renews its onslaught. "With me," she says, louder now. "You will come with me, and I will teach you, and the strength you will have... Oh, my dear. You cannot imagine it."

The difficulty, of course, is that I'm perfectly capable of imagining it. And the horror with which it fills me is something even the most vicious minds would struggle to comprehend.

"I will not go with you," I tell her, and I'm careful to look into her eyes as I say it. Eyes that were once a similar shade of green to my mother's, but are now succumbing to the threads of black that spread across the white like spilled ink. "I want nothing to do with you, or your spirits. And I will do everything in my power to ensure nothing like your monster can ever come through again."

Even as I watch her, the darkness spreads, until the whites of her eyes are overtaken. "You are a foolish girl. As long as you are alive, as long as your heart still beats within your chest, the doorway will never close. They will always seek you out, until your mind is driven to madness."

I look back at Chissick, and his own eyes... I think they are everywhere at once.

"Julian."

He gives me a slight shake of his head, and I know that whatever thoughts he has right now, they are not meant to be heard by one such as myself.

"Julian, do you remember your prayers?"

Another movement, a tightening of his hand on the revolver.

"I need you to save me."

"I..." He stops speaking, his mouth clamped shut, biting off his own words. But then he opens his mouth again, enough to release one small sound that is swallowed up by the suffocating heat in the room. "No."

Beside me, my aunt shifts, her limbs taken over by some new nervousness. "What are you talking about? What are you saying to him?"

"No, Miss Hawes." And again, he shakes his head with all the petulance of a small child. "I won't."

I move closer to him, my gait a shambling and uneven thing. I move until I'm near enough to reach out, to grasp his arm, to lift his hand so that the pistol is between us, the barrel aimed at my chest, quite near to my heart.

"You have to save me, Julian."

"No!" The cry comes from my aunt, but she is rendered useless behind me, unable to act for fear of harming me. And I feel it in her, flowing out from her, the unbridled fear should anything happen to me. Because without me, she will have nothing, perhaps not even her life.

"I couldn't," Chissick says, fumbles, and starts over. "I couldn't do that. I couldn't bear to think of what I'd done."

"And you can bear to watch more people die by the hand of this demon?"

"There has to be another way, there has to be."

"None so quick as this."

My limbs are trembling. I want to exude confidence, I want to convince him, but I'm afraid that I may not be up to the task.

"Thea, what are you doing? Thea!" A hand grips my shoulder, and it is like fire being driven deep into my flesh, burning with an intensity that takes my strength away from me and leaves me crumpled on my knees. I choke on the bile that rises upward, but I cannot stop looking at Chissick, or at the tendrils of shadow that creep from my aunt's fingers and close the distance between the two of them.

"Stop." The word is scraped out of me, and another bout of retching is near enough to undo me. "Don't *touch* him."

"Then listen to me." My aunt stands over me, the shadow still tethered to her hands, but hovering, roiling and twisting in the air, only inches from Chissick's face. "Do what I ask of you. That is all. And I promise you that he will remain safe."

I close my eyes. The pain is so strong, such an unrelenting presence, but I know that I must push through it to reach him. "Let me in," I whisper to him, my voice barely a scratch in the back of my throat.

It is not only my voice, but my hands, the very nearness of me, until he has no choice but to see the things in my mind, the image of his sister, of her final moments, of her naked body, laid out on a table with all the reverence of a doctor's specimen.

And I allow him to see more. I allow him to see my parents, to hear their final words to me, and I look up at him long enough to watch as he cringes at the vision of my mother's slender hands, clawing at the pale skin of her own throat.

He pulls back suddenly, and the separation of our minds is so jarring that I nearly tumble forward onto my chest, my hand grasping at air and finding no assistance. I do not see his face, not because of the poor quality of the light, but because I can no longer look at him.

"You promise?" I say to my aunt, injecting just the right amount of acquiescence into my tone. "No harm will come to him?"

"Of course."

She holds out her hand to me, a gesture I take great relish in ignoring. On my own power, I draw one foot beneath me, and then the other. That I have retained any balance after all this time is a wondrous feat. A slight roll of my shoulders, and it is all I need to stand erect—or mostly so—and I make certain to keep the majority of my figure turned towards Chissick while I watch my aunt, or more importantly, the darkness that slithers through the air, called back to her like a dog on a lead.

"Miss Hawes."

I do not look at Chissick, not even when I hear the click as the gun is cocked. I've never heard that sound before, and it doesn't fill me with the sense of foreboding I had always assumed would come with it.

"Miss Hawes, I am sorry."

There is a second when I think that I want to commit everything about this moment to memory, every sound and smell, the weight of the clothing on my limbs, the dampness of the hair clinging to the back of my neck. But I don't want to remember any of these things. I want it to be over. All of it. And I want it to be done now.

Chapter Twenty-Four

There is no pain. And then, there is all too much.

A cry follows the report of the revolver, though whether it sounds from my own mouth or my aunt's, I cannot be sure. The darkness twists and pulls at the edges of my vision as the pain blooms in my abdomen. There is warmth, as well. On my dress, on my hands, on my skin. I watch as the shadows surrounding my aunt flicker and recede, or perhaps it is the failing of my own sight that tricks me into believing that the edges of her figure have begun to blur. But there's nothing for it. Another twist, a blink, and everything is gone.

***

There is a terrible pressure on my chest, over and over and over. And there are voices, I think. No, no. It is a single voice, soft and low and pleading from somewhere above me.

***

Something lands on my cheek and my forehead. It is cool, and it is incessant, and I cannot open my eyes and I cannot turn my head. My limbs refuse to respond, but there is a jostling beneath me, or else I'm the one being jostled. And then I hear thunder, deep and rumbling and very, very far away. And the air all around smells so clean, and every breath is like torture.

***

I am alone. At this thought, I'm seized with an anguish so acute that the quiet pounding inside my ribcage strikes out an irregular tattoo. Slowly, I pull a draught of cool, damp air into my lungs.

Confusion overtakes me, superseded by a fresh wave of fear. My lungs, my heart, even my mind—damaged thing that it is—are all still functioning. And doesn't that mean I must still be alive? And if I'm living and breathing like so many others, doesn't it follow that nothing at all has changed? Above me, all around me, London still burns. Perhaps the entirety of the world will soon turn to ash, along with the lives that have been and will continue to be sacrificed for my own inability to halt the terror that infects every darkened corner.

I begin to struggle, not only against the shadows that surround me, but also the pervasive silence. My breath scrapes its way in and out of my chest until another sound makes itself known, something beyond my own gasps for air and the erratic beating of my heart. A soft rush of air, not more than an exhale, touches the side of my upturned face. If I will allow myself to listen, there is yet more to occupy my straining ears: a light drumming sound, soft and quick and comfortingly uneven.

I need to look around me, but fear keeps my eyelids sealed. For if I dare to open my eyes, it will be the end of all imaginings, leaving only reality to take hold.

And so I remain there, without the aid of dreams or whispered voices to mark the passage of time, if time is indeed a concept that continues to exist. Without the foul distractions that used to contaminate my thoughts, I have no difficulty sensing the light touch that brushes across the back of my hand. And without any voice to consume my attention, there is nothing to prevent the cry that claws its way from my throat as my limbs are jolted fully into wakefulness.

My bare heels dig into something soft and yielding, while my hands scrabble to disentangle themselves from the blankets that threaten to smother me. My eyelids flutter as I wait for the familiar throbbing to return to my head. It will return, I tell myself, the moment I allow the first fragments of light into my skull, as if the darkness alone had gifted me with some small reprieve.

I continue with my pathetic movements until I've turned my head to the side, my hands still pushing weakly at the covers. I raise my chin, attempt to swallow, and nearly choke as my throat sticks together.

"Here."

A cup of water is raised to my lips, and I choke once more, though some of the liquid runs down my parched throat. My gaze latches onto the chipped rim of the cup before they follow the line of the hand that grasps it, and then I'm looking at Chissick, seated as he is so near to my side.

His chair is pressed into the edge of the mattress, but it isn't the same chair as before, and neither is it the same bed. Because I'm not ensconced in his house, but instead I'm in my own room at Mrs. Selwyn's, in my own bed that creaks and groans beneath even as slight a burden as my own.

He returns the cup to the bedside table, and when he says nothing, I find I cannot bear the silence he's introduced between us.

"Speak," I tell him, my voice a cracked, painful creature.

He takes the time to lick his lips, and I see his teeth appear, long enough to worry the inside of his cheek. "I was beginning to think you would never wake."

I blink again, revelling in the lightness of my eyelids. Until now, I hadn't been aware of the heaviness that weighed upon not only my mind, but upon my body's every movement.

"What..." I say, but there are no other words with which to finish the question. Instead, my gaze darts towards the window, seeking out the source of the incessant drumming sound. There is some light coming into the room, a pale glow that does little to reveal whether I've awakened to a new morning or a night.

"It rained all night," Chissick explains. And with that statement, the unfamiliar sound transforms into something like a well-known melody, forgotten for a while, but picked up again when another person whistles a few notes. "And the air has cooled some," he adds, though I've yet to regain enough sensation in my limbs to notice. "I had worried you might take a chill."

The blankets, of course. They are such a weight upon me, but as I attempt to shift, to move my arms and my legs from beneath them, I understand that it isn't the covers that are holding me in place, but instead my own weakness.

My gaze sweeps in concentric circles that draw ever tighter around Chissick's crouching form. When I settle my eyes on his face, I see that he is watching me. And I wonder if he has allowed himself to take one look away from me for the entirety of the night.

He clears his throat. "How do you feel?"

I doubt there is a language on all the Earth that would convey anything near to the riot of feelings rushing through me. "I don't know," I say. He may expect me to continue, to add some description to this brief speech, but those few words are enough to content him. And I wonder how frail my condition must be that a single thread of speech, so insubstantial as that, will give him satisfaction.

"I imagine you're in some pain." It is not a question, I notice, and it is also spoken with a greater amount of delicacy.

"I don't..." I begin to repeat myself, but even the small movements I've made since waking have ignited a terrible ache in my side, somewhere in the vicinity of my ribcage, I think, but there is such a haze of discomfort around it that I can't identify its source.

Once more, my attention shifts towards the window. "The fires," I say, and Chissick doesn't seem to notice how I deflect his attention from my own damaged condition.

"I've not been out of doors since I brought you here." He looks away from me, a brief flick of his eyes before his shoulders roll back beneath his shirt and his gaze returns to my face. "But I can only assume that with the onset of the rain, the fires have at least diminished somewhat."

I nod slowly. Another question answered, but while I begin to learn—or at least to guess at what may be happening outside, I've yet to tap into any reserve of courage necessary to inquire as to what occurred before I opened my eyes a few minutes ago.

I look around the room as I become more aware of my surroundings. My room is the same, boasting the same sparse, dusty furnishings, the same refuse and debris from several weeks' worth of daily life. And yet this scant space seems to have gained an innocuousness since the last time I laid eyes on it all. Perhaps it's the quality of light from the windows, or perhaps everything has taken on a less suspicious air now that my every thought is no longer accompanied by its own sibilant commentary.

My gaze darts back towards Chissick, as if I expect some part of his visage to have also undergone a change since I last took the trouble to study his features. I notice a bandage on his head—a cleaner one than what he sported the last I saw him—but aside from his injury, there is nothing markedly different about his appearance. Surprisingly or not, he seems to be one of the few things to have remained static since our first introduction.

I'm still lying on the bed, though there is a tightness in my muscles, a rigidity that makes me feel as if I'm poised, ready to bound out of the room like a frightened creature. So I settle my arms more fully onto the mattress, my hands pressing down as I try to shift and pull myself up.

"No." Chissick's reaction is immediate. He half-rises from his chair, both of his hands grasping my shoulders and pressing me back down into the pillow. "Lie still. You'll set the wound to bleeding."

The wound.

I blink up at him, and I know he must read the confusion on my face. And then it returns to me, all of it at once, so that there's no need for him to hold me down since the memories are more than enough to sap what little strength I possess.

There is the pain in my side, and as I shift, I feel a thickness

252

around my middle, and I realise it must be the bandages that have kept me from bleeding to death.

"Miss—" he begins to say, but a quick flutter of my fingers is enough to stop him. "Thea," he finishes, and I close my eyes.

"What happened?"

When he doesn't reply, I look at him. His face is illuminated by the faint morning light, his whiskers taking on a ruddier hue in the pale glow.

"Julian?"

Now it is his turn to shut his eyes, while his mouth appears to work over something, but instead of speaking, he swallows it down and turns his head away. "What do you remember?"

It might be a glimmer of hope I hear in his words, that I won't recall anything that happened once he arrived at my family's former home, that I don't still hear the click of the revolver's hammer beneath his thumb, or the agony in my aunt's voice the moment the bullet pierced my skin. And I could give him such a gift, to lie to him and tell him that I've no memory of anything and allow him to tell me only what he would wish me to know. But I fear we've gone beyond that point, and that any prevarication on my part would only harm us further.

"I remember everything," I say, and watch as he flinches. "Everything until the moment after you shot me, that is."

I hear his sharp inhalation, and the next thing I expect from him is an apology, but I'm surprised when his gaze shifts, his eyes flitting towards some indiscernible point behind me. Only for a second before his attention returns to my face, his features carefully arranged into a pattern designed to prevent me from reading anything displayed there.

"It was..." He shakes his head, his teeth again working at the skin inside his bottom lip. "You fell, and the woman—"

"My aunt."

"Y-Your aunt?" I suspect I could've declared myself Defender of the Faith and not received a more baffled reaction from him.

I nod. If he expects a more detailed explanation than that, he will have to wait until I'm capable of drawing in a breath that doesn't make me wish to cry out in pain.

"Well, your aunt, she began to scream." He pauses, long enough for a shiver to pass through him. "The sound of it was like nothing I had ever heard before. It was inhuman."

I gesture for the cup of water, and grateful for the distraction, he raises it to my lips and slips his other hand behind my head as I drink.

"It was after that, couldn't have been more than a few seconds later, everything went dark. The entire room..." And again, he's shaking his head as he turns the cup of water between his hands. "No, it was as if the entire world went black." A flick of his fingers, and I can sense the panic that must have overwhelmed him. "But it didn't last for longer than a moment, hardly longer than it took me to blink. And it was over, and the woman—your aunt—she was gone."

"Gone?" I feel myself start to rise up, but the sudden flash of pain sends me back down onto my pillow. "She left?"

"I thought that. I even went out after her, into the street, but there was nothing." He shrugs, returns the cup to the table, and settles his elbows on his knees. "I couldn't find any trace of her."

I turn my face up toward the ceiling. If I were to close my eyes, I'm sure I would remember the way the shadows writhed across my aunt's skin, or the way her face possessed an illusory quality, her features as insubstantial as a cloud of smoke. But I don't close them, and in this way I hope the memory will lose some purchase, if only a little.

There is more, I know. But Chissick remains silent for several minutes, his hands clasping and unclasping before he takes to thumping his knuckles on the edge of the mattress.

"When I returned inside, you were right where I had left you." I hear the guilt in his voice, and I wonder how much his own conscience has abused him for abandoning me—if only for a moment—in pursuit of my aunt. "I never realised quite how small you are, until I saw you."

His knuckles continue to strike out an uneven tattoo on the bedside. When his hands still, his eyes seek out mine. "Your heart had stopped," he says, and nothing more.

I draw in a breath, and at that moment, I'm overwhelmed with the thought that for a time, as brief a one as it was, there was no air sliding in and out of my lungs. And then I remember the rhythmic pressure on my chest, and the voice that begged so urgently for my return.

"And?" I prompt him, because I can't allow him to linger over such a remembrance.

"There was blood, so much of it, but I needed to help you, and I didn't know how to go about it."

The rain on my face. "You carried me."

His mouth opens and closes without sound.

"You carried me here," I tell him, so sure of the memory that he can make no argument against it.

"Yes." The word slips out of him, accompanied by a slow nod. "And I sent your Mrs. Selwyn out in search of Trevor."

"Mrs. Selwyn?" This revelation, more than all the others, is nearly enough to bring me fully upright in the bed. Chissick even reaches out to my shoulder, prepared to push me back down, but I settle back into the bed, wincing at the twinge of pain that radiates out from the wound in my side. "I can't remember her ever having left the house."

A slight smile, the first since I've woken, twitches at the corners of Chissick's mouth. "For the right amount of coin, I believe she would take herself all the way to Chowringhee and back." His face resumes a more serious cast. "It was Trevor who patched you up, staunched the wound as best he could. There was nothing left then but to wait and see if you would open your eyes."

I press my head back into the pillow, my gaze skimming over the same ceiling I have spent countless hours examining, the warped and greasy boards having been my anchor in this world as the voices—such cruel and venomous creatures—called out from the next. But now, it is nothing more than an assembly of wood and nails, laced with the abandoned webs of spiders, the droppings of mice that chewed their way between the boards. My head is quiet, my thoughts trickling at a sluggish pace, lonesome and without commentary.

"I should let you rest," Chissick says.

I nod in reply as my eyes continue to pick out the dips and shadows of the room. And I realise the musty darkness that clings to the corners, that huddles beneath the furniture and inside every chink and crack in the walls, no longer holds any threat to me now.

Chapter Twenty-Five

I watch Trevor's hands as they move across my skin. His palms are as broad as meat pies, his fingers as blunt as sausages about to split through their casings. But his touch is gentle, his movements laced with an assurance in his own skills. He draws my attention to his work and secures it without any qualms, though it is my own damaged flesh I've been given leave to study.

"No sign of infection," he mutters to himself. His thick forefinger prods a puckered bit of skin at the edge of the wound. "Seepage?"

I admit, a moment must pass before I realise this question is directed at myself.

"Some, but not for days. And nothing putrid."

He nods, his gaze never leaving the nascent scar beneath my rib cage. I experience the same suspicion as with each previous examination, that my injury holds more interest to him than the person in which it resides.

As he applies the fresh dressing, my stomach lets out an ill-timed rumble of discontent, and I'm no longer left to ponder why my mind conjured images of various edibles as he poked and prodded at my abdomen.

All of my senses have been rendered more acute during the length of my recuperation. Hunger, especially, is often so keen I think no amount of food will dampen it. And my hearing as well seems to have improved in clarity. Or maybe it is the lack of conversation in my head that allows me to now hear other sounds more clearly.

Trevor stands up, washes his hands and arms up to his elbows in a basin set on a chest of drawers beside the window. The basin is new. To me, I should add, considering the amount of chips in its rim and the

QUENBY OLSON

crack in the pitcher's mud-brown glaze. The chest came from
Chissick's house, a piece of furniture he declared hadn't been used
since the previous tenants had inhabited the house, and was in need
of nothing more than an afternoon of strenuous waxing to return it to
its former glory.

With Trevor's back turned, I pull my blouse down over my
abdomen and readjust the waistband of my skirt. Every morning, for
the last four mornings, I have forced myself to dress, to brush and pin
my hair, to achieve some sense of routine; though I have yet to set
foot outside of the room since Chissick brought me here, bleeding from
a bullet wound to my side three weeks before.

"I shouldn't need to look in on you again," Trevor announces as he
rolls his shirtsleeves back down over his forearms, still dripping with
water. "You're healing well, and since the bone doesn't appear to have
been nicked."

I place my legs over the side of the bed and as my heels touch the
floor, there is a tentative knock on the door. Trevor shakes out his
cuffs and looks up as if he could see through the wood that surrounds
him.

"Does he ever go home?" he asks, and pinches at a button with a
peculiar amount of ferocity.

"Not at first, no." I reach up and pick a pin out of my hair, twist an
errant piece of hair around my finger, and secure it back into place.
"He does leave now. Every night, and for several hours each day."

I can't say that I'm comfortable around Trevor. I understand he is
Chissick's acquaintance, and there seems to be some history there I'm
unable to ascertain, but I always feel unwelcome in his presence,
especially as pertains to my connection with Chissick, leaving me with
the overwhelming sensation that I have trespassed across some
invisible boundary no one took the care to demarcate for me.

"Your business," he says, his tone taking on an additional layer of
gruffness, the closest thing to a whisper of which I assume he's
capable. "What he came to see you for? It's finished now?"

There is no way I can answer this, or at least, there is no answer I can think to make that will resemble anything even close to the truth. I look away from him, my fingers fiddling again with the pins in my hair, with a button at my collar, at anything that will prevent me from having to acknowledge the gaze he fixes on me. "As much as it can be."

"So you'll be sending him on his way?"

My hand pauses over the smoothing of a pleat in my skirt. "I think you overestimate the power I exert over where Chissick chooses to spend his time."

A puff of breath, followed by a curse, before Trevor snatches his coat from the back of a chair. "He's damaged, you know."

There is something in the way he says this that shapes it into a warning about my own safety, but it is only Chissick's safety he cares about, and the threat he must believe I pose to it.

The conversation is at an end when Trevor crosses to the door, opening it with a sharp tug I think could remove the entire slab of wood from the hinges, if given leave to do so.

"Jules." There is a nod, a lift of fingers to where the brim of a hat would reside if he were wearing one, and Trevor excuses himself, leaving Chissick alone to scuff his heels in the narrow doorway.

He waits until I acknowledge him. A lift of my eyebrows is all that is necessary, and he enters the room, his hat in his hand, his gait so much as it was on that fateful afternoon—could it have been only a few weeks ago? I admit, I'm reluctant to apply such a short amount of time to all that has occurred over the course of it. And yet here we are: I, seated, waiting for him to state his business, as it were. And Chissick, still unsure of himself, still performing something of a dance, I think. A few steps forward, and then a slight retreat before he builds up the confidence to move forward again.

"All is well?" He tilts his head towards the door, the hall and the stairs and surely the street beyond having already borne Trevor well on his way away from us.

I straighten my shoulders, give myself a subtle check that all is tucked and pinned and fastened back into place. My posture, I hope, is erect enough as I sit on the edge of the bed that no one ignorant of my recent history should be able to guess I still harbour a bullet in my torso, an inch beneath my bottom left rib.

"I believe Trevor is eager to see me retire my role as his patient," I announce, as diplomatically as I can manage.

"So you are healed?"

"I am healing," I amend for him. "As I trust I will be for some time to come."

And then there is nothing but silence between us. I'm torn between wishing to stand, to brush the imaginary flecks of dust from my skirts and test the full ability of all my muscles and various appendages. But as long as I remain where I am, I find I'm better able to hold everything else at bay, and there results no need for me to depart from this room and come face to face with the destruction I know lies beyond these four walls.

But a compromise must be reached, and so I brace my hands on the bowed edge of the mattress and begin to rise. Chissick stays where he is, offering no help towards my effort to find my balance. This is a change in his behaviour that unnerves me, how he watches me as I struggle to my feet, my hands seeking the next piece of furniture as my equilibrium threatens to desert me.

I move along the wall, marvelling at the sound of my footsteps—a sound, I learn, that is taken for granted when the parameters of a small bed become one's entire universe—on the bare floor. When I reach the window, I allow myself to lean forward until I grip the sill to prevent myself from toppling further, and I press my forehead against the glass. A soft exhale escapes me, and a fog of steam erupts on the pane.

The sound of the rain is louder here, and I watch streaks of water cut jagged lines across the other side of the glass. It has rained, if my memory serves, for at least some portion of every day of my recovery.

The dry dust and grime that coated London for so long have been returned to its former saturated state, and the Thames, that great lifeblood of the country, has swelled and risen again.

"'And the floodgates of the sky were opened,'" I mutter under my breath. I close my eyes and revel in the feel of the cool glass on my skin.

"Miss Hawes," he says, standing nearer to me now.

I open my eyes and watch as a few short breaths produce a succession of clouds beneath my nostrils and my parted lips.

"We've found no trace of her," he continues. I keep my back to him, feeling resolute that I will not look at him as long as the whereabouts of my aunt is the topic of discussion. "There'll be a hint, here or there, but it's like chasing after rats before they can disappear inside the walls."

"What of the girls?" I find myself asking, my question sending fresh blasts of steam onto the window. "The ones in the photographs? My aunt said there was more to it, that the pictures were only the beginning, that..." I falter into silence. Before I can even lend shape to all of my questions, I fear I already know the answer.

"They've scattered." He follows those two words with a sigh, and I turn around in time to see the fall of his shoulders that accompanies it. "And if what you said is true, that the peerage is mixed up in it, they'll do their damnedest to make certain they've covered their tracks." His gaze flicks towards mine, the uncertainty that is absent from his expression clearly present in his eyes. "Your aunt? Do you think she's gone?"

I'm sure that by "gone," he's not inquiring as to whether she's departed for a season or two on the Continent. "I believed her to be dead once. I won't allow myself to make the same mistake."

He nods, and I watch as his fingers toy with the edge of his hat, the brim sliding through his hands as he turns it, around and around and around. "I thought there was something unnatural about her, about her presence. I felt as if, when I looked at her, she wasn't quite there."

His glance now has taken on a request, I think. A request for confirmation that he was not entirely alone in what he saw.

I take a step forward, away from the window, towards him. Only a step, but I mean it as a test of sorts, to gauge his reaction to my proximity. And yet, it will also be a test for myself. For it has been three weeks now since the voices have departed from my head. Since then, I have heard nothing, I have felt nothing beyond my own dry and dismal musings. And so, another step. Will he flinch when he understands my purpose? Will he back away from me as one frightened? But he holds his position, his face impassive, leaving me to do nothing more but continue with my meagre progress.

It is when I'm close enough to raise a hand, to touch him, that I stop. I search his eyes, as clear and blue as the first time he looked upon me, but now they are near to glowing under the dim, almost ethereal quality of the rain-soaked light.

I have to steel myself before I reach out to him. Not with any physical part of myself, but with the gentle prodding of before, the softest of touches I can manage while my mind whirls with its new, unconstrained freedom.

I expect the same barrier as before, that he will have shut himself off from me. But instead of being halted before I can even begin, I find it disarmingly easy to slip inside his thoughts. And there, in the length of a breath, before I can think to prepare myself for whatever I may encounter, the whole of Julian Chissick is laid bare.

My senses are flooded with his own memories, all of the scents and colours and emotions that accompany them, everything so much more complex than I would've imagined or have ever experienced. And all of it without a single note of sibilant commentary from within my own head.

I extricate myself before I can go any further, but one moment has already seared itself on my own thoughts, and I feel as if it was my own hand on the revolver, my own sweat-slicked finger sliding over the trigger.

Even the sound of the gunshot seems to ring in my ears, and I reach out to steady myself, my hand touching his cheek, the heel of my palm tickled by the rough hairs on his jaw. "I am so sorry," I tell him. "For everything I've put you through."

The words sound cheap and paltry, considering that I'm begging forgiveness for having stood this close to him before, and all while convincing him to pull the trigger and watch me perish.

"It was at Lord Ryall's that I first noticed it," he says, and I can feel the vibration of his voice through his cheek and upon my hand. "There was a darkness near his body. And then I glanced over at you, and it seemed to flicker and twitch at the corner of my eye."

My thumb grazes the line of his cheekbone. Quickly, I pull my hand away from him.

"His shadow," he continues. "It appeared to move, to detach itself, even though his body remained perfectly still."

I bite down on the side of my tongue, causing my voice to sound strained to my own ears when I speak. "It could've been a trick of the candlelight, a draft from an ill-fitted window."

"Thea."

How I feel like a child when he utters my name in such a way. A poor, confused child. And perhaps that's what I've always been, my own demons hindering any and all necessary maturation.

"And again, when we examined the body of that woman pulled out of the river."

"Sissy," I interrupt him, needing to apply a personality to that discarded life.

"Yes." He closes his eyes and nods once. "I saw how it was drawn to you, but never quite a part of you, as if some part of you were always holding it at bay."

I think back to the weight, to the pressure I carried with me for more years than I care to recall. Like a parasite, feeding off my very soul.

"So, you saw it with my aunt, as well?"

"It was destroying you," he says, with more pain in those four words than I can bear to hear. "And she only wanted to use you, not caring how much it hurt you."

"You understand how thankful I am for what you did." My hand twitches, brushing against my dress, placing the lightest of touches on my bandaged side. "You succeeded where I could not."

It is his turn to reach out, to grasp my hand and turn over my wrist, revealing the scars I will always carry with me. "And you know," he says. "I may never forgive you for it."

I feel the air slide out of my lungs. *He's damaged*, were Trevor's words. And here, I've only gone and broken him further.

"I've something for you," he says all of a sudden, while his right hand disappears into one of the inner pockets of his coat. He retrieves a small leather pouch, tied shut with its own drawstring. "Here. I've been holding onto them since..." He clears his throat. "I wasn't sure what you wanted to do with them."

I accept the pouch from him, the tiles inside taking on an inordinate amount of weight as it rests on my palm. "Thank you," I say, and though I'm tempted to tear the pouch open, to scatter the letters across my bed and see what secrets the letters may have to tell me, I instead place them on the windowsill, my fingers trembling as I pull my hand away from them. "You should leave," I tell him, unable to look at him as I say the words. "You need rest. We both do. And should I need you for anything, I'll be sure to send a note your way."

I turn away, needing to pace, to work off some fresh surfeit of energy that propels me forward. I return to the window, and for several minutes, I simply watch the rain coat everything in a shimmering layer of chill moisture.

"Thea."

I do not respond to him. It isn't until I feel his hand on my arm that I'm able to push away from the sill and turn to face him.

"Shall we go for a walk?"

I glance at the ceiling, imagining all of the water currently pouring down above our heads.

"I have an umbrella," he adds, guessing my thoughts.

And still, I do not speak. The pain is gone now. All of the dark visions that haunted my thoughts, my dreams, my every living moment, have departed from me. My mind is my own, and yet, I cannot shake the terrible fear that something—some cruel, malignant creature—could slip back inside, should I ever relax and let down my guard.

"You should leave," I tell him once more.

He nods. Once, and almost imperceptibly. "But I won't."

I move to take a step forward at the moment he does. And there is his arm, his elbow cocked, his poor hat given a final tap against his thigh before it finds its place on his head.

"Then let us be off," I say, my own coat snatched from the end of the bed before I bury my fingers in his sleeve and he leads me towards the door.

Acknowledgments

I could not have done this without the help from a great many people, a few of whom I will go out of my way to mention here: A.J. Navarre for her tremendous artwork (along with the motivation it gave me to cross the finish line). K.S. Villoso for constantly nudging me along, nit-picking, and reminding me of the myriad spelling differences that exist from one English-speaking nation to another. Amanda Bohannan for her amazing, amazing editing skills. I also can't leave out all of the folks at Breaking Quills and World Tree Publishing for their talents in beta-reading, editing, proofreading, and listening patiently as I nattered on about the most irritating of plot and historical minutiae. To all of these and many, many more...

Thank you

CPSIA information can be obtained
at www.ICGtesting.com
Printed in the USA
LVHW032113011222
734346LV00003B/420